BURNING SEDUCTION

Book 5

VELLA DAY

Erotic Reads Publishing

Copyright © 2015 by Vella Day

www.velladay.com

velladayauthor@gmail.com

Cover Art by Jaycee DeLorenzo

Edited by Rebecca Cartee and Carol Adcock-Bezzo

Published in the United States of America

E-book ISBN: 978-1-941835-14-2

Print Edition ISBN: 978-1-941835-15-9

This is a work of fiction. Names, characters, places, and incidents either are the product of the author's imagination or are used fictitiously, and any resemblance to actual persons living or dead, business establishments, events or locales, is entirely coincidental.

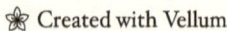 Created with Vellum

CHAPTER ONE

DETECTIVE TRENT LAWSON might have been responsible for putting a lot of men in the Montana State Prison, but he'd never escorted any of them out before—especially someone related to him.

"Your brother is being brought out now," the guard said.

Despite having visited Harmon many times, the barren walls and sterile environment still gave Trent the creeps. He couldn't imagine being cooped up in there. The three years his brother had served seemed like a lifetime.

Dragging his palms down his jeans, Trent was both excited and uneasy about having Harmon back in Rock Hard. He'd thought he'd known his older brother, but apparently Trent had kept his head in the sand when it came to him. Now that he'd served his time for insider trading, it was time for Trent to let go of his anger. At least that was his plan. How well he could execute it was anyone's guess.

He shook his head. There had been a time when he'd worshipped his older brother, but no longer. Harmon had fallen off that pedestal when he broke the law. It was ironic that Trent had been the one who'd been tossed in the Last Opportunity

School just as Harmon was finishing college and graduating at the top of his class.

He's here.

Standing erect, and with his gaze cast slightly downward, Harmon was led out by an armed guard. Before prison, his brother kept his light brown hair perfectly styled, but now it was cropped short. He'd also been on the chunky side, but his brother was thinner now and packed with muscles. Despite the positive change in fitness level, his brother looked older, more worn. Appeals and false hope had done that to him.

Trent inhaled, moved toward Harmon, and embraced his brother for a moment before holding him out at arm's length. "You look like shit, bro, you know that?" Humor was the only way to calm his churning gut.

He held his breath, not having any idea whether he'd be met with anger, cheer, or total elation.

Harmon smiled, and a familiar brotherly rush filled him. He looked behind Trent. "I take it the old man didn't come?"

Trent blew out a breath. "You know better than to ask."

Harmon slung an arm over Trent's shoulder. "As I've been saying, I was framed, but no one seems to believe me, especially Dad."

All criminals claimed they were innocent, but Trent decided to keep that opinion to himself. "Dad's a cop at heart. He'll need irrefutable proof."

Harmon lowered his arm and nodded. "I plan to get some, but I was hoping doing my time would have helped him forgive me."

"You know him. Or maybe you don't. Ever since he became disabled, he's become more ornery."

"Didn't think that was possible. I had hoped we could be a family again, but I guess not." He shoved a free hand in his pocket, holding his few possessions in the other.

As much as Trent would have liked to turn back the hands of

time to before his parents divorced and when Harmon was riding high, Trent was the first to admit that wishing for those days wouldn't make them return. Besides, he wasn't ready to open his heart and be all-forgiving either. He, too, had been betrayed.

They reached his Jeep and Trent jogged to the driver's side, while Harmon slid onto the passenger's seat. "If I forgot to mention it, thanks for picking me up," Harmon said as soon as Trent was seated.

"That's what brothers are for." Even when Trent had visited him in prison, the tension between them had never been this intense. "I found you an apartment, but it won't be available for another week."

"Fantastic, though I won't be a charity case. I'll need to look for a job, even though I had a little money left over after the trial."

He had a lot left over. The lawyer's fees had only put a small dent in his savings. "I asked Pete Banks of Banks Construction if he needed someone for his crew, and he said he could use a man. Since you always were the handy one, I thought it might be a good fit."

"In high school, maybe. I appreciate you helping, but I want to do this my way."

Trent wasn't one to push. He understood pride better than anyone. "Fine."

The hour drive went by quickly, mostly because Harmon kept the focus off himself by asking about Trent's detective work. "You really seem to love your job," his brother said, pride evident in his voice.

"I do. Given where I was thirteen years ago, I certainly wouldn't have pictured that I'd end up in law enforcement."

"The service turned you around."

"True, as did that school for delinquents." Trent drove through the main part of town and couldn't help but wonder what changes his brother spotted. "Look any different?"

Harmon kept his gaze out the window. "Not too much. Glad to see Italiano's Pizza is still there."

"Yup." Harmon used to work there in high school. Trent was seven years younger, and at the time, wasn't aware of anything other than sports and girls.

"There's Charley's Crafts and the Park Hotel." Harmon leaned back and smiled. "It's good to be home."

Trent hoped his brother had the same opinion in a month. Not everyone thought highly of ex-cons. Once past town, Trent made good time to his house. "I picked up a few of your things from Dad's." After Harmon went to jail, Trent had packed up his brother's belongings from his apartment and stored them in Dad's garage.

Harmon smiled, looking like he used to before all this shit came down. "I owe you."

Only for crushing my dreams. Trent pulled into his drive. "Home, sweet home." Harmon hadn't seen it since he'd purchased the house two years ago.

"Nice."

His two-bedroom wasn't large, but it served his purpose especially since he wasn't home much. Between protecting lovely ladies in distress and tracking down clues, he kept busy.

Once inside, he showed his brother to his room and where things were located, but Trent was at a loss what to say. "I promised a friend I'd go to his birthday party, and I'm running a little late. You want to come?"

As mean as it sounded, he almost didn't want his brother to take him up on his offer. There'd be too many uncomfortable questions. It wasn't as if he told the world he had a brother in the joint.

"Thanks for the invite, but I'll pass. I might spend a whole hour in the shower, then veg in front of the tube—something I rarely had the opportunity to do in prison. Besides, you don't need to be dragging around an ex-con."

Trent refused to comment. "I stocked up on beer and food. Help yourself."

"Sounds good. Actually, it sounds fantastic."

"Yeah." Not ready for more conversation, Trent hurried out.

Going to Vic Hart's party empty handed wasn't his style, so he stopped at the Jiffy Mart to pick up a six-pack. Before he went inside, he called the birthday boy.

"I hope you aren't canceling," Vic said without even saying hi. A laugh sounded in the background, along with other chatter.

Trent chuckled. "Are you kidding? I've been working nonstop for three days." *Not to mention picking up my brother from prison.* "I've been looking forward to this, old man." Vic was turning fifty-one. "I'm at Jiffy's, and just wanted to see if you or Ellie needed anything. More booze, chips, dip?"

"Let me ask her." Vic mumbled something. "No, we're good. Just get your ass over here so the party can begin."

"Be there in ten."

The store was empty, which was rare for a Friday night. Since he'd not taken a leak at his house, he headed to the back toward the bathrooms. Once he finished and stepped into the hallway, he heard shouts coming from the front. His instincts kicked in, and he went for his gun. Fuck. He'd left his spare in his glove compartment.

Crouching low, he edged his way between the bread section and candy aisle. Some guy was facing a pale looking clerk, whose hands were raised. Not good. From the robber's slight size, he probably wasn't more than a kid. Jesus. Trent didn't need this tonight, not after what he'd gone through today. His nerves were already on edge.

"Give me the money," the young man grunted.

Trent checked for other occupants but detected no one, and he hoped it stayed that way. When the clerk spotted him, Trent held up his hand hoping to prevent the man from giving away his position. He then slowly reached into his pocket, and when he waved his badge, the clerk's shoulders relaxed. Perhaps now he wouldn't try anything heroic.

The man behind the counter told the kid he'd give him anything he wanted. While the gunman was being placated, Trent eased closer. The cash register dinged open and the clerk slowly removed the money, giving Trent time to move into position.

When he cleared the final aisle, Trent sprinted toward his target, eating up the last ten feet before the kid could react. In one quick move, Trent wrapped his arm around the man's neck, and with his other hand, wrenched the weapon from his fingers. "You're under arrest."

"Fuck you, man. I didn't do nothin'." The kid squirmed, but Trent held him tight. Jeez, he almost sounded like Harmon, claiming he was innocent. Guilt stabbed him. He wondered if this kid would end up spending a large portion of his life in prison.

Trent nodded to the clerk. "Got something I can tie him up with?" His cuffs were in the cruiser, which was back at the station.

"Sure thing," the nervous clerk said, hustling out from behind the counter.

Seconds later, the guy handed him a roll of duct tape. With the boy slammed against the counter, Trent managed to secure the thief's hands. He then stepped away and brandished the perpetrator's gun at him, hoping the weapon was loaded in case he needed to fire a warning shot. "Don't move."

Trent called the precinct and asked for back up. Two units arrived rather quickly, and he could only hope the paperwork would go as fast. He had a party to attend and a certain situation to forget.

* * *

CHARLOTTE HART, VIC'S twenty-four-year-old daughter, went in search of her father in the kitchen. "Didn't you say Trent would be here in ten minutes? It's been forty-five. Do you think we should call him?"

"He'll be here. He probably got sidetracked. Maybe he had to get a cat out of a tree."

Charlotte huffed. Her dad never seemed to take her seriously, especially when it came to Trent "That's not what he does."

Her dad stepped over to her, enfolded her in his arms, and kissed her forehead. "Don't worry, he'll be here."

Her pulse raced. "Does that mean you're in favor of me dating him?" Not that Trent had shown much interest or asked her out. Yet.

"You know how your mom and I feel about that. Trent's job is dangerous."

"Your job is dangerous, yet Mom came back to you." So what if her parents had divorced for five years because of her dad's former FBI gig. Mom and Dad had remarried just last week, and that was all that mattered.

"All I'm saying is be careful. I don't want you to get hurt."

His cell rang and excitement raced through her, hoping it might be Trent calling again. "Is that him?"

Dad nodded. "Hey, where are you? Seriously?" Her dad chuckled. "Murphy's Law, I guess. Get here when you can." He then disconnected.

"What did he say?"

She probably shouldn't be so excited, as that would only lead to disappointment. After all, she hadn't seen him since the Christmas party two months ago. Before that, he'd only called twice after the stalker incident to make sure she wasn't having a meltdown.

"Apparently, he was delayed by a robbery at a convenience store."

Charlotte slapped a hand on her chest. "Is he okay?"

"Yup. Your hero was buying some beer and caught the guy.

He has to fill out some paperwork and will be here as soon as he can."

That sucked, but at least he was safe. She should just forget about him. Dad had told Trent that she'd moved to Rock Hard last week, yet he hadn't made the effort to contact her. She was such a fool, but with a bit of planning, she would change that.

Before she became more upset, the front doorbell rang and a good-looking guy walked in with a food tray in his hand and a six-pack resting on top. Maybe the night wouldn't be a total loss, after all.

Two of the partygoers greeted the newcomer before he made it six feet. "Who's that?" she asked her dad, partly needing him to believe she was willing to focus on others.

"That's Devon Navarro, a cop with the Rock Hard Police Department. We worked together on a case last month. Nice kid. Works hard and is competitive. I think he might go places in the Force if he can keep focused."

Another cop. Damn. Being new in town, though, it wouldn't hurt to meet as many people as she could.

Her mom stepped into the kitchen. "Everything okay?"

"Just getting another beer," her dad said as he slipped a can out of the cooler and escorted her mother back out to the party.

Charlotte picked up a tray of chips and dip to bring out and rushed up to her dad. "By the way, nice going inviting mostly men."

He wagged a finger at her. "Remember, they're all in law enforcement."

That meant they were off limits. She spotted his secretary, Sharon, and a few other women at the party, but most seemed to be attached to a specific man. Charlotte set the tray on the dining room table, but only after moving a few things around to make room for it.

"Hello," came the deep voice behind her.

She spun around. Whoa. It was Devon, the hot cop with the movie star good looks. "Hi."

He smiled and she bet there were a lot of broken hearts in town. She held out her hand. "I'm Charlotte Hart."

He introduced himself. "You Vic's daughter?"

"The one and only."

"Awesome. Where should I set this?" He glanced down to his tray.

How nice of him to bring food. She lifted the beer from on top and made room on the table. "Right here."

"You come down for your dad's birthday?" His brows pinched. "Didn't I hear you lived up north?" He slipped the beer from her hands.

Had Trent talked about her? Or had her dad? "I use to live in Kalispell, but I moved here about a week ago."

His eyes shone. "You going to school here?"

Rock Hard had a good university, and because she was blonde and had a round face, she looked young, but she was twenty-four, not eighteen. "No. I'm opening a branch of an interior design firm that's based in Kalispell."

"Wow. You're a decorator?"

She was pleased he didn't look down his nose at her. Some men did. "Yes."

"Cool." He plucked a beer from the six-pack. "Care for one?"

"Sure. You want to put the others in the fridge?"

"That would be great." He followed her into the kitchen.

Charlotte had to squish a few things to make room for his drinks. Hopefully, her mom wouldn't freak that she'd set things on top of each other. "My dad says you two worked together on a case." She closed the door and faced him.

Devon smiled. "He did?" She nodded. "That was very generous of him. All I did was track down a few leads and make the final arrest of some guy who was harassing your dad's client."

"That sounds like you helped a lot."

"I'd like to think so." He glanced down for a second, almost as if he wasn't used to compliments, something she found interesting.

"I know this might sound strange coming from his daughter, but what is my dad like to work with?" It was only a few months ago that she and her dad had reconnected.

His brows rose as he leaned against the kitchen counter and tipped back his beer. "Your dad's focused and a bulldog. He leaves no stone unturned, so to speak. He's a stand up guy."

She liked hearing good things about him. "Cool."

"You said you were new in town. You like guns?"

That was an odd question. "What do you mean?" She had her concealed weapon's permit, though she needed to practice more if she had any hope of hitting her target.

"The department is having a sharp shooting competition next weekend. You want to come watch?"

She didn't dare ask if Trent would be there. When they'd been at his cabin, he'd asked her if she knew how to shoot a gun, and from his attitude, he was quite good.

"Sounds great." While it wasn't a date, it might be fun. She had a ton of stuff to do to get ready for her grand opening, but she needed to be involved in the community, too. Referrals were a way of life, though she doubted cops would ever use her service.

Just as Devon finished giving her the details about the time and location, two other good-looking men entered the kitchen.

"There you are, Dev." The taller of the two slapped him on the back then glanced her way. "Keeping the beautiful ones to yourself like always, I see." He stuck out his hand. "I'm Mason Everly. I work with Dev."

She smiled. "Nice meeting you."

Devon nodded to the other man. "And this is the guy I plan to beat at the competition—Connor Douglas."

"In your dreams, man."

The three of them laughed. The strong connection between the men made her miss her friends at home. Her mom claimed Charlotte would make new ones, and she hoped she was right.

For now, she'd work hard at her new endeavor and have a good time.

"There you are," her mom said.

"Need me to do something?" *Please say no.*

"Just wanted to let you know Trent's here."

Tingles raced through her. Reacting so strongly wasn't good. Now Charlotte wished she hadn't confided in her mom about how much she liked him.

Devon slipped a hand around Charlotte's waist. "Great. Let's go talk to him."

She couldn't tell from his tone if he liked Trent, or if there was some competition between them.

With his warm hand on her back, Devon led her into the living room. The moment she saw Trent, her pulse sped up. *Stay cool.* She was smart enough to know that men enjoyed a woman who was hard to get, so it wouldn't hurt to have him think she wasn't all that interested.

But damn, she wasn't sure she was that good of an actress.

CHAPTER TWO

TRENT'S GAZE SHOT straight to Charlotte. Holy shit, she looked hotter than when he'd seen her at Christmas, if that was possible. She had on a body hugging sweater dress that accentuated her ample curves, along with booted heels that made her look so sexy. His heart actually pounded. Damn. Her hair was different, too. Instead of keeping it in a ponytail, she'd let it hang past her shoulders, and the blonde waves framed her face, making her even prettier. When she was at his cabin, hiding from the stalker, she hadn't worn a speck of makeup. Now, she was done up with delicate pink lips and smoldering eyes.

Not liking how his cock had turned hard at the sight of her, he glanced away. How had he forgotten she might be here? Trent had been dreaming about her nightly, despite knowing he wasn't the right man for her. Not only was she too young, she was Vic's daughter, and he was highly protective of her. Vic, of all parents, understood how dangerous it was to be a cop, and he wouldn't want his only daughter to be with one. Trent, too, understood that logic. His mom had left his dad for that very reason.

Vic told him Charlotte had moved back to town last week, so of course she'd be at her dad's birthday party. Perhaps Harmon's release had killed all of his functioning brain cells.

Charlotte giggled and Trent returned his gaze to her. As soon as he spotted playboy Devon's arm around her waist, acid burned in his gut. She shouldn't even think of messing with that man. He was a heartache waiting to happen.

Move.

Trying to act as if nothing had happened between them in the cabin, he sauntered up to her and smiled. "Hi, Charlotte. Nice to see you again." He leaned over and gave her a light hug, trying to ignore Devon's arm around her waist. Trent stood back and glanced at the rookie. "Dev."

"Detective."

Trent wanted to wipe the smirk off the man's face, knowing he'd only hurt Charlotte in the end.

A hand clasped on his shoulder, and he turned around. "Sharon."

"May I speak with you for a moment?" Vic's secretary smiled and led him away from Charlotte and Devon.

Her timing sucked. He looked over his shoulder to say he'd be right back, but Charlotte had faced Devon, Mason, and Connor, ratcheting his anger up a notch.

Surely the older woman wasn't trying to pick him up. While he wasn't in the most charitable mood, he admired Vic and wouldn't do anything to piss off his right hand woman.

"You don't stop by anymore. How have you been?" From the gleam in her eyes, that wasn't the real reason she'd pulled him away. She must need information of some kind—or else Vic had instructed her to make sure Trent stayed away from his daughter.

"Good." Ever since the stalker incident that necessitated the need to protect Charlotte, he and Vic had tried to get together for a drink once a week, but of late, Vic had cancelled more times than not, saying he wanted to spend any free moments with his new wife, and Trent couldn't blame him. Vic only had one true love in his live, and she just returned after a five-year hiatus.

Sharon squeezed his arm, her brows pinched in concern. "Are you sure you're okay?"

Trent refocused. She reminded him of the way his mom used to be—feisty, outspoken, and having a flare for the dramatic. "Not really. Can you keep a secret?"

People would find out sooner or later, and he had the urge to talk to someone about it. Seeing Harmon in civilian clothes, acting so normal, stirred doubt in him. While Vic would be a good sounding board, Trent didn't need his friend meddling in the case—a case that had seemed pretty cut and dried at the time. After three years, Trent had time to think about his brother's behavior but could never come up with a reason why Harmon would forsake his upbringing and lie for financial gain. Could his brother be innocent? It was possible, but Trent wasn't convinced he'd been framed, especially in light of the damaging evidence.

Sharon puffed out her chest. "You know I can."

Her effrontery almost brought out his smile. Trent kept his back to Charlotte, fearing that if he watched her look lovingly into Devon's eyes, he'd walk out of the party. "My older brother was released from prison today."

Her mouth opened and then snapped shut. "That's wonderful news."

"For Harmon maybe."

Sharon looked behind him as if she was watching for Vic. She clasped his arm then leaned in close. "Afraid his past will come back to haunt you?"

That was an excellent question, one he'd asked himself repeatedly. "I don't know what I fear. Harmon has always been the elephant in the room whenever I'm over at Dad's."

"I don't see why—not unless you think he'll commit another crime."

"No!"

"Then what's the problem? Family is family. Forever."

His shoulders relaxed. "You're right." His anxiety that something bad would happen was unfounded. Harmon had served his time, and Trent needed to treat him with respect.

Sharon smiled. "Now that that's out of the way, tell me why you haven't contacted Charlotte? She's been in town a week, and I know Vic told you."

So that was the real reason for her dragging him away. Perhaps coming here tonight had been a mistake. The last thing he needed was a matchmaker, especially since he had yet to wrap his head around how he planned to handle his feelings for Charlotte. He told Sharon the first thing that came to mind. "Charlotte is Vic's daughter. I don't want to piss him off."

Vic's secretary chuckled. "He can be deadly, and I know he has some reservations about her dating a cop, but he also wants her to be happy."

"Good to know." Trent needed to mingle, or rather, he needed to make sure Devon wasn't being a jerk to Charlotte. And he certainly didn't need Sharon trying to set him up.

As he turned to check out the scene, Sharon clasped his arm again. "Not so fast, big boy. You like her, right?"

Damned bulldog. He wasn't sure he liked the direction of this line of inquiry. Her kids lived out of state, so perhaps she missed being a mom.

"Charlotte's very nice."

"Just nice?" Sharon's brows rose.

"Sharon Dumont. What's going on?"

She had the decency to glance away. "A few days ago, Charlotte came into the office to see her dad, and we got to chatting. You hurt her feelings when you didn't call."

Shit. He worried that might be the case. "I was her bodyguard, not her date." Though he'd thought about being more.

Sharon lifted a shoulder. "Just saying. Charlotte keeps asking about you, and I think you two would be perfect for each other. She's young, pretty, and single."

The Rock Hard Police Department should hire this woman. She'd make a great interrogator. Before he had the chance to voice his reasons for not asking her out, the front door opened and his boss, Dan Hartwick, came in wearing a suit—of course.

Sharon's eyes lit up, and it was as if Trent wasn't even in the room. She turned back to him. "If you'll excuse me, I need to harass Dan."

Dan? From what he'd heard, Dan wanted nothing to do with her. She was a loose cannon, not to mention uptight–Dan didn't date—though he never discussed why. His past seemed to be a taboo subject.

Trent looked around for Charlotte but couldn't find her. Thinking she might be in the kitchen, he headed that way, but no sooner had he taken a step than Vic appeared, coming toward him. Trent wasn't in the mood for a lecture from him about his daughter, so he pretended as if he needed to use the bathroom and hightailed it down the hallway. Two bedroom doors sat ajar on the right, while the one door on the left was closed. It seemed logical this was the bathroom. As he twisted the knob, the door flew open and he almost tumbled into Charlotte.

Down boy.

* * *

CHARLOTTE'S BREATH CAUGHT, and her stomach did all sorts of odd twisting, not to mention what was happening between her legs. She'd seen Sharon chatting with Trent and didn't need to guess what that conversation was about—her. Her dad's secretary seemed determined to have Charlotte find true love, and she believed Trent was that man. Charlotte couldn't agree more.

"Excuse me," Trent said, his gaze never leaving her face.

Her pulse soared. "No problem. I'm finished." What a dumb thing to say. If she hadn't been done, she wouldn't be leaving.

As she stepped into the doorway, Trent didn't move, and when her eyes connected with his, her heart beat frantically. She wanted this man, and from the way he was looking at her, he wanted her, too. Or did he? Maybe the blood pounding in her ears had halted all rational thought.

"I really need to thank you," she said as her hands touched his abs and started a slow glide up his body.

"For what?" he asked.

When his hands clasped her waist, she figured it was as good as a green flag. Some invisible force seemed to lift her arms and wrap them around his neck. She stood on her tiptoes and kissed him—something she'd wanted to do for months.

When he didn't jerk away, anticipation weakened her, and her heart slammed against her ribs. Then his tongue slid along the seam of her lips and she thought she'd been delivered to the pearly gates themselves. Hungry for him, she opened up and plunged in. Not only did he smell of pine and musk, he tasted like mint. The incredible intensity lasted about two seconds before Trent broke the contact, and devastation claimed her.

"I didn't mean to do that," he said, hesitation or maybe confusion lacing his voice.

She laughed. "Well, I did."

"Charlotte, listen." He scrubbed a hand down his chin.

She wasn't in the mood to hear his excuses why he hadn't called or that he wasn't interested. She didn't like lies, and from the way he just kissed her, he'd be telling one—though perhaps he wasn't ready to believe there was something brewing between them.

Charlotte waved a dismissive hand. "I'm good. You don't need to explain. I just wanted to say thank you for saving my life. That's all."

Plastering on a smile, she stepped into the hallway and forced herself not to run back to the party. Part of her was thrilled to have experienced that much of Trent, but the other half was a bit disappointed. She could guess all of his reasons for staying away, but she wanted to prove to him they were all unfounded. Trent was a lot like her dad—noble, protective, and passionate underneath the gruff exterior.

As she entered the living room, Sharon was speaking with Dan Hartwick, Trent's boss who'd she'd met at the cabin after that terrible man had tried to burn it down with her and Trent inside. Now, Charlotte would have to wait to find out what Sharon had spoken to Trent about. Wanting to keep busy, she located her mom in the kitchen.

"When are we going to give Dad his gifts?"

"We could do it any time. You want to help me with the candles?" Her mom nodded to the cake covered in chocolate guns.

"Sure." Anything to avoid thinking about Trent since embarrassment was beginning to seep in.

Kissing him had been foolish, though highly stimulating. What she wouldn't give to know what he thought of their brief encounter, though his erection told her plenty.

Her challenge now was to figure out a subtle way to make him chase her.

CHAPTER THREE

As CHARLOTTE PLACED the tile samples next to the hardwood planks at the back of her new store, her mind wandered back to Trent. Dad's party had been four days ago, yet Trent hadn't contacted her, not even to say he enjoyed seeing her again. If nothing else, she thought he would have called to discuss their brief kiss. He had to know she'd felt his reaction.

Since he wasn't going to make the first move, her only option was to go after him. Her problem was that she hadn't thought of a way to do so without appearing desperate. She would have asked Mom, but she and Dad had left two days ago for their second honeymoon in Hawaii. Even if they'd been home, her interest in Trent would get back to Dad, and he'd give some reason why she couldn't date him. It didn't seem to matter that she was an adult and had been living on her own for years.

Before she could worry about her love life, she needed to finish up on her store, as she wanted to have it up and running by next Monday. Only then could she start planning her future with the man of her dreams.

Time was her worst enemy. All last week and most of this week, she'd spent every waking hour creating flyers and pounding the pavement, trying to drum up business. In hindsight, opening a new store in February might not have been the smartest move. It was cold and snowy, making it hard for customers to get out, but she wanted to be all set by spring, the time of year when people wanted to make over their homes.

By five, her body was beat, but her mind remained active. Even as she sorted through sample materials, she thought of ways to attract Trent. He was a cop and apparently was quite good with a gun. It made sense he'd appreciate a woman who could shoot, or at least one who was knowledgeable about weapons. When she'd taken her classes for her concealed weapons permit, she'd enjoyed her time at the range, so she wouldn't have to fake her interest.

Wanting to show Trent that she understood what was important to him, she packed her gear and headed home to pick up her gun. She'd been meaning to stop by the range in Kalispell, especially after the man who wanted to harm her dad had come after her, too, but then Patty, her boss, and she had begun brainstorming expansion plans, and practicing had been put on the back burner.

Once she collected her weapon, she drove back to the range. Inside, Charlotte purchased some ammo and found a spot at the far end. Only four of the ten slots were taken, and each of the men looked very serious about his shooting.

Charlotte's skill was a bit rusty, but that was even more reason to practice. She loaded her Walther PPK .380 ACP, slapped on the headgear, and took aim. Damn. Her hands shook as she slid off the safety. Keeping her arms level, and her gaze down the sight, she pulled back the trigger. Instantly, a small hole appeared on the edge of the paper, and she was pleased she'd even hit the target. The recoil, though, was stronger than she remembered.

Determined to improve, she widened her stance and tried again. This time, her aim improved somewhat.

"Fancy meeting you here," came the muffled voice behind her.

Charlotte set down her weapon, spun around, and whipped off her earmuffs. "Trent! What are you doing here? I thought you'd be working." Her pulse soared at the unexpected meeting.

He lifted one shoulder. "This is working—kind of." His shoulders sagged. "I probably should be tracking down some clues, but I wanted to blow off some steam."

She didn't dare hope it was because he was sexually frustrated after their amazing kiss. "From?"

"My brother moved back to town."

Oh. "That's not a good thing?" In all the time they'd spent together in protective custody at his dad's cabin, he'd never once mentioned he had a brother.

Trent pressed his lips together as if he was trying to decide his next move. "Harmon's been in prison for the last three years."

Her heart nearly snapped. She couldn't imagine the pain of having someone you cared about in jail. "May I ask what he was in for?" *Please don't say murder or some violent crime.*

"Insider trading."

"That's not so bad. At least he didn't kill someone."

He chuckled. "You could look at it that way." Trent nodded to the target. "Let's see you take another shot."

"So you can give me pointers?" She meant her comment to be cute, but it came off defensive. In truth, it was hard for her to take direction.

"I am an expert marksman," he said without sounding arrogant.

This time she smiled, so as not to appear so bitchy. "Okay, but you helping me is like me coming to your house and giving you interior design recommendations."

His eyes sparkled. "Would you?"

She'd totally do a makeover if it meant she could spend more time with him. "Sure."

Trent flashed a quick smile then moved to the stall next to hers. It was for the best that he left her alone, but it was damn hard to concentrate with such hotness next to her. Even in his protective gear, he looked sexy as hell. Those broad shoulders and powerful arms would be able to hold the gun with ease.

Pop, pop, pop.

Charlotte really wanted to check out his score, but instead, used some discipline to practice. Inhaling, she focused on hitting the bull's eye. After ten more shots, her arms grew weary, and she brought the paper target toward her.

"Not bad," Trent said, suddenly materializing next to her.

"Thank you. Let's see yours." None of her shots would have been lethal.

He grinned and pressed the button to bring the target toward him. Eight holes were all clustered in the center. "What do you think?"

"Damn, you're good. Are you going against Devon this weekend?"

"Nah. He's good, but I don't need to feed his ego should he win."

She couldn't imagine anyone being better than Trent. Suddenly, she pictured his strong arms around her, helping her aim, and decided to break down and ask for his help. "Maybe I could use some pointers."

He chuckled. "You sure your ego can handle it?"

"What's that supposed to mean? I might be independent, but I'm willing to accept guidance."

He grinned. "Let's see how well you take instruction then."

She moved the target back into position. "I'm ready."

"Okay. Show me your grip."

She faced the target and clasped the handle. Immediately, his hands slid around hers. "The grip is one of the most important aspects to shooting. Slide your hand up as high as you can."

She did as he asked, and she had to admit, it felt more comfortable. "What about my other hand?"

"With the heals pressed together, wrap your non-dominant hand around the other and squeeze tight. Like so." He demonstrated on his weapon, and then helped her line up her fingers appropriately, his touch causing sparks of desire to pool in an inappropriate place.

"I vaguely remember my instructor telling me this." Only she'd never really paid attention.

"Show me your stance."

She widened her legs and lifted her arms. Trent moved behind her and placed his arms around her shoulders to guide her. His scent unnerved her, but she inhaled to calm her racing pulse.

"Good. Once you line up the two sights, focus on the front one."

I can do this.

"Got it," she said.

He leaned down, cheek to cheek, and readjusted her aim a bit. Never had her old instructor been this close, and boy was she now happy she'd asked for Trent's guidance.

"Lastly, take up the slack in the trigger, and once you come against the wall, slowly press it, nice and even."

He stepped back. The lack of his body contact tore at her. Wanting to impress him, she squeezed her left hand, inhaled, and shot. While the recoil was strong, it wasn't as intense as before and excitement filled her.

"Not bad—for a girl."

She loved that he seemed to enjoy teasing her. Charlotte placed her weapon on the counter again, tore off her ear protection, and stuck out her tongue. Trent laughed, just as she'd hoped.

He brought the target toward them. "I'll be damned. You came within an inch of hitting his heart."

"I have you to thank." Without his help, she might have spent weeks here and never made such progress.

"It was all you, girl."

A loud grumble emitted from her stomach, and she placed a hand on her belly. "Sorry."

He glanced at his watch. "I have to pick up Harmon at Italiano's Pizza when he gets off his shift in an hour. Want to catch a bite to eat?"

"Sure." Excitement sizzled in her veins. It was the best offer she'd had since coming to Rock Hard. Too bad, she hadn't put on any makeup, and her clothes were baggy, making her look more like a hippo than a sleek, sensual woman, though Trent didn't seem put off by her appearance.

Italiano's was only three blocks north of the gun range, so they decided to walk. While it was cold, having Trent's arm around her mitigated all discomfort.

Inside, the place was packed, but they managed to snag a small table along the window. Charlotte looked around. "Which one is your brother?"

Tension tightened the lines around his eyes. "Harmon's one of the cooks in back." He placed the napkin on his lap. "How's your store coming along?"

Note to self: Harmon is a touchy subject. "Good. I'm waiting on some samples to arrive."

"Tell me again what it is you do, exactly?"

She laughed. They had talked a bit about what she did for a living when they were hiding in his dad's cabin, but she'd never gone into detail. "With some luck, people will ask me to decorate some portion of their house, and I'll bring them to my shop and let them pick out samples. It gives me a good idea what's important to them."

"Cool. What's the hardest part of your job?"

"That's easy. If a couple is involved, them agreeing on a style is often the worst. Invariably, one wants contemporary and the other insists on rustic."

"I'm not sure I could handle that level of indecision."

"It's challenging, but fun."

Their waiter came over and asked what they wanted to drink. Trent ordered coffee, so Charlotte did, too. They chatted some more about what she had left to do before opening her store, and as much as she wanted to question him about Harmon, she could tell it wasn't something he wanted to talk about, especially with them sitting in the restaurant where his brother worked. Harmon might have been given the job because he didn't mention where he'd been the last few years, or else having Trent as a reference helped.

"So what case are you working on?" she asked.

He dipped his chin and lowered his voice. "If I tell you, I'll have to kill you."

She loved it when he was in a fun mood. "That bad, huh?"

"Actually, it's been rather boring around the station. We haven't had any real excitement since your dad came to town, and we had to locate those gun toting terrorists."

"Dad said you took a bullet in the leg trying to stop them."

He waved a hand. Then as if the pain suddenly flared, he rubbed his thigh. "All in the line of duty."

The waiter returned with their drinks and they ordered their meals. "I want to hear the whole story about my dad and your involvement. Start from the beginning."

He laughed. "You sure? Your dad's injuries were severe."

"I know." She'd asked him about it, but he hadn't elaborated much.

For the next hour, he regaled her with how her dad, using the name Jonathan Rambler, would sit for hours in front of this warehouse pretending to be homeless, all the while collecting vital information about these terrorists.

Charlotte loved hearing about her father and what he was like. "I don't know how my dad survived the beating and the fire."

"It was touch and go. If it hadn't been for Jamie and Max Gruden, the flash drive wouldn't have been delivered to the right hands, and we wouldn't have caught the bastards. A large part of the townspeople would have died in the explosion."

The waiter cleared their plates, and then brought over the

check. Both of them pulled out their credit cards at the same time. Trent placed a hand on hers. "I got it."

"You sure?"

"Yes."

She was thrilled. He must have considered this a real date.

"Hey!" This came from a tall man striding toward them.

Charlotte turned and stared into the face of a man who looked remarkably like Trent. His hair was shorter and a little darker, but he had the same strong jaw and appealing green eyes. She held out a hand. "You must be Harmon."

"Sure am." He turned to Trent. "Am I interrupting?"

Trent shook his head. "Nope. We just finished. I came to give you a lift home."

"Great."

As Trent stood, his cell rang. He slipped it from his top pocket and checked the screen. "It's Cade Carter. He's a detective from work. I'll only be a sec."

From the way the tension radiated across his forehead, the news wasn't good.

"Hey." Trent turned his back, and Charlotte couldn't make out much of the one-sided conversation. He finished quickly then glanced between the two of them. "Something came up at work." Trent faced her. "Is there any way I can impose on you to drive Harmon back to my place?"

She'd love to see where her mystery man lived. "No problem."

Harmon placed a hand on his shoulder. "Is it serious?"

"Deadly. Someone was murdered."

CHAPTER FOUR

CHARLOTTE STOOD THERE, stunned, as Trent hightailed it out of Italiano's. Someone was dead?

"From the look on my brother's face, it's like he knew the person," Harmon said, his gaze focused on the closing door.

"I hope not. Poor Trent."

"Come on." As they left the restaurant, Harmon held open the door.

"My car's parked behind the gun range. Hope you don't mind the walk."

"Not at all."

For most of the way, they walked in silence.

"Does my brother always leave a beautiful woman when his job calls?"

What a sweet man for asking. "I don't know." She still hadn't come to terms over what Trent must be going through. His leaving didn't upset her. If she'd been with her dad, he would have run out, too.

"So, you two aren't dating?"

She wished. "No. Trent was my bodyguard a few months back when my mom had a stalker. Actually, the stalker was trying to get back at my dad for him putting his father in jail."

Harmon chuckled. "Sounds like you and Trent have a lot in common."

"Why's that?" She wanted Harmon's take on the enigmatic Trent. When they reached her car, she unlocked the doors.

He slid in. "Didn't Trent tell you Dad's a cop?"

"No." There was so much she didn't know about him.

"Dad's retired now, but for as long as I can remember, our father was a workaholic, and always on the job. All he thought about was solving crimes. In the end, it cost him his wife and his health."

She hissed. The apple didn't fall far from the tree. "Do you think Trent is trying to be like your father?"

Harmon chuckled. "Good question." He pointed to the cross street. "Head toward SR 25. Trent's place is on Mountain View. As for being like Dad, who's to say? Our father had high standards—too high perhaps—and Trent does, too, from what I can tell." His voice trailed off.

"Were you ever tempted to go into law enforcement?"

Harmon chuckled. "No. I'd rather use my brain; not to mention, I wanted to stay alive. Chasing the bad guys wasn't my thing. I took after my mom in that regard. She was a math teacher in Rock Hard for years until she left."

From the sadness in his tone, the break-up was painful, and Charlotte could relate. "Do you plan on living with Trent?" she asked, wanting to change to a more upbeat topic.

Now, he laughed. "Hardly. One of us would probably end up killing the other. In case you haven't noticed, Trent's not the sharing type."

She hadn't seen that side of him in the cabin, though they had been there under stressful conditions. "I really don't know that much about him." *Other than what has been in my dreams.*

"I guess he didn't mention that he found a rental place for me, but it won't be ready until next week. I'm looking forward to getting my life back in order, like having a driver's license and buying a car."

She wanted to ask what happened to all his stuff after he was arrested, but that would be overstepping her bounds since she didn't know him. Harmon directed her to the turn off, and shortly thereafter, she pulled into the drive. "Here ya go."

"You want to come in, or do you need to run home?"

"I'm temporarily living with my folks until my apartment is ready, but they're on their second honeymoon, so I have a bit of time. Besides, I'm filled with questions about what Trent was like as a little kid."

He smiled. "I'll tell you whatever you want to know."

She believed him. Harmon Lawson seemed like an open book, quite the opposite of Trent. If they didn't look alike, she never would have guessed they were brothers.

Trent's house looked cute from the outside—a one-story brick home with black shutters and neatly cared for shrubs in front. As soon as Harmon let her in, he immediately rushed over to the table and picked up the paper and some dirty dishes.

"Sorry, I didn't clean up before I left for work."

She recalled the few days she and Trent had been in the cabin, and he seemed rather neat. "No worries."

"Want to help me make some coffee?" he called from the kitchen.

She could use a cup. "Sure."

Together they managed to find everything, and soon she had a steaming cup in her hands. He nodded toward the living room. "Let's sit." Harmon took the chair and she sat on the sofa.

She placed the steaming coffee on the coffee table to cool, wanting to take advantage of Harmon's willingness to share. "So what can you tell me about Trent as a kid."

"He was a hellion."

Her brows rose. "You're talking about Trent?"

"Hard to believe, I know." Harmon leaned back. "Dad demanded we both work hard, whether it was at school or when doing chores about the house. Our father insisted that Mom shouldn't have to be a slave to the family, even though he wasn't around a lot. I think his guilt made him be so strict. Could be why Trent rebelled."

"I can't see him doing anything bad."

"He did. He might not have harmed any one and was always kind to animals, but he did smoke weed and once spray painted the side of an abortion clinic. He was only fifteen at the time, and claimed it was because one of his friend's sister had been harmed there."

She could understand that. From what her dad had told her about Trent, he always seemed to fight for the underdog. "What did your dad do when he found out?"

"Sent him to a school for troubled kids. It was kind of like juvenile detention expect that it wouldn't go on his record."

Now that her drink had cooled a bit, Charlotte sipped her coffee and loved the burst of flavor on her tongue. "This is really good."

Harmon winked. "It's a special family blend."

She leaned back. "I have to say I'm a bit curious. You seem so different from Trent."

"I'm seven years older and had Mom to run interference for me. I was in college when she left Dad, whereas Trent was only eleven. He had to split his time between both parents. It was rough."

That could affect a kid big time. She knew all too well. "Given all you've been through, you seem so...normal. I would have thought you'd be bitter and combative." Her idea of prison life had come from the movies.

"I won't deny that I was quite angry at first. Everyone I met in jail claimed to be innocent, but I really was framed. Hell, I hadn't been at the job long enough to be jaded to hand out insider information."

She wanted to be sympathetic to his cause, but if his own brother wasn't singing his innocence, she felt she couldn't either. "Who do you think framed you?"

From the slight chin tuck, he hadn't expected her to ask that question.

"I worked at Ardton Investments run by Bill Goddard and Frank Hamilton. Jayson Kendall worked with me, but he came to the firm after I did."

"Do you think one of them framed you?" She didn't understand how insider trading even worked.

"I've had three years to think about it, and the answer is yes, but which one of the three is anyone's guess. I always figured Bill Goddard was out to get me for some unknown reason, but I had no proof."

"That had to be beyond frustrating." The cheer that had surrounded Harmon suddenly disappeared, so she set her half empty cup on the coffee table and stood. "I have a lot of work to do, so I best be going."

"You don't have to leave."

She imagined he was lonely, especially after being in jail for three years, but she didn't feel right being there alone for too long. "I'm opening my shop in a few days and have a lot to prepare."

"I understand. I sure did enjoy talking to you. I also appreciated the ride."

"Any time."

* * *

TRENT STEPPED NEXT to his partner Cade Carter who was in the bedroom with the corpse. "He looks different dead," Trent said. "Did you know he used to be my brother's boss?" *Fuck, fuck, fuck.*

"I thought the name sounded familiar."

"Any idea when he died?" Given his state of rigor, he had to have died more than twelve hours ago. Trent glanced over to the sobbing redhead in the corner who was probably the victim's wife.

"We're waiting for the coroner to give us the time of death."

Trent nodded toward the woman. "What did she say?"

"Mrs. Goddard was at her sister's last night to help out with the new baby. She came home about an hour ago and found him dead."

"Bloody mess." The body had a knife protruding from his chest. Given the amount of blood pooling around him, he didn't die right away. Black fingerprint powder covered the handle. "You get any prints off the murder weapon?"

Cade shook his head. "No. The killer must have worn gloves."

"What's your take?" Trent asked looking around for signs of a struggle.

"Given the smashed window in back and the mess left in the office, it looks like a robbery gone bad."

Trent's heart pounded fast, praying Harmon hadn't had anything to do with this. He checked the victim's hands, but didn't see any defensive wounds. "Doesn't look like he put up a struggle."

"No. And nothing's been disturbed in this room."

Something didn't make sense. "What was taken?"

"Mrs. Goddard hasn't composed herself enough to tell us, but the file cabinet in Bill Goddard's office is mostly empty and papers are strewn all over the place."

Trent couldn't imagine coming home and finding a spouse murdered in bed. "Was the point of entry a window or a door?"

"Back door. The pane was smashed in with a rock. And no, there were no prints on the handle."

"Breaking glass is loud. Mr. Goddard must have been a sound sleeper. We should have the medical examiner run a tox screen to see if someone drugged him. Who's canvasing the neighbors to see if they saw anything?"

"Devon Navarro."

Devon did good work, but at the moment Trent wasn't all that enthusiastic about working with the guy. However, if the playboy was on the case, he couldn't be bugging Charlotte. "You take the wife's statement yet?" he asked in a low voice.

Mrs. Goddard was sitting with a woman who could be her sister. They both had the same color hair and were about the same age, take or give five years.

"I haven't taken her full statement. I was leaving that pleasure to you." Cade cocked his brow.

"Thanks." This was the worst part of his job—speaking with the relatives of the deceased. Wanting to put this past him, Trent pulled out his pad and walked over to her. "Mrs. Goddard? I'm detective Trent Lawson. May I ask you a few questions?"

She nodded to the other woman. "Deb, can you get me some water?"

"Sure."

While Lawson was a fairly common name, he was surprised she didn't ask if he might be related to Harmon. Then again, she might not have been involved in her husband's business.

Mrs. Goddard inhaled and sat up straighter. "I'm not sure what I can tell you. I found Bill like this."

"Start with where you were from say, yesterday to right now, assuming you feel up to going over what happened."

"Like I told the other fellow, I went to Deb's last night for dinner. She's been having a hard time with the baby, so I said I would help, I spent the night there since Bill wasn't supposed to arrive home from a business meeting until late last night."

Trent made a note in his pad. "And then?"

"The baby started fussing, so I stayed until four. I returned home an hour ago and found Bill in bed. Dead." She broke down again, and Trent had to wait until she composed herself.

Deb returned with the water, and with shaking hands, Mrs. Goddard sipped the drink.

"Do you know of anyone who would want to harm your husband?"

She looked up and grimaced. "Detective, probably every client who lost money at Bill's firm would be out to get him."

"Do you have a list of his clients?" She acted as if the cops knew what her husband did for a living.

"I'm not involved much in what he does, but his partner, Frank Hamilton, might know."

Trent didn't need to write down that name, but he'd be sure to visit the partner. "When you get a chance, I'd appreciate you looking around to see what was taken besides some office stuff."

"I will."

The poor woman had been through enough. He turned to her sister. "Is there any way she can stay with you for a few days? This needs to remain a crime scene for a short while."

"Of course." She wrapped an arm around the grieving woman's shoulders.

For the next hour, the crime scene unit investigators did their thing while he and Cade planned their next move.

"I'll have to question Harmon, you know." Cade said.

Trent had been dreading that from the moment he found out who'd been murdered. "I understand. To my knowledge he was at my house asleep."

"Could your brother have slipped out without you being aware?"

"Anything's possible though he doesn't have a car, and I keep the only set of keys to my Jeep with me on the nightstand."

Cade shifted his weight. Suggesting someone's relative might be guilty of such a heinous crime was never easy. "Then let's hope Harmon can give us some insight regarding this guy."

Trent shrugged. "It's doubtful as he's been out of the loop for so long."

By nine, the coroner had come and gone and the crime scene unit was packing up. Cade stretched. "Let's head out. Heaven only knows we have a ton of stuff to do tomorrow."

"Amen."

They both headed out. About the only positive thing to come out of the evening was that Trent hadn't been focused on Charlotte as much.

Once he returned home, he sat in the drive for a moment trying to sort out how he wanted to break the news to his brother. Hell, Trent didn't know if his brother would cheer or be pissed. In theory, Bill Goddard held the key to proving Harmon's innocence.

When he entered the house, Harmon was watching television, and he immediately clicked it off. "You okay?" he asked. "You look beat."

"Let me shower and grab a coffee. We need to talk."

"About?"

Trent held up a hand. "I need a minute."

He was thankful when Harmon didn't push it. The shower wasn't long enough, but he didn't want to delay the painful questions any longer. When he came out still rubbing his hair with his towel, Harmon had fixed a pot of coffee.

"Thought you could use some." Harmon nodded to the cup on the coffee table.

"Thanks."

"What do you need to talk about?" His hand raced to his chest. "Oh, shit. It wasn't Dad was it?"

It took Trent a minute to figure out what he was asking. "No, Dad's still alive."

"Thank God. For a moment I thought that was why you ran out of the restaurant."

He hadn't meant to scare Harmon. "I ran out because a crime had been committed and I was needed. Someone murdered Bill Goddard."

Trent studied his brother's facial expression, but he gave nothing away. Their father had trained them well.

"Can't say I'm sad."

Trent nodded. "Thought you might feel that way, and as much as this pains me to ask, where were you last night around midnight?" Yes, Cade would be the one asking that question officially, but he wanted to study Harmon's reaction. The coroner had put the time of death between midnight and two a.m.

In a flash, his brother's expression changed from fairly placid to livid. "What? You think I killed him?"

Trent's blood pressure soared. "I didn't say that. You had a reason to want him dead. I asked his wife the same question. Doesn't mean I think she did it."

"I was here. With you. In my bed. Asleep." He ground out each word.

"Okay. I believe you." He did.

Harmon drew his cup to his lips, drank some of the coffee, and then set it down. "Well, fuck. Now, I might never prove I was framed."

CHAPTER FIVE

CHARLOTTE WAS ARRANGING her samples on one of the tables near the back of her store, when a knock sounded on the front door. Since she wasn't open for business, she was surprised to see a well-dressed woman peering in.

Charlotte stopped what she was doing and hurried to greet her. "I'm not open for business until next Monday."

The woman's shoulders slumped. "Oh." She looked around Charlotte and into the store. "I have a job I need done quickly and was hoping you could help."

Her pulse raced. Just because all of the samples weren't in yet didn't mean she couldn't find out what this woman wanted. "Sure. Come in. Excuse the mess."

The rather wealthy looking lady glanced around and smiled. "It looks wonderful to me."

The tension in Charlotte's shoulders released. "Come over to my work station and tell me what you're interested in having done."

The lady held out her hand. "I'm Elaine Goddard, by the way."

"Charlotte Hart."

For the next hour, Charlotte listened to the woman's needs.

Turned out, their tastes were quite similar—a contemporary flare with some antiques blended in. The woman had drawn the room she wanted redone in great detail, and even showed Charlotte pictures of the space.

"It will take me a few days to draw up some plans and gather all of the samples. Then we can go over my designs and you can pick which one suits you."

Mrs. Goddard smiled then withdrew a check from her purse. "That sounds wonderful. Will a thousand dollars be enough for a retainer?"

Charlotte worked hard to keep her mouth from dropping open. Holy shit. Now she could buy a few pieces of furniture she'd been eying for her apartment. "Yes, thank you."

Elaine stood. "I'll be expecting you in a few days." And then she was gone.

Charlotte couldn't believe she already had her first client and had yet to open. Excited beyond belief, she studied the dimensions of the room Elaine had given her and then began a preliminary sketch of the new design, ideas flooding her brain.

After several hours of bending over the drawing table, her body ached, but she was pleased with the concepts she'd come up with. Wanting a break, she decided fresh air was just what she needed. That, and she wanted to share her good news with Sharon. Charlotte debated calling Patty, her boss up in Kalispell, but she thought it best to wait until she had the "before" and "after" pictures to show her.

Five minutes later, she was parked in front of her dad's private investigation office and stepped inside. Sharon jerked her head up. "Oh, hello. You startled me. I wasn't expecting anyone with your dad out of town."

"Sorry. I should have called."

"No. I'm happy for the company."

Charlotte looked around. He sure could use a makeover in here. "Am I interrupting?"

Sharon swiveled her computer screen to face her, showing a solitaire game. "Nope."

Charlotte laughed. "I'm glad. I wanted to share some good news."

Sharon stood and dragged over one of the seats from across the room. "Do tell."

"I haven't even opened and I have my first client!"

Sharon clapped. "Your mom and dad are going to be very proud."

"I hope so."

"You want some coffee?" Sharon asked. "You look like you could use some."

Charlotte dragged a hand through her tangled hair. She hadn't even taken the time to check if she was presentable. "Sure. By any chance do you know of any young men who might be willing to help move out some furniture from my client's home?"

"I bet I could find a few people for you. Need anything else?"

"I'll need a contractor and a good carpenter, even though Dad suggested I ask Alex Hendrix, a friend of his. He owns a construction firm and might be willing to help, but I want a backup in place in case he's too busy."

Sharon made notes on a pad in front of her computer. "Give me a day or two to see who I can find. I bet there are plenty of University boys willing to earn a few extra bucks."

"Great."

While Sharon fixed the drinks at the table against the wall, she looked back over her shoulder. "Has Trent contacted you?"

Just hearing his name made her pulse jack up. "Funny you should ask. We ran into each other at the shooting range a few days after Dad's party."

Sharon brought over two cups of delicious smelling coffee. "How did that go?"

"He gave me some pointers."

"Ooh. Did he wrap his arms around you?" Sharon leaved forward.

"A little." Charlotte could still feel the delicious pressure, and if she closed her eyes, she could smell his spicy scent. Trent was all man. "Because it was close to supper, he suggested we go to Italiano's. His brother works there and Trent needed to give him a lift home." Charlotte wondered if Sharon knew about Harmon.

"How's his brother doing?"

"Good. Did Trent mention him?"

"In passing. So are you going to see him again? Trent I mean, not the brother."

Her shoulders sagged. "I don't know what to do. At the end of dinner he was called away on a case, and I haven't heard from him since. It's been a couple days. What you think I should do?"

Sharon planted a hand on her chest. "*Moi?*"

"You, too, are out on the prowl." It didn't matter she was about her mom's age. "I saw the way you were eyeing Dan Hartwick. What's up with that?"

Sharon wagged her finger. "Let's not change the subject. Dan and I are a work in progress. I'm interested in him, but I can't say he feels the same way about me." She blew out a breath. "Actually, he probably considers me a thorn in his side."

"I doubt that. From what I've seen of the man, he is a bit uptight." Darn. Here she thought Sharon had at the answers. "You must have some ideas what I should do. You've been married."

She leaned back in her seat and wrapped her hands behind her head. "My motto has been if you want something, you have to go after it."

That was what Charlotte thought she'd been doing. "I believe Trent likes me, but—"

"Oh, he likes you all right. When you were talking to those other cute cops, I could almost see the smoke coming off the top of his head."

Excitement sizzled in her veins. She thought she'd caught

him stiffening when Devon had his arm around her. "Even if he does, it seems as if work is more important to him than dating."

Sharon smiled. "He sounds like Vic."

"Dad's with Mom now. What did she do to change his mind?"

Sharon lowered her arms. "Your dad never stopped loving your mother, so when she came back into his life, he knew he had to change."

So much for learning the secret of love.

Before she had a chance to pick Sharon's brain again, the office door swung open, and who should walk in, but Trent Lawson himself. She couldn't have been more surprised, and from the way he was staring at her, he hadn't expected her either.

"Charlotte, Sharon."

Sharon grinned. "What can I do for you, Trent?"

"I wanted to see when Vic was coming back to town. I need his services."

"He and Ellie are supposed to return a week from today, but you never know with those lovebirds." She winked at Charlotte. "Do you need me to schedule you an appointment?"

"That would be great. Thank you."

He faced Charlotte. "Been back to the range?"

"I wish. I've been too busy trying to open my store."

He smiled. "Let me know when you want another lesson."

Her heart flipped. She should say she'd be willing to go now, but if he turned her down because he had to work, she'd be embarrassed. Trent turned toward the front door, and Charlotte felt her chance of seeing him again slip out of her fingers.

"Hey, Trent," Sharon called.

Trent spun around. "Yes?"

"Charlotte stopped by because she has some really good news."

As much as she appreciated Sharon trying to put the two of them together, she could land Trent on her own terms. How though, she didn't know. She was about to say her news was no big deal, but then stopped because his whole demeanor had changed.

His brows rose and a small smile came to his lips. "Oh yeah? What's that?"

If Charlotte told him the details right away, he would congratulate her and be on his way. She needed to be smarter than that. "How about after your shift ends, you stop by my house for a drink and I'll tell you?" Her palms were actually sweating just asking him. Being this brave was not her style, but she was at a loss as to what else to do.

Trent held her gaze for a moment. "I can do that. I'll text you when I'm done, since I'm not sure when I'll be finished wrapping up the case for the night."

"Sounds perfect."

Trent flashed her a quick grin and Charlotte's pulse soared. As soon as the door closed behind him, she let out a small yippee.

"I'm proud of you," Sharon said.

Reality slowly filtered in. "Do you think he agreed just to be polite?"

Sharon's brows pinched. "Why would he do that?"

"I don't think I'm really what he's looking for."

"Oh, really? What kind of women do you think wants?"

"Trent is so fit and I'm, well, not." She smoothed her palms down her pants.

"Charlotte Hart! You should be ashamed of yourself. You are a beautiful young woman and Trent would be lucky to have you."

That was sweet of her to say. Sharon was overweight, too, so it would be rude to talk about being too curvy. "You're right, and since Trent will be stopping by, I need to go and get ready. Wish me luck." She pushed back her chair and gathered her things.

"Stop by anytime."

"I will, and thank you."

CHAPTER SIX

When Trent had walked into Vic's office and spotted Charlotte looking rather sleepy-eyed, something inside of him snapped. He'd worked hard not to think about her these last few days but all of his efforts had fallen apart when he neared her. Something about the woman turned him inside out. It had started when he'd protected her at the cabin, and she'd been so brave. Nothing seemed to faze her—that was until he dropped her off at his cousin's, and she'd finally broken down. To be honest, he'd been glad to know she was human after all.

Trent still wasn't sure why he'd agreed to stop over at her house after work, since from the way Charlotte had looked at him, she wanted to pick up where she left off at her Dad's birthday party—kissing him. Hell, he wanted that, too, but there were a ton of reasons why he couldn't—or rather shouldn't.

It was too late now to back down. He'd already called her and told her he was on his way. He'd picked up a bottle of Malbec wine from the store, thinking the good news meant they needed to celebrate. Even though it was a Wednesday night, this felt like a real date, and with the week he'd had, he needed some release. By release, he meant some down time. That was all.

Sure.

Trent promised himself he would share only one or two glasses of wine, congratulate her, and then head home. Being in Vic's house should be enough to squelch his desires. Hell, it wouldn't be fair to Charlotte to date her for a few days, and then have to disappear when duty called. It didn't matter that many people had relationships in which the partners were separated for periods of time. It still troubled him that he'd abandoned her at the restaurant and then had to ask her to do him a favor. Charlotte deserved so much more.

He pulled in front of Vic's house and checked the mirror to make certain he looked okay then rubbed a finger over his teeth to polish them. Now he regretted not stopping home and shaving, but he didn't need Harmon grilling him. His brother had already asked about Charlotte, and Trent told him he didn't have time for a relationship. To say the least, that didn't go over very well.

No sooner had Trent knocked than the door eased open. The harsh lighting from the party was gone, and in its place were two softly lit lamps. His cock stirred at the sight of Charlotte's glowing blonde hair. Good sense told him to turn around, but the devil of old sat on his shoulder, encouraging him to stay. From the way she was dressed, she had seduction on the mind. Boy, was he in trouble now.

"Hey. You look pretty," he said as he stepped in.

"Thanks." The light was too dim to tell if she blushed.

He held out the bottle, not trusting himself to hug her. If he touched her, he feared he might do more. "I thought we'd celebrate whatever your good news is with this."

When she clasped the gift, their fingers brushed, and his breath caught. He was a goddamn detective with nerves of steel, yet this woman seemed to have a way of making him come unraveled.

"You want to help me open this bottle?" she asked.

"Sure." Trent followed her into the kitchen and couldn't help but watch her ass sway. Charlotte looked hot in her tight pants and body-hugging shirt. He wasn't sure he'd be able to keep his hands off her, but he had to. "Where are the glasses?"

"In the cabinet above the sink."

Trent was happy to have something to do while she searched for the corkscrew. He retrieved two crystal goblets then slipped the opener from her fingers. In a matter of seconds he had the wine open.

"Let's sit in the living room and I'll tell you about my news," she said.

He wasn't expecting anything epic, but he was happy to share in her good fortune. Not wanting to be too close to her, he took the chair across from the sofa, and from the way her jaw tightened she wasn't happy with his choice. Clearly, she didn't understand how hard it was for him to sit there and not take her into his arms. He sipped his wine to be polite then set the glass on the coffee table between them. "So tell me."

She smiled and his damned out-of-control cock hardened.

"I haven't even opened the store and I have my first new client!"

That didn't really surprise him, as there weren't many interior designers in town. "Is it a big job?" He wasn't sure what he was supposed to say.

"Kind of. This woman knocks on my storefront door and asks if I'd be willing to redo her husband's office and replace it with a cozy retreat for herself."

He didn't know anything about decorating and had never been all that interested in learning, but since this was Charlotte, he did want to know more. "Is the husband okay with this?"

If he had his own man cave or office, he wouldn't want his wife to change it.

"I don't think he's in the picture anymore. Mrs. Goddard didn't think it would—"

His nerves shot to high alert. "Elaine Goddard?"

Charlotte set her glass on the coffee table and worry crossed her features. "Yes, do you know her?"

He wasn't sure how he was going to approach this topic. Mrs. Goddard wanting to redo her husband's office only a few days after his death was an interesting turn of events. "Remember when I had a run out on you and Harmon at the restaurant?"

"I couldn't forget that."

As much as he wanted to say that the dead man used to be Harmon's boss, he didn't need Charlotte interfering in that case. Knowing the sassy woman, Charlotte would start asking Mrs. Goddard questions, which could bring more trouble to his brother. Furthermore, he wasn't able to tell her much about the case as it was an ongoing investigation, but he wanted to caution her. "The man who was murdered was Bill Goddard, her husband."

Charlotte slapped a hand over her mouth, her eyes going wide. Damn.

"Why didn't she tell me?"

"Good question, though I imagine the mere mention of his death would have caused more tears to flow. As for why she asked you to redecorate so quickly after his death, I can only guess that having her husband's personal effects around could be very painful for her." Or else she wanted to erase some evidence.

"I can see that." Her voice trailed off and he wanted to wrap his arms around her, but he refrained. "Are you thinking she had something to do with her husband's death?"

For her own safety, he had to give Charlotte a few more details. "I can't discuss the case, but I can say that Mrs. Goddard seems to have an airtight alibi of where she was when her husband was murdered."

"Seems to have?"

He waved a hand. "It's what we say. We take nothing for granted."

"That's good to know since I wouldn't want to be alone with a possible murderer." She laughed, but it didn't hold a lot of joy.

"Perhaps she didn't tell me because she thought I wouldn't go into a house were a man had been killed." Charlotte looked off then chugged a good portion of her wine. "I can't believe what that poor woman must be going through. I'm so glad I'm able to help her in some small way."

He loved her compassion, but if she wasn't careful, she could end up in trouble. "Just be mindful when you're in her house."

Charlotte sat up straighter. "You just said Mrs. Goddard wasn't a suspect."

He should have kept quiet. "We don't know why Mr. Goddard was murdered, but we're hoping whatever the murderer was after, he found it. We don't need him coming back."

Charlotte tipped back her glass and finished the contents. "Way to scare me."

Now he felt like a real shit. "I'm sure you'll be fine."

What he wanted to ask was for her not to take the job, but Charlotte would never go for it.

She stood and picked up her empty glass. "I need some more to drink."

Wanting to be helpful, Trent stepped over to where Charlotte was standing, and slipped the glass from her fingers. "You relax. I'll pour you some more."

As he headed into the kitchen, he chastised himself for even mentioning there could be danger in the house, but dammit, he was a cop who happened to see evil in too many places. He also had never overcome his protective urges towards her. If he knowingly let her go back into the house and something bad happened, he'd never forgive himself.

Trent quickly poured the wine, returned, and handed her the glass. Charlotte was now seated at the end of the sofa with her back leaning against the arm, looking way too seductive, despite her face being too pale. "Are you sure you're okay?"

"I'll be fine." She smiled, but her lips trembled. "So, are you going to the sharpshooting competition on Saturday? Devon told me he plans to beat Connor Douglas."

Trent didn't like the way her eyes lit up when she said Devon's name, but he figured it was her way of not talking about the possibly scary situation. "I don't plan to. I have this case that needs attention." He raised his brows, which seemed to bring a smile to her lips.

"Doesn't Devon have cases he has to work on, too?"

Caught. "Yes. In fact, he's working on the Goddard case with me."

She planted a cute little hand on her hip. "Then how come he can take the time off and you can't?"

She sounded like Harmon. "Because I take my job seriously." And because if I go to the competition and see you there, I might do something stupid—like ask you out and then take you to bed.

Charlotte crossed her legs, and he swore she ran her lips around the rim of the glass on purpose to seduce him. "Are you the only detective who works hard?"

She was trying to bust his chops. "No."

"So tell me, Detective, what drives you? Are you trying to prove to your dad that you are the better son?"

It was as if she'd punched him in the gut, and his anger shot up. "You don't know what you're talking about." His damn voice came out too sharp. Now she'd know for sure she'd broached a very sore topic.

Charlotte stood. "Is that so? I know something about ambition and working too hard. Remember who my father is." She stepped closer, looking like she was on the warpath. "I know what it's like to see a man so driven that he ignores all the people he loves the most."

It was time to leave. Trent stood and faced her. "Congratulations again on starting your new business. I hope it works out very well for you." He forced his voice to stay even.

Charlotte set her glass down and closed the gap between them, her gaze firmly latched onto his face. He couldn't have moved if he'd wanted to. When her palms slid up his chest, he grabbed her wrists. "Charlotte?"

"Yes?" She licked her lips in a very alluring way.

"What are you doing?" He knew, but he needed to stall. His body was screaming for him to kiss her, but the rational part of him was spitting out all the reasons why he shouldn't.

"What does it look like?" Her eyes twinkled. "Don't tell me you're afraid of me?" Her sultry tone made his cock harden even more.

He inhaled and gave her his best stare. He had no idea what had triggered her change. One minute she was angry, or rather insulted, and the next she looked like she was about to devour him. "Should I be?"

"No, but that doesn't mean you aren't. I think you're afraid that you'll have fun with me if you let down your guard."

Her blue eyes, soft mouth, and fresh smell mesmerized him. "I have the willpower of steel."

"Is that so?"

"Yes." *Except around you.* He hoped she couldn't see that his heart was pounding in his chest. She was entering dangerous territory and he had no idea how to stop her.

"Then I guess you won't mind if I test my theory."

"Theory?"

His grip on her wrists loosened and she slid her arms upward, cupped his face, and kissed him. Just like he'd experienced during her drugging kiss before, his brain told him to step out of her grasp but his body wasn't getting that message. He had the sense to know that Charlotte held a lot of power over him and that he needed to be strong, but for once in his life, he didn't want to listen to reason.

He hadn't meant to let her pry his mouth open, but before he knew it, their tongues were twisting and entwined in a passionate embrace. Her full, sensual breasts pressed against his chest as her thumbs caressed his cheeks. He couldn't breathe, but he'd be damned if he broke the contact.

Trent needed to show the little girl that she was no match for him. He was a dangerous workaholic and no good for her. Taking back the control, he let his hands roam down her back and cup her ass. As her tongue plundered into his mouth tasting of bold, rich wine, he squeezed her butt, loving the fullness.

Unfortunately, the more he kissed her, the more she seemed to want from him. Somehow she managed to lower her hand and cupped his balls, and as much as he wanted to strip her naked and fuck her hard right there on the floor, he wouldn't.

Using all his willpower, Trent stepped back. "We can't."

He was certain she had no idea how hard it was for him to say those two words, but he wouldn't do this to Vic or to the lovely Charlotte. Her breaths came out fast and the urge to kiss her pink swollen mouth again surprised him in its intensity.

"Admit it. You're afraid."

She had no idea she was the match that set him on fire. "The only thing I'm afraid of is hurting you."

"I don't think you're capable of hurting anybody. Harmon told me you never harmed anything in your life."

He'd harmed his family. After Harmon left for college, his mother divorced his dad, and Trent always wondered if he'd been more affectionate, would she have stayed? He blamed himself for her leaving. Then when Harmon was arrested there was the guilt that he hadn't done everything he could to prove his brother's innocence. It didn't matter that the case belonged to the FBI. He could have done something.

Charlotte reached up and dragged a knuckle down his cheek. "Where did you go?"

Her comment startled him. "Go?"

"You seemed deep in thought."

He couldn't confide in her. If he did, it would be giving her a piece of his heart, and she deserved more. "I was."

As gently as he could, he removed her hand from between his legs, and then refused to think about how good that had felt.

"Good night, Charlotte. If at any time you feel uncomfortable being at Mrs. Goddard's house, promise you'll call me?"

She smiled as if he hadn't just broken her heart. "You can count on it, Detective."

Before he did anything reckless, Trent grabbed his coat and rushed out, praying she didn't run after him. If she pleaded with him, he just might give in.

CHAPTER SEVEN

CHARLOTTE STARED AT the door still not believing Trent had walked out on her. Her entire body was on fire, and it was like the man had just dumped a bucket of ice on her. Damn him. What was wrong with Trent?

Charlotte plopped down on the sofa and polished off her second glass of wine. Even though he'd stomped off, the man had enjoyed that kiss. She'd bet her life on it. His hands had been like hot pokers on her body, and she could still feel his touch. And then there was the kiss itself. He enjoyed exploring her mouth as much as she had his. His breath had come out fast, and the fact his cock was hard was proof that he wanted her—bad. Something was going on inside that head of his, only she didn't know what.

Trent was noble, and like her dad, probably thought his job was too dangerous to have someone in his life. While there were risks, she wasn't going to let that stop her. Hell, one of her friend's dads had a piece of meat lodged in his throat and nearly choked to death. And he worked in an office.

Too bad she didn't have any idea how to get it through that thick skull of his that she didn't care if he was a cop.

From the little bits and pieces she'd gathered about her

parents' reunion, her mom had been anything but enthusiastic about being with Dad again. Perhaps that was what made him want her even more. Playing hard to get might be Charlotte's only option with Trent, but she didn't want to go that route. If her dad had been more honest with her mom, they might never have divorced.

Until Trent came to his senses, she needed to focus on doing the best job she could at Mrs. Goddard's home, hoping for more referrals. If she and Trent were meant to be, it would happen—with some help on her part, of course.

* * *

ON SATURDAY, CHARLOTTE finished her final designs just in time to head out to the sharp shooting competition. About twenty people, some cops and some family members, stood or were seated behind the glass partition ready to watch the show.

Charlotte studied the backs of the six men readying to participate and recognized a few of them. Devon was fourth from the left, Connor stood next to him, and Cade Carter, who she recognized from her dad's birthday party, was in the first stall.

Sharon had said she was going to be there, but at the last minute had to cancel because her cat had taken sick. Charlotte bet if her dad had been in town he'd have come, and if the competition hadn't been limited to cops, her father might have entered. He'd have won, too—not that she was prejudiced or anything.

A voice bellowed over the intercom announcing the competition was about to begin. The men picked up their guns and readied themselves. With all the firepower, she was happy to be behind the glass partition. Despite the barrier between them, when the orange light flashed above their targets, and the guns went off, the sound reverberated, making her wish she'd worn ear protection.

Because she was so far from the target, she was unable to tell who had the better score. Everyone seemed to have hit the black circle. While she didn't know Devon very well, she hoped he was pleased with his performance.

"Hello," said a voice behind her.

Her heart nearly tripped over itself. What was Trent doing here? Charlotte spun around and his gaze on her face was like sunshine on a dreary day.

"Hi, I didn't expect this to see you here." He'd said he wasn't coming. Every time Trent was near, he threw her off balance, and Charlotte needed a moment to calm down.

"I came to see *you*."

She couldn't believe it, especially after how they'd left things a few days ago. Her pulse raced, and her mouth seemed unable to respond. His beautiful green eyes shimmered, and all she wanted to do was to sink into those pools of desire. No wait. Had something bad happened? Probably not or he wouldn't look so lustful.

"About what?"

He lifted one shoulder. "Felt bad about how I keep running out on you."

For real? Joy streaked through her. This was too good to be true. She was about to ask him to elaborate when another round of gunfire exploded, preventing anyone from carrying on a conversation. Trent smiled and turned her around. It was almost as if he could tell she was going to ask something personal. Dang. At least with him behind her, she was able to inhale and compose herself. This must be round two as only three men remained.

"I see Devon survived the first cut," he said, his lips too close to her ear. His breath tickled the hairs on her neck and sent shivers of delight right between her legs.

He must have thought she'd come just to see Devon. "So it seems."

"Who are you cheering for?"

So that was the reason for the visit. Charlotte debated what to say then decided to go with the truth. "No one in particular."

She'd come to study their expert form and execution to help improve her shooting. Since Devon had asked her, she thought it only polite to show up because she'd said she would.

When Trent stepped next to her, her shoulder touched his arm. He smiled, and sparks of need raced through her. She really needed to gain some control of herself, especially if this relationship wasn't going anywhere—or was it?

For the next few minutes they watched the pool go from three men down to two. Finally, the targets were pulled down for the judges to check the scores.

With his weapon down and his ear protection off, Devon turned around, spotted her in the crowd, and waved. She glanced up at Trent and his posture stiffened. Stupid man. Trent had to know she only had eyes for him.

Charlotte had no idea how long it would take the judges to choose a winner, but she wanted to stay long enough to learn the outcome. While they waited, she turned toward Trent. "Any news on the case?"

A small smile spread across his face, and he slowly shook his head. "You know better than to ask, Ms. Hart. There was one thing I forgot to mention, however."

"What's that?"

"Did you know that Mr. Goddard was Harmon's boss at Ardton Investments?"

She searched her brain but came up empty. "No, I had no idea. When your brother and I were talking, he mentioned who he worked with and who he thought might have framed him, but I honestly didn't pay attention to the names. Do you think this will affect his ability to prove his innocence?"

Trent stared at her for a long minute. "What makes you so sure he wasn't involved in insider trading?"

"I can't be sure, but I'm pretty good at reading people." She failed to keep the challenge from her voice. If Trent didn't believe his own brother, the proof must have been damning. Her heart sank for both of them. At least, Harmon had done his time.

Trent's face softened. "I hope you're right. It's the cop in me that wants to question everything."

Her father was the same way.

Trent placed his palm on her back and twisted her toward the glass enclosure. "Dan Hartwick is about to make the announcement of the winner."

As much as she had been interested in who won, she wanted to learn about Trent more.

"Ladies and gentlemen, thank you for coming out. It is very important that the fine men of Rock Hard Police Department do their best for its citizens, so I am pleased to announce that the winner of this year's indoor sharpshooting competition is Connor Douglas."

Devon and Connor shook hands as the audience applauded and cheered.

Trent's hand returned to her back. "Care to join me for dinner?"

She hadn't expected the invitation—now or ever. "I'd love to, thank you." Today had turned out better than she'd ever thought possible.

"Do you mind walking?" he asked.

"Not at all."

As Trent escorted her outside, she thought Devon had called her name, but right now, all she wanted to do was be with Trent. Charlotte tried to tamp down her expectations about their date and prayed she wouldn't blow it. The last two times she'd been the one to kiss him, and that had ended badly. She hoped that if he came back to her place tonight, she'd be able to control herself.

She looked up at Trent. "Do you think you could've beaten Connor?"

"Doubtful. I have every intention of spending some time at the range each week, but I seem to be too busy."

Trent didn't look happy about working all the time. "Have you considered slowing down? Or maybe even working as a private investigator?"

His brows rose. "Do you think I'd be happy doing what your dad does?"

She honestly hadn't given it a lot of thought. "I know my father is a lot happier not working for the FBI because now he can pick and choose the cases he works. I think having my mother in his life again has changed him. Dad wants to spend more time with her. I wouldn't be surprised if he hires someone to lighten his load."

"I'll keep that employment opportunity in mind, but I like to think that as a cop, I'm doing some good for society."

His attitude was admirable. They arrived at the Steerhouse and as soon as they stepped inside, she could see this was a really nice place. "Do you come here often?"

"You mean do I take my dates here?"

She wasn't sure what she was asking. "Maybe."

"No. I don't date all that often."

The hostess seated them quickly since it was still early for dinner, and the waiter rushed over and took their drink order.

"I'll have a glass of the house red wine," she said.

"Beer for me." Trent leaned back in the seat. "I don't know what to do about you, Charlotte Hart."

Oh, shit. "Do?"

"I like you. In fact I like you a lot."

I knew it! She almost jumped out of her seat. Keeping calm was almost impossible, though she didn't know why he seemed so concerned about the situation. "You have a funny way of showing it sometimes." Damn. She just couldn't seem to keep her mouth shut. Her mom always accused her of speaking her mind too often, and she was right.

He unrolled the white linen napkin, removed the utensils,

and placed the cloth on his lap. "Here's the thing: you deserve better."

Her jaw dropped. "How can you say that?"

"I'm good at my job and am able to protect people, but I'm not really good with emotions. You'd only get hurt in the end."

She wished he'd stop saying that. "How about letting me decide?"

He blew out a breath and glanced to the side. "I know Harmon mentioned our dad was a cop."

"He did, and he also said your father had high standards for himself, which you inherited."

His eyes slightly widened. "Harmon said that?"

"Yes. Your dad was a workaholic and that in the end it cost him his health and his wife. Is that what you're aspiring to?"

"Fuck," he said under his breath. "I'm not trying to be like my dad. I know I have my faults, but helping people makes me feel good."

"Helping people makes me feel good, too, but it doesn't mean you have to give your life for the job. There are more important things than work." *Like someone to love.*

The waiter delivered their drinks, and Trent tipped back his beer. "I'm not sure if I can change. Being ambitious is built into who I am as a person."

His answer seemed too simple. "What about your mother?"

His green eyes darkened. "I guess Harmon didn't tell you the whole story. My mother was killed a year after she divorced my father. I was only twelve."

Pain stabbed her gut. She wished she hadn't asked. "I'm very sorry."

He dragged his thumb down the label tearing the paper into shreds. "I was at her house complaining about having no cookies to eat. I whined so much that she gave in and went to the store. On her way, some criminal avoiding capture slammed into the driver's side of her car, and she died immediately."

"How terrible. Were you with her?"

"No. I stayed back at her house."

A strong ache coursed through her. "I can't imagine what you went through. What did you do when she didn't show up?"

"It was all a blur. I called Dad, and eventually, he came and picked me up. I can't imagine what he went through though, having to tell me my mother was dead." He looked up to the ceiling and pressed his lips together. It looked as if the guilt was still eating at him. "All because I wanted a bag of cookies."

"It wasn't your fault. You couldn't have known she'd be in a accident."

He returned his gaze to her and tapped his skull. "I know that up here, but in my heart, I regret it every day."

Trent needed to give himself a break. "How did Harmon take the news?"

"He was at school at the time. He came home for a week after she died, but then threw himself into his studies. It was his way of coping." Trent leaned forward on his elbows. "Cops put their life on the line every single day. We chose our profession knowing full well we could be snuffed out at any moment, but my mother didn't deserve to die that way."

Charlotte reached out and cupped his hand. "No one deserves to die that way, but bad stuff happens." His pain seemed to radiate from deep within. "You were just a kid, but even as an adult, you couldn't have prevented it."

"I guess." He huffed out a breath. "I never understood what really happened between her and my father to make her leave in the first place. Dad never would talk about it. When I asked my mom, she just said she couldn't take the long hours and never knowing if dad would come home at night. At the time, I didn't really believe her. I always thought that if I had been a better kid, she might have stayed."

The agony streaming across his face tore at her heart. Charlotte shook her head. "I felt the same way. Only it was with my dad."

He looked hard at her. "How? You told me a few things about

the situation in the cabin, but I thought Vic left your mom because his job was too dangerous."

"That's what he told us, but after he left, I wondered if I hadn't complained to my dad so much about missing my birthday parties and him not spending Christmas with us, he might have stayed. Like you, I thought if I'd been better, he wouldn't have walked out of our lives. I was older than you, but I still thought the world revolved around me. At the time, I had no idea that my father was willing to give his life for this country, and that his leaving had nothing to do with me.

Since the incident with the stalker, Dad and I have talked a lot. His biggest regret was not seeing me grow up. I'm just thrilled we were given a second chance."

She sipped her wine to clear the clogging in her throat. When she looked up, Trent had a small smile on his face that she could best describe as passion.

"Harmon was right," he said. "We do have a lot in common."

CHAPTER EIGHT

TRENT HAD NEVER connected with someone as much as he had with Charlotte. She really seemed to get him, in part because they both had a parent who had issues dealing with his job. Somehow in telling his story, Trent could see that he, too, had been quite full of himself by thinking his mom's death had been his fault. That guilt, along with being a cop, made him keep his distance from women. In hindsight, that might have been a cover up for some deeper issue. Charlotte was right in another way, too. People died for all sorts of reasons, yet he thought it ironic that his father was still alive despite having been in many shootouts.

After dinner, Trent told Charlotte that he wanted to follow her home because he needed to make sure she made it safely, and that while she'd only had two drinks over a two-hour period, her reflexes could be impaired. The truth was that he wanted to follow her home because he hoped she'd invite him in.

Trent pulled to a stop behind Charlotte's car in front of her house and rushed to open her car door.

As she slipped out, she looked up and smiled. "Do you want to come in?"

"I was hoping you'd ask," he said, mentally pumping his fist.

This time, if Charlotte kissed him, he wouldn't stop her. Hell, it would take all of his willpower not to rip off her clothes and make love to her for hours on end.

He escorted her onto the porch where she stuck her hand into her purse and then frowned. "I know the front door key is in here someplace."

He was about to ask why she didn't keep it on the same ring as her ignition, but he didn't want to imply she wasn't capable of handling herself. He hoped she found it, as he didn't want to have to take her back to his place since Harmon would be there. Tomorrow his brother was thankfully moving into his own apartment.

She lifted the key in her fingers. "Ta da!"

"Good job."

In seconds, she had the door open. When she flipped on the rather glaring overhead light, he appreciated the soft lamps she'd had on before.

Charlotte would probably offer him coffee or perhaps another beer, and then they'd talk about her new business or one of his old cases, as she seemed fascinated by the scope of his job. As much as he enjoyed chatting, once he'd decided that he wanted Charlotte, his patience had run out. The urge to undress her one piece at a time was driving him crazy.

They both slipped off their jackets, and as she placed them on the back of the sofa Trent moved toward her. "Did I tell you how hot you look tonight?"

She might not be wearing a sweater as tight as the one she had on the other night, but her soft pullover showed off her curves just as well.

She grinned and stroked her chin. "I can't recall. Maybe you did."

"If my words didn't sink in, then perhaps I need to show you." His cock turned rigid at the thought of kissing her.

"Oh, yeah?"

Charlotte moved close and placed her palms on his chest, the heat from her fingers searing through the shirt to his skin. He wanted to kiss her so badly he could taste it, but he didn't want to rush her. It didn't matter that she'd come on to him twice before. Life had taught him that he should take it slowly, but damn, whenever he was around Charlotte, his common sense seemed to vanish.

She grabbed hold of his shirt, and when she tugged it out of his jeans, all he could think of was getting her naked and then sucking on those luscious tits.

"I thought you'd be more comfortable this way." She dragged her fingers close to his throat and lightly brushed his chest hairs. "So soft."

He wiggled a bit. "It's a little tight around the neck. Do you think you can do something about that?"

She bit down on her lip in the sexiest way possible. "I can try."

Slower than dripping molasses, she threaded the top one he'd buttoned through the hole and then moved down to the second one.

"That feels much better. Please keep going." His mouth was dry, and he should ask for a beer, but he didn't want to stop the seduction.

She stepped even closer if that was possible and looked up at him. "If I didn't know any better, I'd say you were trying to seduce me, Detective."

Hell, yeah, he was. "And if I am?"

As she ran a finger down the length of his shirt and unbuttoned it from the bottom upward, her scent distracted him. The woman had totally bewitched him.

"How do I know I can trust you?" she asked, looking rather innocent.

Once she finished unbuttoning his shirt, Charlotte slipped her hands under the material and slowly dragged her palms downward, testing his resolve.

"Trust me?" Either what she was doing to him had messed with his head or she was trying to be coy.

She wrapped her hands around his waist and pressed her body against him. "If I recall, you always walk out on me after I kiss you."

Ah. He'd apologized for that hurtful action at dinner—a few times. "I don't remember any such thing." He raised his chin, trying to look offended, but he probably failed.

"Hmm. Then is it safe to say that if I kiss you, you won't run away?"

Trent couldn't keep his hands off the little temptress any longer and threaded his fingers through her hair, his palms cupping her cheeks. "I say give it a go and hope for the best."

Her hands slid down to his butt, and this time it was her turn to squeeze each cheek. "How about you kiss me?"

"Do you think you can handle what might come afterward?" His damned heart was beating way too fast.

She slid her hands around to the front and popped open the top button of his jeans. "You won't know unless you try."

That was all he needed to hear. Trent leaned over and kissed that sassy mouth of hers. For one night, he wouldn't think about whether he was good enough for her; he'd just enjoy the moment. When she slid her tongue into his mouth, his need exploded, and the urge to take her hard nearly did him in. Charlotte deserved to be loved and not fucked, but right now he wasn't sure if he could go slow.

As their tongues dipped and parried, she seduced his mouth. Needing air, he broke the kiss. "I'm not running out on you this time. I promise."

She grinned. "You better not."

Trent dragged a finger between her breasts. "To ensure I stay, perhaps you ought to take off your top."

She laughed, and the pleasure shot straight through him. "You want to help?"

"Fuck, yeah."

CHARLOTTE COULDN'T BELIEVE she was about to make love with Trent Lawson, the man she'd been dreaming about for months. Sure, it was great that he'd protected her when someone was out to harm her, but it was the way he treated her that she really loved. Trent was kind and considerate, and she bet he'd be that way in bed, too. He acted as if he was always in control, but now she could see that he was dealing with inner demons and was probably afraid to let loose.

He dragged his hands under her sweater, and when he cupped her breasts, every nerve in her body shot to life. Needing to see more of him, she popped open the rest of the buttons on his jeans. She meant to keep her focus on his face so that she could tell what he was thinking, but his hard cock sticking out let her know what was on his mind. "Someone's happy to be free."

"You have no idea."

He slid his hands around her back and unhooked her bra in a second. When his thumbs reached in front and strummed her nipples, her legs weakened. His very touch sent her spiraling.

"Somebody likes to be stroked, I see."

"Maybe." From the way her fingers were trembling and her breathing was too fast, he had to know she was lying. "Perhaps if you take off my sweater you might have a better idea if I'm enjoying it."

As if a pistol had sounded, signaling the start of a race, he whipped off her top and tossed it on the back of the sofa. Cool air pebbled her nipples.

"Excellent suggestion," he said. "Now where was I?"

Charlotte slowly lowered the straps and let her bra drop to the floor. "I think you were about to lick these."

He grinned and cupped each breast. "You are so gorgeous. Perfect in every way."

Her heart skipped a beat at his words. She was a bit heavy

and had worried he wouldn't find her body attractive. Perhaps she'd been wrong.

"Let's get you more comfortable," he said.

Still holding her tits, he maneuvered her backward until her rear bumped into the side of the sofa, forcing her to sit on the arm. He then leaned over and suckled one nipple while he strummed his thumb across the other tip. Shards of bliss radiated across her body, and she dropped her head back to revel in the pleasure then had to grab his shoulders to keep from falling. What she really wanted to do was latch onto his cock. But her time would come.

He nabbed the hardened peak between his teeth and pulled it taut before moving to the other side. Each tug lit up her body, and she wanted to beg him to take her right then and there. She didn't though, because she wanted this moment to go on forever.

She dragged her palms up to his head and clamped onto his scalp. "I like to suck on things, too," she said a bit too breathy.

Trent lifted his head. "I'm a firm believer in equal opportunity." He stepped back, kicked off his shoes, and stepped out of his jeans. "You want to give him a go?"

She dragged a finger down his covered dick. "I'd like to try him out."

"I'm all yours." He held out his arms.

She grinned, excitement sizzling in her veins. Still seated, she dipped her thumbs into the waistband of his briefs and tugged them down. What popped out had her mouth opening in total awe. "He's huge. I hope I'm not in over my head."

Trent chuckled. "I can be gentle. Or not." He stepped out of his briefs and kicked them to the side.

Wanting to taste him, she drew his hard shaft toward her and rimmed the edge of his mushroom-shaped cock with her tongue, loving his slightly salty tang. He groaned and then grabbed a chunk of her hair.

"Better not take too long if you want me to reciprocate." His words came out tight.

The thought of him licking her pussy had heat pooling between her thighs. Pumping her hand up and down his cock, she licked the tip.

"Suck on it."

She loved how his voice sounded more like a growl. Wanting to please him, she drew him deep into her mouth, and as she swiped her tongue around and around, the tension on her hair tightened.

Wanting to see how far she could push him, she rolled his balls with her palm, eliciting a soft moan. When the tip oozed a bit of cum, Charlotte feared she might have pushed him over the edge too quickly. Letting go, she dragged her tongue up and down his length.

"Enough." Trent stepped out of her reach then lifted her leg and tugged off each shoe. He drew her to a stand and unbuttoned then unzipped her pants. "Did you wear something special underneath your jeans for me?"

She laughed. "I didn't expect to see you today, remember?"

"If you had, would you have worn a bit of frill to entice me?"

Keeping things a bit mysterious seemed a better choice. "I'm not telling."

Trent licked his lips, dragged down her pants then whistled. "I like virginal white."

"Virginal, huh?"

He chuckled. Holding onto his shoulders, she stepped out of her jeans. Now dressed only in her panties, she wrapped her arms around her belly.

Trent eased open her arms. "None of that. I love the way you look, especially your womanly curves."

Warmth flitted up her cheeks. "Thank you." She had never been insecure about her looks until she'd met Trent. For him, she wanted to be perfect.

"Hold still, and let me love you the way you deserve."

Charlotte couldn't wait.

CHAPTER NINE

Trent dropped to his knees and slipped off her panties. "A true blonde." He grinned.

"You match, too."

"I hope so." He had her sit back on the sofa arm then spread her legs wide. "I can't tell you how often I've dreamt of being here with you like this."

Her pulse raced. "After you dropped me off at your cousin's house, I didn't think you ever thought about me." She wasn't looking for a compliment but rather the truth.

"You have no idea." He dragged his palms up her thighs and opened her folds with his thumbs.

The first swipe of his tongue had her reeling so much, she didn't care that his comment gave away nothing. Clutching the arm of the sofa, she inhaled deeply, trying to hold on as he flicked her clit back and forth, electrifying her. Her breaths came out faster and faster. She wanted to tell him to slow down, that she was close to tipping over the edge, but the intense joy running rampant inside made her keep quiet. With her free hand, she dug her nails into his shoulder.

"I need your cock." Begging sounded unsexy, but she couldn't help it. Trent's velvety swipes were heating her core to the boiling point.

He looked up at her and smiled. "Just take it easy. I've got a long way to go."

She'd never last. "You couldn't handle it when I was sucking on you."

He lifted one shoulder. "You're right. I'm weak around you."

While nice to hear, it didn't help slow her need. He threaded a finger deep into her pussy and swirled around causing chaos to descend. The tension inside her escalated, and she closed her eyes to keep control. If it hadn't been forever since she'd had sex, and if this hadn't been Trent, Charlotte might have been able to last. When he pressed on her G-spot, she lost it. As her orgasm swept over her, a strange gurgling noise rushed out of her mouth.

Trent withdrew his finger, looked up, and smiled. "That feel good?"

He didn't need to ask. "It would feel a lot better with something thicker, bigger, and harder inside me. Got anything like that?" She flicked a glance to his throbbing cock.

Trent stood, the corner of his mouth lifting. "I think I can accommodate you."

He bent down, pulled out his wallet, and retrieved a condom. He waved the packet. "Cops always come prepared."

She laughed, wondering if that were true, or if he'd gone to the competition with the intent of seducing her. She was on the pill, but it was better to be safe than sorry. "May I?"

He ripped open the foil. "Sorry. I don't trust you not to work your magic on me." Once he extracted the condom, he rolled it down his cock.

He drew her to her feet, twisted her around, and pressed lightly on her back. Bent over, she palmed the sofa arm. Standing behind her, he widened her legs with his foot and anticipation coiled deep within her. Her insides clenched in desperate need of him. "Hurry."

Trent cupped her breasts as his chest met her back. His

heated body and his strong fingers overwhelmed her. The moment he wedged his cock between her legs, a rush of electricity soared through her. This was her every wish come true.

She wiggled her ass, hoping he'd understand what she desired. He pinched both nipples and a quick blast raised her need to a new level. It almost wasn't fair that he could touch her and yet she couldn't enjoy him.

No wait. Charlotte dropped down onto one elbow, freeing up a hand then reached between her legs and stroked his cock.

"Watch it there. It's about to go off."

"So am I."

Trent placed the tip of his cock at her entrance and eased in about an inch. Just that much heated her from the inside out. He slid her hair across her neck and placed tiny kisses on her shoulder, leaving a trail of scorching bliss in its wake.

He inhaled deeply. "You smell so fucking good."

Not able to wait any longer, Charlotte pressed her hips back, which drove his cock in halfway. Her inner wall stretched and fluttered around him, and when she tightened her hold, he groaned. She was getting to him. If only she could last a little longer they could ride this divine wave together.

He massaged her breasts as he slowly forged into her the rest of the way, sending erotic pulses to her whole body. As often as she had dreamed about this moment, she'd never imagined it could be this good.

"I want all of you," Trent said as he drove into her hard.

"Ah, yes." Her body soared as shutters racked her, and she held her breath, waiting for the pulses to subside.

With each thrust, Charlotte flew higher and higher. Fingers of lust lit her insides and she clamped down hard on his cock. The divine friction brought her climax closer, forcing her to lower her head and grip the sofa tighter. His hands slipped to her hips and held her tight as he pounded into her over and over again. Their bodies slickened with sweat, their grunts and moans took on a romantic rhythm.

"I can't wait any longer," he huffed.

She was so lost in her spiraling journey that she could barely answer him. "Uh-huh."

He held on tight, thrust into her once more, and then exploded. The powerful pulsing jettisoned her toward her climax, and a wave of emotion swept over her.

His hands slipped upward and then he wrapped his arms around her, his breath coming out hard. A minute later, Trent finally pulled out, but Charlotte was too tired to move. He returned a minute later with a warm cloth and wiped her clean.

"You want me to carry you into the bedroom?" he asked.

Charlotte dropped onto the sofa not caring that she was naked. Her muscles had totally fatigued. "How about a drink first?"

Trent grinned. "You got it."

* * *

ON SUNDAY, WHEN Trent called and said he'd be spending the day helping Harmon move into his apartment, Charlotte told him that was fine. What she didn't mention was that she, too, would be at her new place waiting for her furniture to be delivered from Kalispell. Having gone through the moving process before, she understood that it was a dirty, nasty job, and there was no way she wanted Trent to see her in her cleaning attire.

Possibly because Sharon felt bad for not showing up at the shooting competition, she had offered to come over and help with the unpacking.

"I'm really sorry for skipping out on you," Sharon said as she opened a box labeled dishes. "Who won?"

"Connor beat Devon. It was rather exciting." At least the part she'd actually watched had been.

"Dan was there, wasn't he?" Sharon didn't make eye contact, but Charlotte could tell the question was important. From Sharon's dreamy voice, she was as hooked on Trent's boss as

Charlotte was on Trent, and she hoped neither of them would be disappointed. "Yes, Detective Hartwick was the announcer."

She snapped her fingers. "Damn. I should have gone, and just so you know, I'm not in the habit of standing up people, but my kitty had an emergency."

"I understand. We can't control everything in our lives." She stood back and studied the placement of the dining room table. "Actually, it turned out for the best."

Sharon placed the last dish in the dishwasher. "That so?"

"Yup. Trent showed up."

Sharon raised her brows and smiled. "Didn't you tell me he said he wasn't going?"

"He said that, but then he felt so bad for running out on me after I kissed him at Dad's birthday party that he stopped by to apologize." That wasn't the complete truth, but Charlotte wasn't about to mention that after she'd invited him over to her house to celebrate getting the Goddard job, he'd done the same thing.

Sharon finished stacking the dishes then opened a new box. "And what did this apology entail?"

Charlotte did a last minute adjustment on the table and then came into the kitchen. "He took me to dinner at the Steerhouse."

She straightened. "Oooh. He must've felt really bad. That's only the most expensive restaurant in town."

She'd noticed how pricey everything had been. "I figured. Then after dinner, he claimed he wanted to make sure I got home safely, so he followed me back to my house."

Sharon stopped unpacking the next box. "I may not be as good reading people as your father, but from the light in your eyes and the smile you've been fighting, I'd say you succeeded in seducing him."

Charlotte couldn't hold it in any more. "Yes, and it was amazing." She practically jumped up and down.

Sharon hugged her. "I'm so happy for you. Maybe I'll be getting pointers from you in the future on how to land a man."

She laughed. "I can't exactly say I've *landed* Trent. As soon as he has to do something for his next case, I will play second fiddle, but I'm all right with that. I understand ambition and the need to do what you have to."

"You've learned well from your parents. Noble men are hard to find."

"I know."

"So what's your plan?"

Charlotte really hadn't thought about it in that way. "I need to concentrate on doing the best job I can for Mrs. Goddard, and when the time's right, Trent and I will be together."

"And if he doesn't call for a few days?" Sharon opened the cupboard next to the oven and put away the pots.

"I don't really expect him to. He's working on a murder case. I imagine he'll have to talk to a lot of people and fill out reams of paperwork. If I'm too pushy, he'll run. I think he feels enough pressure in his life."

"Smart. How do you think Trent sees the relationship? Do you think he wants you in his life, or are you merely a booty call?"

"A booty call? No. At least, I don't think so, though when we're near each other, we can't seem to keep our hands off one another." Charlotte shook her head. "Sorry. That was too much information."

Sharon laughed. "I get it. I was young. Once."

"Trent seems like the serious type, and not a guy who does a one night stand. He has some issues to work through, and I'm willing to wait for him."

Sharon closed the cabinet door, picked up a cloth, wet it, and swiped it across the counter. "I can see you have a lot of your mother in you."

"Thank you. I'm trying to be a little more tolerant than she was, though. Having a child to raise had to have been hard. I'm lucky that Trent's not with the FBI or going undercover."

Sharon pulled out more pots and pans from the box. "What

happens if he has to protect another witness, one that might be beautiful and young?"

A pain stabbed her in the heart. "If that's going to happen, I hope it's after Trent and I have been together for a while. Everything is new right now, and we're trying to understand each other."

"How old did you say you were?"

Charlotte laughed. "Twenty-four."

"You're wise for your age." Sharon was about forty-five, but acted as if she was ninety or something.

Charlotte finished taking out the rest of the pots from the box. "I think it's because it was mostly me and my mom for so long. Much of the time, Dad was gone. With her working a lot, I had to be independent. I just hope that I don't inherit my mom's stubborn streak when it comes to men."

Sharon smiled. "I think you'll do just fine."

Charlotte crossed her fingers. "Let's hope."

CHAPTER TEN

AFTER HELPING HARMON move all day, Trent was hungry and his back ached. He thought about calling Charlotte during one of their breaks, but he wasn't sure what he'd say. Thanks for the amazing sex? I appreciate you listening and understanding about my guilt-ridden childhood? I'd like to be with you more, but I have a killer to find?

Fuck. This might be why he didn't have a steady girlfriend. Knowing the right thing to say and do often eluded him. Not to mention, there were never enough hours in the day to do a good job and have a relationship. Something had to give.

After he showered and grabbed a bite, it was past nine. If he called Charlotte, she'd probably suggest he come over for a nightcap, and he didn't have the willpower to turn her down. Knowing them, one thing would lead to another, and he wouldn't do that to her. Charlotte wasn't the type of woman a guy only saw just to have sex with. While she'd never come out and said she was looking for the white picket fence and two kids, he could tell that was what she dreamed of. Family was important to her.

He wasn't all that experienced in understanding the dynamics of a family unit. Growing up, Harmon was always doing his thing, too busy to play with a little brother. His dad worked all the time and his mom left when he was in fifth grade. In the end, Trent learned that the police force was his family, and that they'd always be there for him. Did he yearn for more? Fuck, if he knew.

The next morning, when he arrived at work, he had to fight to keep focused. He'd rather think about Charlotte than finding a killer.

"You get a hold of Frank Hamilton yet?" Dan Hartwick asked, suddenly appearing in front of his desk. Trent swore the man had the ability to materialize at will.

He jerked out of his reverie. "I have an appointment with him at ten. He's been out of town since the murder."

"So, he's not a suspect?" Dan's brows pinched.

"He flew to New York on the seven a.m. flight the morning after Bill died, so he's not in the clear. In fact, he looks like our most likely candidate. He's back in town now."

"Were you able to dig up any dirt on him?"

"Not much. I spoke to Harmon, who thought Frank was the more honest of the two partners, but my brother didn't really trust either one of them."

Dan nodded. "Good luck then."

A few minutes later, Trent gathered his stuff and headed out. He'd be going right by Charlotte's store and the urge to stop was strong, but he didn't want to be late to Ardton Investments. Besides, once he started chatting with her, he might not want to leave.

Trent parked in front of the marble clad building and headed inside. He didn't want to think back to the time when he used to come here to visit his all important and rich brother. The ache still dug at him.

The receptionist was new—or at least since his brother had worked there—and she told him to wait in the reception area while she went in search of Mr. Hamilton. Out of habit, Trent's gaze shot to the office where Harmon used to work, occupied now by someone new. Instead of two bosses and two brokers, there was now one boss and about six brokers, implying the firm was doing quite well.

Shortly after the receptionist stepped into Frank's office, he rushed out and held out his hand. "Trent, good to see you again. I wish it were under better circumstances. Come on inside."

Trent was taken aback. He'd expected a cooler reception. After all, Trent had practically accused Frank of setting up Harmon. To his credit, Frank had been quite shocked that Trent's brother had been involved in something illegal. When he told Harmon later on about Frank's reaction, his brother reminded him that stockbrokers were often the best actors in the world.

Frank motioned Trent take a seat in front of his desk. "I'm still in shock over Bill's murder. Do you have any clues?" he asked, sitting down and straightening the items in front of him.

"We're working on it." He wasn't about to give anything away.

Trent would have asked where Frank was at midnight the evening Bill was murdered, but most likely Frank would say he was asleep in bed next to his wife. The funny thing about late night murders was that it was easy to sneak out of a house, kill someone, and be back before anyone knew it.

He dismissed the thought as soon as he remembered that Cade had asked him what Harmon had been doing at the time of the murder, too.

"How can I help?" Frank asked.

"I'll begin by asking who would want Bill dead?"

Frank slightly shook his head. "That would be any client who lost a lot of money, I suppose."

He sounded like Bill's wife. "You wouldn't want to share that information with me, would you?"

Frank leaned back in his seat. "Detective, you know better than to ask. My livelihood would evaporate if I handed over the names of our clients."

Trent expected that answer, but he needed to ask anyway. "Do you think there exists a client who would be irate enough to murder?"

"I hope to hell not. I sure don't want to end up like Bill." He visibly shuddered.

"Who stood to gain the most by Bill's death?"

Frank placed a hand on his chest. "Are you asking if I'm in Bill's will, or if the company is now mine after his death?" Trent hadn't expected such defensiveness.

"It was merely a general question." It was always better to remain non-committal.

Frank stabbed a hand through his slicked-back hair. "Bill and I did not discuss each other's wills, though I imagine everything would go to Elaine. As for the company's assets, she'll get half of the profits for the rest of the year, and then her income stream ends since I'll be the one doing the work from this point forward."

Trent wasn't getting far with this line of questioning, though he didn't really expect to. "Let's talk about Elaine Goddard."

"What about her?"

Trying to act casual, Trent stretched out his legs. "If she were to benefit from her husband's death, say from his life insurance policy, do you think she would be capable of killing him or having him killed?" Just because she was at her sister's the night before, didn't mean she couldn't have snuck out.

Frank's face colored. "Anything's possible. Can't say their marriage was a match made in heaven."

Trent didn't remember hearing about any discontent before, though there was probably no reason anyone would have brought it up. "Was Bill unfaithful?" Perhaps a jealous lover did him in.

"I think you're barking up the wrong tree, Detective. Try Elaine."

"She's having an affair?" Perhaps it was her lover who decided to do in Bill. Christ. Trent had more suspects than he knew what to do with.

"I can't speak from experience. I tried to stay as far away from her as possible. Perhaps you should ask Harmon."

Trent's blood pressure shot up. "Harmon's been in jail for the last three years. He was released just last week."

"I am very aware of that, Detective, but when Harmon was at the firm, Elaine set her sights on him."

Trent's gut tightened. "What are you suggesting?"

"All I'm saying is that Bill's wife is trouble. She has a way about her to get people to do things for her. Now if you'll excuse me, Detective, I have trades I need to place."

Trent knew that was all he was going to extract from the man today, so he stood. "Thank you for your help. I hope you understand that I need to ask you to remain in town until we find Bill's killer."

His eyes widened. "Am I a suspect?"

"Everyone who knew Bill Goddard is a suspect. Good day."

* * *

EVEN THOUGH CHARLOTTE'S designs were solid, she was a little nervous about showing her work to Mrs. Goddard. She was confident that Patty, her boss back in Kalispell, would say they were the best she'd ever done, but since this was the first time she'd been out on her own, Charlotte wanted to make a good impression.

Charlotte rang the bell at the Goddard home, pleased that the sophistication of her design seemed to match the exterior of the house.

Footsteps sounded and a moment later a very elegant looking Mrs. Goddard opened the door and smiled. "Did you have any trouble finding the place?" she asked as she motioned her inside.

"No. My GPS was spot on."

Mrs. Goddard nodded to the folder in Charlotte's hand. "Are those for the new room?"

"Yes, and I can't wait for you to see what I've come up with."

"Me, neither. Let me show you to Bill's office and then we can take a look at what you've done. I hope my dimensions and photos were good enough to give you an idea of what the place looked like."

So did Charlotte, but if she had to redo the design, she would. Usually, she asked to see the place first, but Mrs. Goddard had been in such a hurry that Charlotte had agreed to do the drawings sight unseen.

Her client led her down a small hallway and then through a set of double doors where light from a bay window streamed in. Excitement filled her. "It's really a lovely space."

"I'm hoping someone can use Bill's sofa, chairs, and desk."

The furniture looked like fine leather and the desk could have been handmade. Charlotte still couldn't believe Mrs. Goddard wanted to get rid of everything. "You sure you want me to take all of this? You don't want to try to sell a few things?" There were books, a computer, plants, and beautifully framed photos, much of which looked valuable.

Mrs. Goddard waved a hand. "Bill decorated his office and picked out all of the furniture." She pulled out a handkerchief from her pocket and dabbed her eyes. "It's too painful for me to look at his things any more. I've even arranged for someone to come in and clean out his closet. I just want his stuff gone."

The poor woman. "I understand. Now that I've seen how much you have, I can let my movers know the scope of the project."

"Thank you, dear. Let's go back to the dining room where you can show me your plans."

For the next half hour, Charlotte explained how she thought the room could best be configured. In the three years since she'd been doing design work, Mrs. Goddard had to be the easiest client to work with. She seemed very excited about all of Charlotte's ideas.

"You said you were going to be able to clear out Bill's office tomorrow?"

"Yes, I can have my people in here by nine. I can't imagine it will take them more than an hour or two to clean out the place." Thankfully, Mrs. Goddard had decided to keep the hard wood floors and the drapes, making Charlotte's job easier.

"Excellent. And when can you start painting?"

Charlotte liked the beige walls, but Mrs. Goddard said she preferred a sea-foam green, as it helped relax her. Wanting to please her, Charlotte said she would come up with a slightly different palette that she was sure her client would be happy with.

Mrs. Goddard kept glancing to the clock on the wall and Charlotte figured it was time for her to leave. She had a ton of things to do before tomorrow anyway. Charlotte stood. "I'm very excited to start on this project. I'll see you tomorrow."

Charlotte slipped back into the car, her mind going a million miles an hour, trying to figure out if the beautiful sofa and chairs would fit in her small apartment. Mrs. Goddard had seemed quite pleased when Charlotte had asked if she could take the furniture for herself.

Coming to Rock Hard had been the best decision Charlotte had ever made. She couldn't wait to tell Trent all about it.

CHAPTER ELEVEN

"THANKS GUYS, FOR all your help." Sharon had found the college men for Charlotte, and they'd done a fantastic job this morning moving all of Mr. Goddard's possessions. They took several bags to the trash, donated a ton to the women's shelter, and delivered the cream leather sofa and two chairs to her place minutes after she'd arrived home.

"Anytime," the largest of the three said.

She gave each of them a big tip. "I'll be sure to call you on my next job."

They all grinned. To them, this was probably easy money. They'd flirted with her all during the job, and while she was flattered, none of them interested her, even though they seemed nice and uncomplicated.

I want Trent, damn it.

Charlotte closed her front door and headed straight to the shower. Every bone in her body was fatigued, and she smelled bad from all the hard work of packing up Mr. Goddard's books. She planned to ask Harmon if knew of anyone who might want the financial books.

Once the water warmed, Charlotte stepped under the relaxing flow, and as she soaped up her hands, she closed her eyes and pictured Trent rubbing his palms up and down her body. Her nipples hardened as she dragged her fingers over the tips. She then imagined Trent on his knees with his fingers sliding in and out of her pussy. When he'd touched her all over, he'd sent her into the outer stratosphere, and she could almost feel his hands on her now.

Because she had a client list to build and he had a killer to find, the timing wasn't the best, but deep in her heart, she believed she was the right woman for him. The question was how to prove it to him.

Born with a logical mind, she understood the first step was to get Trent over to her new place. She didn't want to wait too long before she invited him over, since he might already be a bit upset that she hadn't told him she was moving in. Once he'd mentioned he had to help his brother on Sunday, she didn't want to him to have to make a choice.

Excited to learn if he was free tonight, she finished her shower and then toweled dry. Knowing that men always liked it when a woman made a home cooked meal, she'd asked Sharon for some advice. Her father's assistant claimed if she could just get a man to taste her food, she might be able to land him in bed. Charlotte adored Sharon, and the fact she had helped save her father's life had endeared her to Charlotte even more.

After Sharon had helped with the unpacking on Sunday, she'd written down two fairly simple recipes she claimed all men liked. From the ingredients, the meal sounded wonderful. Charlotte had gone shopping Sunday night and purchased what she needed, figuring Trent would be over at some point.

If he couldn't come tonight, she'd make some spaghetti for herself and prepare the fancy dinner another time. Before she dressed in something sexy for him, she called to see if tonight would be *the* night.

"Charlotte, are you okay?" Worry laced his voice.

She smiled at the overprotective man. "Why wouldn't I be?"

Trent waited a beat before answering. "No reason."

Even if there had been, he might not share it. "I'm not sure if I mentioned it, but I moved into my own apartment Sunday, and wondered if you'd like to come over tonight?" She hoped she didn't sound too needy, but she wanted to be with him again. The one time they'd made love only served to wet her appetite.

Besides jumping his bones, she wanted to learn more about him, and she bet he'd be willing to play a game or two of chess like they had when they were up in his dad's cabin. If, after a few glasses of wine, they ended up in bed, even better. Charlotte was well aware it would take some work to break through his tough exterior.

"I should be finishing up here at the office in about a half an hour. Does that work for you?"

Pinpricks of joy sizzled over her skin, and moisture pooled between her legs. "It does if I can make you dinner."

"You don't have to. I can pick up something on the way."

Sometimes men could be a bit dense. "I have to eat, and I thought you might like to share."

Finally, she heard the chuckle she'd been waiting for. "Sounds fantastic. Can I bring a bottle of red or white wine?"

She had several in her wine rack, but Trent was the type who wouldn't like coming empty-handed. He'd even brought a six-pack to Dad's party. "White would be fantastic. I'll start dinner whenever you arrive." She then gave him the address, and he said he knew the building.

"See you soon." He sounded excited, and her energy doubled. She couldn't wait to seduce him.

* * *

TRENT WAS THRILLED that Charlotte had invited him over to her place. That way, if anything should happen, it wouldn't look as if he only wanted her for sex. He wished he could spend hours chatting with her, finding out what she liked, but every time he came near her, his libido soared out of control. If only he knew what it was about her that drew him to her, he might be stay calm.

With the white wine in hand, he knocked on her door, pleased she'd found a place in town since it was safer than being in a house on the outskirts. While the man who had been after her was now in prison, Trent still had the urge to protect her.

The moment Charlotte opened the door, all thoughts of her stalker disappeared. His pulse raced and a few other body parts reacted. She had on a pretty skirt that showed off her long legs, along with an almost see-through blouse that made him want to rip it off. Clearly, she'd dressed to entice and wasn't concerned her attire was better suited to summer than winter. He'd have to think about some gruesome detail of his case all during dinner in order to keep his hands to himself.

He stepped inside, closed the door, and held up the bottle. "Would you like me to open the wine?"

His smoothness meter had dipped to zero. As much as he wanted to hug her, he didn't trust himself. She slipped the bottle from his fingers and smiled. Damn if she didn't know what she did to him.

"There's no hurry. I want to show you around first."

Duh. That was why she'd invited him, and all he could think of was eating quickly and then being with her. "I'd love to see your place." He slipped out of his jacket and placed in on the back of the dining room chair.

While the kitchen was small, he liked that it opened up to the dining room. She set the bottle on the counter and returned. "I only moved in two days ago and haven't had time to do much in the way of decorating."

"Looks great to me." He'd always planned to put up pictures in his place, but he never seemed to have the time.

"I'll show you where I do my work first. I was so excited to get two bedrooms."

As they walked past the living room, he checked it out. It was simple, yet nice. He loved the large sofa and very comfortable chairs, but he'd pictured her buying something a bit more rustic. These pieces had more of a masculine flair. "It looks comfortable in here."

"You like the sofa?"

"Yes." He wouldn't mind making love with her on that.

"Those three pieces belonged to Bill Goddard. When I redid his office, his wife insisted I give away everything, and she seemed delighted that I wanted these pieces."

He whistled. "She could have made a lot at a consignment shop."

"I know, right? She said the transition to being without him would be easier if she wasn't surrounded by his things." Charlotte threaded an arm through his. "You can enjoy it after dinner."

His cock hardened. He hoped she was thinking of a repeat performance like the one they'd had on her dad's couch.

Her office was small, but given the number of windows, it would be filled with a lot of light during the day. She had a desk and a long table that was covered with fabric swatches and other assorted decorating items. He should make his spare room into an office. "I like it."

"Thank you." She opened the door between the two rooms. "My bath is a bit small, but it works for me. Lastly, this is my bedroom."

Trent had to work hard to hold in his groan. As soon as he saw the large bed piled deep with pillows, his mind shot to a place where it didn't need to be. "Nice." He sucked at knowing the right thing to say.

Charlotte turned and faced him. "You want to help me cook dinner?"

I'd rather help you undress. "Me? I can do the basics, as I demonstrated in the cabin, but if it's fancier than scrambled eggs, hamburgers on the grill, or spaghetti, you might be on your own."

She laughed. "We'll try together. Sharon promised me it was a no fail recipe."

He'd heard Vic brag about his assistant's cooking. "Then I'm game." He followed her into the kitchen and caught himself staring at her ass. He needed to take his mind off of sex. "How's the decorating gig going?"

She swiveled around and his gaze latched onto her breasts—breasts that he could see quite well through her rather translucent top.

"We paint tomorrow, and then I can start doing my magic."

"You're moving quickly." He always had suspected Charlotte of being a hellfire when it came to her job. "What's Mrs. Goddard like to work with?"

He told himself he wasn't trying to find information about the possible suspect, but that wouldn't be completely true. Getting Charlotte's perspective would be extremely helpful. His team had cleared the scene the day after the murder, and the next day, the woman was knocking on Charlotte's store asking her to redecorate.

"Easiest woman I've ever worked with. She sweet and nice and doesn't fuss."

He laughed. "Perhaps I should go into the decorating business." Most of the people he ran into were hostile, either by their attitude or by wielding knives or waving a gun.

She raised her brows. "I say, go for it." She grinned. "How about opening that wine now?"

Charlotte had a knack for making him laugh. Happy to have something to do, he brushed past her and picked up the corkscrew she'd set out on the counter. In a flash, he had the bottle opened and two glasses of wine poured. "Now what can I do?"

She ran a finger across a piece of paper that contained some written instructions. "How about you get me the bottle of capers in the refrigerator?" She sipped from the wine and groaned, as if it was the best tasting drink in the world. He swore she did it on purpose.

"Capers?" he asked. He'd seen those mentioned on a menu, but he really didn't know what they looked like.

"I'm putting them on top of the fish."

"Ah." That didn't help.

Once he opened the refrigerator, he scanned each shelf, but didn't see anything that might be a likely candidate. A second later her hands landed on his waist and his cock shot to life.

"Excuse me." She reached around him, and her breasts brushed his arm. She then lifted the small glass bottle from the shelf on the door. "These are capers," she said waving it at him.

Clearly, Charlotte found his lack of knowledge humorous. He wouldn't be surprised if she'd set him up. "Okay, master chef, let's see you do your thing."

He stood close to her and pretended to be studying her technique, when in reality he was inhaling her scent and admiring her sensuous curves. She diced the capers and sprinkled them on the fish. Not wanting to look like a fool, he didn't dare ask what kind it was.

She poured some crumbs on top as well as some cheese, and then popped it in the broiler. "Dinner in few minutes."

"It really looks good," he said.

"It does, doesn't it?" She stepped over to the refrigerator and retrieved two tomatoes, some lettuce, croutons, and a bag of diced stuff and then placed everything on the counter but the tomatoes. "Can I interest you with cutting these?"

"Can do. I'm quite good with a knife, or so I've been told."

He withdrew a sharp blade from a butcher block and went to work on his assignment. As they worked in companionable silence, he remembered the good times he and his mom had preparing meals together. When a wave of sadness descended, he pushed aside those thoughts and glanced over at Charlotte who was staring at him. "What? Do I have something on my face?" He swiped at the imaginary food particle.

"No. You looked lost in thought again, and I feared you might cut yourself."

Charlotte was being polite. They both were aware he had too many issues. He set down the knife, rinsed his hands, and then dried them. He stepped close to her and cupped her face. "I don't know what it is about you, but I keep having these memories of my childhood whenever I'm near you. I'm sorry that I often seem distracted."

"Is there anything I can do to help?" Her lips slightly parted.

"I can think of something."

Like let me kiss you.

CHAPTER TWELVE

IF SHE DIDN'T know better, Charlotte would say that Trent wanted to kiss her. Oh, hell. So what if the fish burned and they were forced to go out to dinner. She wasn't one to miss an opportunity.

She placed her palms on his chest. "You said I could help? What would that be?"

"This." Trent leaned over, and the moment he planted his lips on hers, her insides heated and her heart did a rapid tattoo.

She thought because they'd made love before that her reaction to his kiss wouldn't be this intense, but she was wrong. Charlotte wrapped her arms around his waist and then dragged her hands up his back, melting against his body. Even through his cotton shirt, she could feel his strong muscles as he twisted against her.

This time she waited for him to open his mouth and invite her in. When he did, she groaned and nearly devoured him. Trent tasted of the wine mixed with a hint of mint, and here she thought he'd come straight from work. He must've taken some time to get ready, and that pleased her.

His hands roamed along the sides of her breasts, and as his thumbs brushed her nipples, intense pleasure skidded through her. His hard cock was evident underneath his jeans and she couldn't wait to strip him naked.

Then reason intruded. Always being so eager to make love with him might not be the best strategy. Sometimes making a man wait worked better—or so Sharon had claimed. Charlotte broke the kiss and stepped back, her breath coming out fast. "Dinner will be ready soon."

He glanced to the side. "You're right. You've gone to all this work and we shouldn't waste the food." He stabbed a hand through his hair.

Poor Trent. She almost gave in and told him it was all part of her plan to make him fall in love with her, but she refrained.

She licked her lips, inhaled, and guzzled half her glass of wine. Attempting to appear cool, she located two bowls, finished making her salad, and then held them out. "Want to dump your tomatoes on top?"

"Sure."

Perhaps breaking the kiss hadn't been the smartest move, as it now seemed the tension between them had escalated. Planning everything so carefully might not have been the right path to take. Darn.

She needed to say something. "Mom and Dad come home tomorrow."

"Great. Have you heard how things went?"

"Mom texted only once to say Hawaii was beautiful. I think they were probably too busy having fun to call." Her mom never came out and said it, but from all the giggles and whispers that had come from their bedroom while Charlotte had stayed there, her parents certainly enjoyed making love. She visibly shivered, not wanting to think about *that*.

He laughed. "I'm a bit surprised your dad took the time off to go on a honeymoon."

"He's changed since he left the FBI." The oven timer sounded. "Fish is ready." Thank goodness, as it would give them something to do.

Once he helped her take the food over to the table, she dug in and moaned. "This is so good."

Trent seemed to inhale the fish. "Really good. Next time I see Sharon, I'll thank her."

"Me, too. So how did the move go with Harmon?"

"Fine."

She was disappointed he didn't elaborate. "How is he adjusting to being a free man?" She thought about stopping by Italiano's and seeing him, but if he had been in the back, she wouldn't have been able to speak with him.

Trent drank half his glass of wine then set it down with too much force. "I'm worried about him."

She stopped eating. "Did something happen?"

He twisted in his seat to face her. "That's just it. He seems the same as before he was arrested."

"This is bad?"

"Fuck, if I'd been in prison for three years because someone framed me, I'd be spitting mad, yet Harmon seems to be taking this framing shit in stride. Assuming he's as innocent as he claims."

"When I spoke with him, he thought the person who framed him could only be one of three people, and now one of them is dead."

Trent leaned back in his seat. "I really wanted Harmon to be innocent, but maybe he really did do what he was accused of. It's the only thing that would explain why he appears so...calm."

"Perhaps prison changed him. Sometimes in life you have to accept things and just move on."

Trent jammed a lot of the fish in his mouth. When he finished, he nodded. "Maybe."

She ate her fish and was halfway through her salad when an idea struck. "You want to know what I think?"

Trent pushed back his chair. "Hold that thought. Let me bring the bottle over here. I want to hear this."

As he was getting the wine, Charlotte gathered her thoughts.

As soon as he sat down she held out her glass for more fortification. "Don't you think it's a little coincidental that the day your brother is released from prison that his accuser is murdered?"

A flash of fear crossed his face. "It occurred to me, but Harmon was in my house when Mr. Goddard died."

"I know, but the killer doesn't know that. This person might be the one who framed Harmon before and is trying to do it again. Maybe three years of his life wasn't enough for this guy."

"So you think the murder has something to do with wanting more revenge against my brother?"

She shrugged. "I don't know what to think. My dad says there is no such thing as a coincidence."

"Usually that's true. Do you have a suspect in mind?"

"I'm not privy to the details of the case, but from an outsider's point of view, I'm agreeing with Harmon—in part. It's either the other boss, or the young man who worked alongside Harmon." She raised a finger. "Or it could be Mrs. Goddard."

He glanced aside as if he was trying to formulate his next question. "I've spoken with the other boss, Frank Hamilton, and I will be speaking with the man who worked alongside my brother, but Mrs. Goddard was at her sister's house the night of the murder."

"Are you sure?"

"I'm not sure of anything. Why are you pointing the finger at her? I thought you liked her."

"I do, but I think it's odd that she wants to ditch all of his possessions. It's like she didn't really love him."

"You might be right. I'll check into her some more."

Charlotte was thrilled that Trent took her opinion so seriously. "I can see you have your work cut out for you." Once they both finished, she picked up her plate and stood. "Would you be interested in a game of chess?"

He sucked in a breath, and the concern regarding his brother that had filled his face a moment before had disappeared. "I don't think my ego can stand losing again."

She laughed. "If I recall, I won two games and you won two."

"I'd like to leave it that way. I could be persuaded to play a game of cards." He raised his brows.

He'd played right into her hands. "We never did get to play strip poker at the cabin, now did we?"

"Did I agree to that?" Trent grinned. "How about I clear the table while you scrounge up the cards?"

"Deal."

She rushed into her office and removed the deck from her desk drawer, having anticipated they might end up playing. She'd also collected a ton of buttons over the years, and thought they could use these as chips. With only six pieces of clothing, she figured she'd be naked soon.

* * *

TRENT WANTED TO kick himself. What had he been thinking agreeing to play strip poker? It might be what he wanted, but he could see disappointment ahead for them. At some point in the near future, he'd agree to come over and have dinner with her, and then something would come up at work, and he'd have to cancel. Just because Charlotte would understand, didn't mean it would be fair to her. Whether he wanted to be with her or not, his work had to come first—or so he always believed.

He would have played chess with her like they had at the cabin, but when Charlotte was adamant that his brother was innocent, he wanted to do something more intimate. That kind of faith was hard to come by in a woman—or in anyone. He'd give anything for this relationship to work, but common sense told him it wouldn't.

"Got them." Charlotte strutted toward him, pulled up the chair across from him, and sat down. "Five card stud?"

"Your game, your deal."

"I hope I remember how to play." She placed the bag of buttons between them. "You want to split these in half?"

Only Charlotte would think of using these as markers. "You got it."

While he counted them out, she shuffled the cards then stretched out her long legs, looking all too enticing. Trent didn't know if he wanted to lose on purpose or actually try to win. He had a feeling she'd like it better if he played fair. No matter who lost, they'd both be naked and doing what they wanted in the end.

She placed the first card face down in front of both of them then followed it with one face up. She had a queen of hearts showing and he had a ten of spades. Since he had the lower valued card, he picked up a button and placed it in the center. "I bid one."

She lifted up her downed card and bit her lower lip. Damned if she wasn't doing that on purpose to distract him. "Here's my one and I'll raise you one."

He was game. Trent tossed in another button. His pair of tens would probably win in the end anyway. She dealt each of them another up card, but none of the ones showing matched.

"Do you have anything good?" she asked.

"I'm not telling. Let's see if you get something good with the third card."

She placed another card face up. When she checked her down card again, she grinned, but he couldn't tell if she was faking it or not. If she was, she was good. He bet two buttons this time and she matched him. By the time she dealt the fifth card, he believed he'd win unless she had a hidden queen.

Charlotte flipped over her downed card. "I've got nothing. Let's see yours," she said, acting defeated.

He turned over his ten of clubs to show her he had a pair and then smiled. "I win."

"Darn. You want to take off my shoe?" She lifted her leg and wiggled her foot.

He didn't buy her disappointment. "Can I take both of them?"

She tilted her head and raked her gaze up and down his body. "You can if I get to pick which item to take off when you lose," she said with a delightful gleam in her eye.

"Deal." He slipped off her right shoe and then her left, but instead of letting go, he massaged her instep and she moaned.

"Are you trying to end this game quickly?"

Yes. "Is that what you want?" he asked.

"I think it depends on how long you're going to keep rubbing my feet."

He chuckled. He'd never met anyone like Charlotte before. She was good for his soul.

Trent released her foot. "I like a challenge. I want to see if I can have you naked before I lose one piece of clothing." He didn't believe he would, but it was fun to tease her.

"Not a chance." She picked up the cards, shuffled them, and then handed the pack to him. "Your turn to deal."

He might have chosen a different game but five-card stud only took a few minutes to complete. He dealt the two cards— one face down and one up. Once more he had the lower hand, and tossed in his button. Charlotte glanced at her second card, and then threw in three more.

"You're that confident?" he asked.

"Yes." She almost giggled. So much for her ability to bluff.

With two cards, the best she could have was a pair of jacks, but he was willing to see it through. After he'd dealt a total of four cards, she had a potential of two pairs, and this wasn't looking good for him. He blew on the cards for luck and then dealt the final one. When he placed that Jack of Diamonds on her side, he couldn't believe it.

Charlotte jumped up. "I won, I won! Stand up so I can take something off."

He had a feeling that she wouldn't just stop at one piece, and that was fine by him.

CHAPTER THIRTEEN

CHARLOTTE COULDN'T BELIEVE her luck. She debated whether to remove his jeans first or his shirt. Because his shoes were in the way, she took the easy path. "Stand up, please."

Trent obeyed. "What's it going to be?"

It was more fun if she strung him along, so she stepped in front of him, ran her gaze up and down his body, and then walked around him. "Your shirt."

Not wanting him to help, she moved in front of him, eased his shirt from his jeans then slid her hands underneath the material, enjoying the sensuous feel of his hard body.

Trent placed his hands on her hips. "Do we have a time limit?"

As much as she wanted to explore him at her leisure and drive him crazy, if she lost the next round, no telling how long he would take. Then again, the whole purpose of playing was to have foreplay before enjoying each other in the most carnal way.

"Should we?" She'd like to know what he thought. If she assumed he was interested in sex, and wasn't, she'd be devastated.

He grinned, providing her with his answer. "I'm game."

Lust pooled in her veins. Since she wasn't sure what he meant, Charlotte decided to do what she wanted. As slowly as she could, she undid each button, making certain to drag her hands up and down his chest after each one.

His groan came out long and loud. "You do realize the longer you take, the more time I'm going to spend on you."

Yes! "That so?"

Once Charlotte opened his shirt, she eased the material down his muscular shoulders, and the urge to nibble at his biceps overwhelmed her. Leaning over, she took a mock bite, and then laughed.

"I like a feral woman." Trent shrugged out of his shirt. "Be forewarned. Turnabout can be a bitch."

"You can lick and bite me all you want." She really only meant the lick part.

He chuckled. "Since you took so long removing my shirt, I think it's only fair that I take off your top."

As fun as it was to play cards, this was far more exciting. "Okay."

"Close your eyes and keep them shut," he demanded in a tone that caused her pussy to moisten. Trent Lawson could turn her on without even touching her.

Thankfully, her blouse had no buttons so this shouldn't take long. Then again, this was Trent. Not wanting to make it easy on him, she stood still.

"How about placing your hands on your head?" he asked.

She shifted her weight to one leg then raised her arms. "How can you take off my top with my fingers locked?"

"Who says I want to take it off right away?"

He was a sly one. When his warm hands suddenly slid under her blouse, she jumped.

"Easy there."

"I wasn't expecting that."

"You have to be prepared for anything," he said.

Charlotte didn't know what he was going to do, but lifting her bra above her tits hadn't been one of her choices. As he lightly brushed each nipple with the pad of his thumb, need sizzled through her. His breath then cascaded down her neck, right before his teeth nabbed her earlobe.

"I can't seem to get enough of you," he whispered. He cupped her breasts and dragged his lips down her neck, inhaling deeply. "You smell so good, too."

His words sent goose bumps across her neck and shoulders. "Thank you."

He must have moved to a different place because his breath was no longer hovering over her skin. After lifting her shirt and bra higher, he then sucked on her nipple, causing her to draw in a breath. Delight and excitement collided. Trent then nabbed the other tip between his teeth and drew it taut. When desire flamed and spread from her belly to her clit, the urge to lower her hands and cup his head nearly undid her, but she wanted to show him that pleasing him was important to her.

He lifted both breasts and pressed them together. "You are amazing."

"I bet if you were naked, I'd be able to say the same thing about you."

Trent laughed. "You'll have to wait a little longer before that happens."

"I thought you were taking off my blouse."

His hands grabbed both her wrists and lowered her arms. "Is someone in a hurry to have my cock?"

The mere mention of making love with him had electric bolts charging up and down her spine. Keeping her eyes closed, she lifted her chin. "Should I be?"

"If you can't remember how fantastic it was, then I guess I'll have to refresh your memory."

"You can try." Pulling off the indifferent attitude had never been her forte.

In less time than it took her to inhale, her blouse flew off. He unhooked the back of her bra, dragged the straps down her arms, and then palmed her breasts, lightly brushing her tender nipples. She could feel the tips harden as contractions rippled between her thighs.

"It's my turn now," she said as need coursed through her.

His body heat disappeared. "Works for me. To make it easier on you, I'll remove my boots."

She opened her eyes and watched him take them off. Unless he went commando, he had two items of clothing on and so did she. Let the fireworks begin.

Charlotte stepped closer. "Wanting everything to be fair, how about if you close your eyes and not move until I tell you?"

His brows rose, as did his lips. "And if I say no?"

"I'll stop my seduction." Two could play at this game.

His eyes closed. "You drive a hard bargain, lady."

She smiled and was happy he couldn't see her. Charlotte moved toward him and quickly undid the buttons on his fly. "I think you will be pleased with the result if you do as I ask."

"I hope you realize what happens if you spend too much time loving my cock."

"It'll explode before I want it to. Trust me, I'll be careful."

She dropped to her knees and dragged down both his pants and his briefs.

"Hey you. I think you took off two items at once." Humor laced his tone.

"Whoops." When his jeans pooled at his ankles, she tapped his leg and he lifted his right foot and then his left.

Now that he was naked, she leaned back on her heels to admire him. Not only did he have a fantastic cock, his legs were thick and strong, and everything about his body was in perfect proportion. The only thing marring his skin were a few scars that appeared to be bullet holes, but now wasn't the time to ask for details.

"Are you going to just stare at me?" he asked with his eyes still shut.

She chuckled. He had to have peeked. "You're nice to look at."

He grabbed his cock and scrunched his brows. "I think it's turning purple, so you better get to it."

Charlotte fell to the carpet laughing. In a flash he was on top of her, tickling her. Tears leaked out of her eyes as she grabbed his hands.

"You think that's funny, young lady?"

If she didn't give in, he might never stop. "No, you're condition was highly serious. I wanted to help."

Trent released his grip, and then pulled down her stretchy skirt and panties, despite her being curled into a ball.

"We're both naked, so now were even," he said.

"What happens next?" Of course she knew, but she wanted to see what he'd do.

Trent reached behind him, picked up his jeans, and stuck his hand in his pocket to withdraw a condom. "This is next."

Oh, yeah. "How about letting me put it on?"

He grabbed her wrist, drew it to him, and then placed the foil packet in her palm. "Go for it, but be quick."

"It'll be easier if you lie on your back."

"You're the boss." It was clear from his sexy smile that he didn't believe that for one minute.

Trent stretched out and then wrapped his hands under his head. God, he was a beautiful man. She could look at him for hours.

Who am I kidding? She couldn't keep her hands off him for even a minute, and once she touched him, she'd have to have him.

Charlotte made a big show of opening the foil wrapper but had no intention of placing it on his cock right away. Kneeling, she edged her way toward him, opened his legs, and crawled between them. Instead of dragging the protection over his cock, she leaned over, and sucked his rigid dick deep into her mouth.

Both of his hands grabbed her shoulders and squeezed. "Careful now. I'm on edge."

"I should hope so," she mumbled with his cock in her mouth. "I'm naked and willing."

He laughed. "You are something else, Charlotte Hart."

His words warmed her through and through. Wanting to tempt and tease him, she stroked his shaft lightly while her tongue did a dance around the tip. He groaned and dug his fingers into her shoulders, hard enough to excite, but gentle enough not to hurt.

"Harder," he said with authority.

Charlotte almost laughed, but she feared she might not be able to handle the retribution if she didn't do as he asked. When a bit of cum leaked out of the tip, she decided it was time. "You're lucky I'm taking mercy on him."

"Mercy, you say? It's called self-preservation. You would have gone to bed dissatisfied if you'd continued for much longer."

Trent was so much fun, though she believed he had the control of steel. Regardless, she rolled the rubber down his length. If she wasn't in such need, she would have straddled his face and asked him to lick her. Instead, she positioned herself above his cock and prepared to ride him.

Trent clasped a hand on her hip and lifted up, driving into her. "I couldn't wait."

Her breath caught as his wide girth stretched her to the max. It didn't matter that she was slipperier than water on glass. Cascading pleasure tripped up her spine, forcing her to wait for the spasms to end before lifting up.

Once she gained some control, she leaned over and offered him her breasts. Trent instantly nabbed a nipple between his teeth and when he tugged hard, a sharp ache drove straight to her clit. He cupped her other breast and waves of delight washed over her. His teeth, his fingers, and his hard cock were almost too much for her to handle. Sizzles of ecstasy shimmered all over her as heat built inside.

"Ride me," he said between sucks and twirls on her tits.

Given his size, and the way he was breathing hard, he seemed ready to burst. If they hadn't been flirting all night and then touching, she might have been able to last, but Trent seemed to have the key to her lock.

Charlotte lowered her face and lifted his head to kiss him. Trent let go of her hips and slammed his fingers through her hair and gripped her head hard. The kiss that followed spoke of passion and what she thought a future would be like.

He groaned then rolled her over so that he was on top. "You've driven me too far."

With his eyes closed and his mouth open, he thrust into her, pounding her pussy with desperate and needy strokes. When his cock filled her to the hilt, Charlotte dragged her nails down his back and screamed his name.

Lust, passion, and pure ecstasy slammed into her from every angle as her orgasm claimed her. Not wanting their time to end, she clasped his hips and lifted up, helping to drive his cock in farther.

Heat filled the condom as his dick expanded and pulsed, stretching her even more. Her breasts tingled and her swollen lips demanded to be kissed. When she opened her mouth, Trent dipped his head and possessed her once more.

Spent and slick with sweat, he slid to the side and pulled her onto his chest. Every muscle relaxed, and she dropped her cheek on his shoulder, content to lie there forever. "Is it my imagination, or are you getting better?" she asked.

He laughed and lightly patted her butt. "Better? Both times have been wonderful."

Yes, they had been. Trent was like her drug. "I think you could improve if you wanted to."

He rolled her off him and lifted up onto his elbow. "That so?"

Not at all, but she wouldn't confess that to him. Charlotte

waved a hand. "I'm tired now, but if you catch me at a later time and want to try again, I'd be game."

He chuckled, clearly seeing through her lie. Trent rose to his feet and padded into the kitchen. Water ran, and he returned with a towel to clean her up. She was sticky all over. "Want to shower together?" she asked.

"Will we fit?"

"We can try."

CHAPTER FOURTEEN

TAKING A SHOWER with Charlotte didn't help calm his need for her one bit. As much as Trent enjoyed soaping her body and rubbing his hands all over her luscious curves, it only made him hornier. Because she was probably sore from all his hard pounding, he decided it wasn't wise to make love with her again tonight.

After a lot of touching and pure enjoyment, they finally stepped out of the shower and had fun drying each other off. Trent didn't want to leave this warm and welcoming home, but it was late, and he had some paperwork to do before heading into the precinct tomorrow.

Charlotte quickly changed into something more casual than her hot and sexy outfit, which was probably a good thing, as it was hard enough to stay away from her.

As he stepped from the bathroom, he glanced into her office once more, and stilled. From this angle, he spotted an Ardton Investments' sticker plastered on top of one of her two computers.

"Where did you get that laptop?" Trent asked as he moved into the room.

"Mrs. Goddard gave it to me, but don't worry, she erased the files."

He highly doubted someone like Mrs. Goddard had the computer know-how to permanently delete them. "She probably just dragged them into the trash."

Charlotte's mouth opened. "Nope. I checked." She went over to the computer and clicked on the trash icon. "See? It's empty," she said triumphantly.

"Doesn't mean the information is gone. This computer might be evidence in Mr. Goddard's murder."

"How so?"

Trent had several working theories about what Mr. Goddard might have done to warrant being killed—assuming it wasn't from being in the wrong place at the wrong time. Blackmail topped Trent's choice, along with revenge. Possibly there was evidence on the computer that would lead him to the killer. When the computer had been at the Goddard's home, he had no probable cause to confiscate it. Now that Mrs. Goddard had seen fit to give it away, the computer became a lot more interesting.

"I'm not at liberty to say." It wasn't that he didn't trust Charlotte, but she might let something slip to Mrs. Goddard. Knowing the way Charlotte's mind worked, she might even try to stick her nose into something where it didn't belong, especially since she had a concealed weapon's permit and didn't seem afraid to use her gun. Trent would never live it down if something happened to her.

"I get it. Dad never could tell us much when he was working on a case either."

He couldn't believe how understanding she was. "Then you won't mind if I take this into the station to have it checked out?"

"Yes, I mind." Her anger flared, but only for a moment. She looked so damned cute with a slightly red face.

He waited a beat to let her think about what he said. "Are

you positive nothing can be retrieved from the computer? Not even the FBI could get anything off it?"

She looked to the side and blew out a breath. "You're right, but is the Rock Hard Police Department sophisticated enough to restore deleted files?"

"They are."

"Do I have a choice? I mean you probably could get a warrant for it."

He wanted to be honest with her. "I could, but I'm hoping I won't have to."

"When do you think I'll have it back?"

"When we're done looking." He appreciated she didn't put up a fuss.

She punched him in the arm and then smiled. "If they harm it, you owe me another computer."

He didn't want to promise something he couldn't deliver. "We'll be careful."

"As long as we're talking about Mr. Goddard's things, would you mind taking this box of his books to Harmon? I'm hoping he'll know who might be able to use them."

"Sure."

* * *

TRENT YAWNED, BARELY having slept last night. He kept wondering how things could have become so out of control with Charlotte. She'd seduced him, plain and simple, and he'd let her, because he wanted what she had to offer.

Being with her had felt so right, but what if he'd been called into work while they were playing strip poker? He wondered if he would've been able to leave, and it bothered him not knowing how he would have reacted.

Trent needed to let it go for now. He had a killer to catch. As he walked into the station, he spotted Cade in his office studying some papers. Trent delivered Mr. Goddard's laptop to the tech department then knocked on Cade's door and entered.

Cade looked up, his eyes wide. "Look who the cat dragged in."

He didn't look that bad. At least he'd shaved and changed his clothes. "Didn't sleep much last night. Had a lot on my mind." He'd been talking to Cade when he'd received the call from Charlotte to come over, so his partner knew where he'd been last night. Trent pulled up a seat in front of a desk and sat down.

"Thinking about Charlotte, I take it?"

Cade was too damned perceptive, but Trent wasn't in the mood to elaborate. "That and other things."

Cade smiled. "Trust me, it gets easier with time."

"What does?"

His friend and fellow detective leaned back in his seat, looking smug. "The sleepless nights, the hard-ons, and not being able to focus on the job."

Trent sat up straighter, not liking that his partner hit too close to home. "I'm doing just fine."

"Sure you are."

Trent needed to get this conversation back on track. "You find out anything from Jayson Kendall?" Trent hadn't seen him at the firm when he'd spoken with Frank Hamilton, but perhaps he was on vacation.

Both he and Cade believed the murder was connected to Harmon somehow since the timing of Goddard's death was too coincidental. While they couldn't know for sure, it seemed like the killer wanted the police to think Harmon had killed the man since Goddard had accused Harmon of insider trading.

At the time of his brother's arrest, only four people worked at the firm—Bill Goddard and Frank Hamilton who were the owners, and Jayson along with Harmon who did most of the grunt work at the firm, from bringing in clients to doing research.

Jayson had come onboard about two months after Harmon

had, and his brother claimed his coworker was a good guy. Harmon didn't think the new kid on the block had what it took to frame him. Jealousy didn't seem to be the motive either. According to Harmon, Jayson was having a hard time handling his own clients. He had no reason to want Harmon gone.

"Yes, but it was a bitch to find him. He's no longer with Ardton Investments."

So that was why Jayson wasn't in the office. "Who's he with?"

"Works at the bank now in the mortgage department. Said he didn't like lying to people."

"Good to know." That alone didn't exonerate him.

Cade opened a folder on his desk and glanced down at it. "When I realized Jayson didn't work there, I interviewed the rest of the staff. All were hired after Harmon left."

"Which lessens the likelihood that any of them would have the motive to set up Harmon for the murder. Did they have any insight into who might have wanted Goddard dead?"

"No. The only remotely interesting tidbit was that one of the new hires, John Samuels, was promoted after Bill's death. With Jayson's departure, John took over Bill's clients."

"Not the best motive for murder. Someone had to be promoted. I don't see anyone in the firm wanting Bill dead. Not only would his death cast a pall over the whole firm, the firm's income might be affected."

"Agreed."

He wondered why Frank hadn't mentioned Samuels' promotion. Perhaps he didn't think it was relevant. "What do we know about Samuels?"

"Not much. I ran his name, along with the others, into our databases but they all came up clean."

This seemed like another good job for Vic. Trent certainly didn't have the time to follow him around for days on end. "Did anyone beside John benefit from Bill's death?"

Cade shook his head. "Not that I could tell. Frank will now

be the sole owner of the firm, but again, is that enough motive to kill Bill? And if it is, why wait until now?"

"Good question. I spoke with Frank, too, but nothing seemed out of place. You said you talked with Jayson?"

"Yes, no sooner had he said he had no idea who would want to harm his old boss, than he began talking about the night Mrs. Goddard's brother spilled the beans about his company's merger." He leaned on his elbows. "What do you know about that Christmas party?"

Trent shot to high alert. Did Jayson know something that he'd kept secret? After all, this was the infamous night when the insider information had been divulged. "I wasn't there, but Harmon, of course, was. The FBI handled the case, but my brother claimed that Elaine Goddard's brother, Richard Delaney, had gotten drunk at their annual festivity. Richard, Hepfield Electronics' accountant, never would say what set him off that night, but he started bragging about how Hepfield Electronics was going to buy out another company, and that the merger was sure to drive up the price of their stock by at least ten percent."

Cade whistled. "And in theory, Harmon let that sensitive material leak to a client, and said client benefitted."

"Yes. Did Jayson have anything new to add?"

"Not about that, but about something else that happened that night. Were you aware that Jayson walked in on Harmon and Mrs. Goddard doing the tongue tango?"

Tongue tango? A wave of injustice slammed into him. "Harmon never said anything about that. My brother may or may not be guilty of trading company secrets, but he'd never do anything with a married woman." His mom accused their dad of that very thing, and while Trent never believed it and Dad denied it, it was what started the divorce. "Harmon knew better than anyone how damaging that could be to a family."

Cade shrugged. "Perhaps he was too embarrassed to tell you, or was afraid that you'd judge him."

"I don't buy it. Did Jayson tell Bill what he saw?"

"He said he never mentioned it to his boss for obvious reasons, but that he did speak to Elaine's brother."

"I bet that didn't go over well. I'll ask Harmon about it, and then I want to talk with Richard Delaney. Perhaps his memory has improved."

"I doubt it, but let me know what you find."

Trent pushed back his chair. Harmon wouldn't be at work for another hour. It was time for a heart-to-heart conversation.

After a short drive to his brother's apartment, Trent grabbed the box of books for Harmon that Charlotte had given him, hiked up to his brother's door, and knocked. "It's me."

The door opened to a smiling Harmon, but the look of joy disappeared as soon as he saw Trent's scowl. "What's wrong?"

Trent stepped in, set down the heavy box, and motioned they sit at the kitchen table. The hint of coffee beans in the air implied his brother had already made a pot. "Got some coffee to spare?"

"Sure. What's in the box?"

"Just some old books." Trent wanted to discuss something else first.

"Oh, shit, did something happen to Dad?"

"Stop, will ya. He's fine. You should go see him."

"I will. Soon." Harmon poured a cup, brought it over, and sat down across from Trent. "I'm listening."

"What can you tell me about the night Richard Delaney spilled his guts about Hepfield Electronics?"

His brows pinched. "Why are you asking me about this now?"

"Some new information has come to light."

Harmon straightened, a sparkle appearing in his eyes. "Really? I can't tell you any more than what I've been touting for the last three years. Richard was drunk, spouting off about his company's merger. I was there, along with Bill, Frank, and Jayson. Like I said before, a few of Bill's clients had been invited to the party, but I can't remember if they were in the living room at the time. If they were, any one of them could have leaked the information."

That was what Harmon had said before. Trent had spoken to Bill during the trial and learned the names of those clients, but none of them admitted they'd heard anything. "What do you remember about Elaine Goddard that night?"

Harmon stared at Trent. "Oh fuck, what did she tell you?"

"It's what Jayson told Cade that has me worried. He saw her kissing you."

Harmon waved a hand. "She was even drunker than her brother and came on to me. She wished me a Merry Christmas then threw herself at me. Trust me, I did not return the affection. Do you really think that I would have an affair with a married woman?"

"No." Harmon had a lot of women after him and didn't need to chase anyone. Besides, he was the better looking of the two. "Did you see Jayson in the room during this display of affection?"

"I wasn't looking around. I was trying to be polite and get away from Elaine without making a scene."

Trent drank his coffee. The rich aroma and bold taste really hit the spot. "I forgot you always did buy the best blend."

"It's one of my few indulgences."

Trent leaned forward on his elbows. "Suppose Bill saw you kiss Elaine or found out about you making out with her. In order to put a stop to it, maybe he framed you to get you out of the picture." Bill Goddard was a rich and powerful man but wasn't particularly attractive.

"It's possible, but why wouldn't he have just confronted me? He could have threatened to fire me if I ever saw his wife again, when in fact, he never acted as if I was a threat for the few months afterwards."

"Maybe he didn't want to let you know he was upset. If no one knew he was angry with you, when your client benefitted from the stock trade, they wouldn't glance his way."

"It's a great theory, but with Bill dead, you'll never be able to prove it."

"I'm not so sure. Remember I mentioned that Mrs. Goddard hired Charlotte to redecorate Bill's office?"

"Yes. Did she learn something?" The lines around Harmon's eye tightened.

"I don't know yet, but Mrs. Goddard gave away all of Bill's possessions." He nodded to the box. "Charlotte packed up some of his books. She asked me to bring these to you. She thought you might know of someone who could use them."

"Tell her thank you. I'll check the dates on these books to see if our library would want them."

He finished off the delicious brew. "I find it rather odd that someone would be in such a hurry to throw everything away, especially after all their years of marriage."

Harmon dropped back against his seat. "I don't know. If my spouse had died tragically, I might not want to have her things around."

Trent didn't buy it. "You wouldn't keep a favorite painting of hers, or her most cherished book?"

Harmon smiled. "I see your point."

"Besides the books, she gave away Bill's computer to Charlotte, claiming she deleted all the files, but I'm hoping our tech gurus can find something of interest."

"I can't imagine Bill would keep any damning information on his computer. He was smarter than that."

"You'd be surprised what we've found on home computers. Remember, people don't expect to die. I don't know what we'll find, but I want to look." He wrapped his hands around his empty cup. "What can you tell me about Elaine Goddard?"

Harmon's chin tucked under as if he was at a loss for words. "I can't say I knew her very well, but I did know Bill, and he wasn't a very emotional man. It's hard to be in the kind of business we were in and give out hugs and kisses. If I had to speculate, I'd say theirs was a rather loveless marriage."

"Did he tell you that? Or did she?" Trent didn't like to act on pure guesswork.

"Neither one said anything. Since Bill is a dead end, pun intended, you might want to find out what the neighbors thought about their relationship. Maybe Elaine was only staying around for the money. If he was being a jerk, maybe she offed him."

Trent didn't think she'd killed her husband. "Women don't usually stab their victim. It takes a lot of force."

"Maybe she drugged him first."

That was a possibility. "The coroner is checking for drugs, and then I'll know, but let's say she did kill Bill. What's her motive? Her source of income would stop."

"True, unless he had a huge life insurance policy. That, or she couldn't take it anymore. Some women just snap. If she knew the cops would be looking in my direction, she might have decided to take her chances. I bet Bill had quite the nest egg saved up, too."

"I'll see what I can find, but do you believe Elaine Goddard is capable of killing her husband? Divorce is much simpler."

"Perhaps she had a pre-nup, though after all of the stories I've heard in prison, nothing would surprise me about what people are capable of."

This whole line of thought had just made Trent's job harder. "Thanks for letting me talk this out."

"You bet."

Trent stood. "I need to get back, but if you think of anything that Elaine said, or Bill for that matter, about the relationship, let me know."

"You can count on it."

CHAPTER FIFTEEN

CHARLOTTE HAD JUST enough time to put the finishing touches of paint on Mrs. Goddard's new room, rush home to shower, and then head to the airport to pick up her parents.

No sooner had she pulled up to the arrival door than her parents walked out hand-in-hand, each dragging a suitcase behind them. Charlotte was thrilled they looked so happy.

She jumped out of her car and opened her trunk. "Did you have a good time?"

"Yes," they said in unison then smiled at each other.

From the lustful look they exchanged, perhaps it would be wise not to ask for too many details about their second honeymoon. She hugged her mom first since her dad was busy loading the suitcases. Once he finished, he embraced her.

"Is Rock Hard still in one piece?" he asked.

"Yes." She'd tell them about Bill Goddard's murder after they had time to unwind.

Knowing Dad, he'd want every gory detail, and then try to tell her how Trent should run the investigation. Sometimes having a father as a private investigator and an ex-FBI agent wasn't always the best thing.

Charlotte couldn't wait to get her mom alone so she could

tell her about her budding relationship. The entire strip poker event, however, definitely needed to stay private.

On the way home, they called in a to-go order at Italiano's since her mom said there was nothing edible in the house.

"I'm sorry," Charlotte said. "I didn't even think to stock up the fridge for you." Once she'd moved out, she hadn't looked back.

"That's okay, hon, I'm too tired to cook anyway."

Fifteen minutes later, Charlotte pulled in front of the restaurant in a slot designated for take-out. "Be right back," her dad said as he pushed open the door.

As soon as her father disappeared inside, Charlotte faced her mom. "Trent and I have been seeing each other." The bubble of excitement had been building for too long to stay quiet.

Her mother's face remained unreadable, though Charlotte understood why her mom would worry. A cop's life was fraught with danger. "How's that going?"

Charlotte was a bit disappointed that her mom didn't act thrilled, but she'd expected that reaction. "He's like Dad in some ways, and quite unlike him in others. For the most part, Trent's able to express his emotions."

"Your father's a changed man now." A knowing smile filled her face. "He can be quite expressive when properly motivated."

"Mo-om!" She so didn't need to hear that. The divorce, coupled with him leaving the FBI, had forced him to see the light.

"Just be careful," Mom said.

"Of what? That Trent might hurt me emotionally, or that someone who wanted revenge against him could come after me, just like they did against us?"

Her mother's shoulders sagged. "I was thinking of both, but you're a grown woman. I shouldn't be telling you what you already know. Just do what feels right for you. If you're happy, I'm happy. No matter who you're with, you could be hurt, I suppose." Her mom leaned back against the seat. "For the longest time, I was too cautious with your dad, mostly because I had you to take care of. Perhaps if I'd been more understanding, things might have turned out differently."

"But you had a second chance. You two seem to have figured things out now."

Light returned to her eyes. "Yes, we have indeed."

Her dad returned with three large bags and slid into the back seat. "It's cold out there. Two weeks in Hawaii spoiled me."

"I imagine it would." The aroma made her stomach rumble. "Smells divine."

Before she broached the subject of Bill Goddard's murder, Charlotte wanted to have a peaceful dinner, though she saw no reason not to share her good news about the job. For all she knew, Sharon had already texted her dad about it. "While you were gone, I landed a new client!"

"That's fantastic, hon," her dad said. "How's it going?"

Charlotte detailed how the woman's husband had died, and that she wanted to toss all of his furniture. "She let me keep several awesome pieces. She seems really pleased with what I've done so far, and since she's wealthier than sin, I'm hoping she'll recommend me to her friends."

Her mom reached out and squeezed Charlotte's thigh. "I can't tell you how happy I am. It means you'll stay in Rock Hard."

"I'm not leaving any time soon, that's for sure." She planned to stay for more than just her job, however.

* * *

IT MIGHT BE from a lack of sleep, or his guilty conscience was working overtime, but Trent wanted to believe nothing had happened between his brother and Mrs. Goddard during that fateful Christmas party. What a travesty it would have been if Bill Goddard thought Harmon was a threat to his marriage and then followed through with setting him up as the fall guy for the insider trading scam. Jumping to conclusions, though, wasn't Trent's style, despite wanting Harmon to be innocent.

After he'd spoken to his brother yesterday about Elaine Goddard, Trent had returned to the office because he'd been unable to get a hold of her brother, Richard, to confirm Jayson's story. Before he approached Vic about doing some surveillance, Trent wanted to learn as much as he could about both John Samuels—the man who'd replaced Bill—and Richard Delaney.

Trent had debated calling Charlotte last night just to hear her voice, but she'd told him she was picking up her parents from the airport after work. As much as he wanted to know how things had gone, if he spoke with her on the phone, she'd have convinced him to stop over, and then they'd end up making love again. Probably any thirty-one year old male would have jumped at the chance to delve into luscious Charlotte's body again, but for both of their sakes, he needed to take things slow. Right now, his life was in flux, and he didn't trust himself to make good judgments where she was concerned.

Besides Cade and one other detective he could think of, too many of the men in his department had issues with their marriages because of the stresses of their jobs. If they didn't, it often meant they weren't doing their job to the fullest.

A few hours later, he'd gathered all he could about John Samuels and Richard Delaney. It was time to head over to Vic's office for his appointment and hire him to tail Samuels.

As soon as Trent arrived, Sharon looked up and grinned. "There he is! Charlotte's protector."

"Former protector." Sharon always seemed to focus on what he'd done during that one fateful week. Unless something happened to Charlotte again then he'd protect her just as fiercely as before.

"How are you and Charlotte doing?"

Trent inwardly groaned. "You tell me. Has Charlotte been telling tales?"

Her cheeks pinkened, matching the streaks in her hair—hair that had been blue just a week ago.

"No, but Vic mentioned you were seeing his daughter."

"Did he now?" Charlotte must have spilled the beans. In truth, he'd be a little disappointed if she hadn't told her parents they'd seen each other a few times.

"Go on in and see the man. He's waiting for you," Sharon said, the grin still taking up residence on her face.

Trent headed down the hallway, knocked on Vic's office door, and stepped in. His friend slipped off his glasses and smiled. He was tanner and looked like he'd put on a few pounds, weight Trent thought he could use. "How was Hawaii?"

"Beautiful, but a little busy for my tastes. Reminded me too much of Washington DC during rush hour."

"Ouch. And the beaches?" Someday he'd like to go there, but he doubted he'd have the patience just to sit on the sand and listen to the surf. Then the image of having Charlotte with him surfaced, and he imagined what he'd like to do with her on the hot sand.

"Fantastic, but I would've liked it if the water had been warmer. The waves were terrific though, but I bet you didn't come here to ask about my honeymoon. Charlotte mentioned the night your brother returned to town, his former boss was murdered. Want to tell me what happened?"

Since Vic understood confidentiality better than anyone, and Trent wanted to hire him to do some surveillance work, he had no problem sharing the intel. For the next hour he detailed everything he knew.

Vic leaned back in his seat and tapped his fingers on the desk. "You want me to watch John Samuels or Richard Delaney?"

"Samuels. I'll interview Delaney and then see what Frank Hamilton is up to."

"What do you expect to find?"

"I have absolutely no idea."

***

CHARLOTTE HAD SPENT all day Thursday going store to store locating the perfect furniture and the best artwork for her new project. In the end, she was thrilled with her choices. Every piece seemed to match Mrs. Goddard's sophistication and her vulnerability. The greens, blues, and peaches all blended to make a soothing room.

To Charlotte's delight, the stores promised to deliver everything by three that afternoon, which was perfect. The paint would be dry and the area rug she'd ordered would already have been laid down. Rather tired and a bit anxious to finish the job, she hurried to Mrs. Goddard's home to begin the final phase of decorating.

Once she was shown inside, Charlotte went to work cleaning every surface before the major pieces arrived. Within an hour the van showed up, and the men unloaded everything, saving her a lot of time arranging the pieces herself.

Mrs. Goddard tapped on the closed door. "May I see the room?"

Charlotte liked to have the reveal only when it was totally done, as it made for a bigger impression. She poked her head out the door. "Not yet. It shouldn't take me more than an hour or two to put everything in place and hang the pictures. Is that okay?"

It was her house, and Mrs. Goddard could do what she wished.

"Sure." She smiled. "I feel like it's Christmas. I can't wait to see it. Let me know when it's ready."

"I will."

Charlotte loved the design process, picking out the fabrics and trying to make designer magic, but it was putting everything together that really had her creative juices flowing. Fortunately, the expensive furniture arrived assembled.

As she arranged the artwork on the shelves, she wondered

what it would be like to have a big home like this someday with children running around. As much as she dreamed that Trent would be by her side, she wondered if there was room in his life for a relationship. Her dad had put off having the family he wanted until he was no longer able to work at the FBI. She hoped Trent didn't want to wait that long.

Thinking about the future would only distract her, so she focused on the job instead. Charlotte hustled from one end of the room to the other, looking at the arrangement from every angle until she was satisfied. She couldn't wait to see the excitement on Mrs. Goddard's face.

Charlotte exited the room, closing the door behind her to make it more of a surprise. She walked down the hall. "Mrs. Goddard?"

"Are you ready for me?" Her excited voice floated in from the kitchen.

"Yes."

When they reached the door to the retreat, Charlotte opened it, and as she stepped out of the way, she gently clasped Mrs. Goddard's shoulder so that they wouldn't bump.

The woman winced and grabbed her arm.

"I'm sorry," Charlotte said. Sheesh. She'd barely touched her.

"It's okay."

Charlotte didn't believe her since pain still raced across her face. Perhaps she'd recently had shoulder surgery. As soon as her client stepped in the room, she covered her mouth. "It's amazing. You captured everything I wanted in the room."

Charlotte was thrilled by her response. "Thank you. Sit in the chaise lounge and see how comfortable it is. I think you'll really like it."

Mrs. Goddard eased her way over to the lounge chair, taking her time to study the two paintings on the wall and the assortment of art spread around the room. "This is so beautiful. Too bad Bill can't see how you've transformed his room."

Charlotte doubted he'd appreciate losing his office. She

followed Mrs. Goddard across the room, and as she leaned over to sit down, Charlotte couldn't help but notice the yellow bruises right below the woman's collarbone on the opposite side of the sore shoulder. These could have come from a seatbelt bruise if she'd been in a car accident. Given it was on her left side, she'd have been a passenger. However, it wasn't Charlotte's business to ask what happened.

From the yellow and green hue to the skin, the bruises looked about a week old, and if they hadn't come from an accident, all she could think of was that Mr. Goddard might have caused them. Charlotte knew nothing about the man other than he was Harmon's boss, and that he might have been responsible for setting him up.

"You're right," Mrs. Goddard said. "This chaise lounge is incredibly comfortable. I never could have done this without you." She swung her legs over the side and stood. "Let me get your check for the balance of the job before I fall asleep here."

She hustled out and Charlotte looked around once more to enjoy the beautiful room. Less than a minute later, Mrs. Goddard returned and paid her.

"I added a little extra because you worked so hard and so fast. I plan to tell all my friends about you."

Joy and satisfaction filled her. What a nice woman. "Thank you."

As soon as Charlotte left, her mind began to spin. She wanted to tell Trent about the unusual bruising on Mrs. Goddard's body. Since it was a Friday night, and Charlotte had a large check in her hand for her first solo job, she wanted to celebrate. Naturally, she wanted Trent to be there with her.

Calling and asking him over to her place might backfire, since he always seemed so focused on his job. Trent had said their two interludes together had been nothing short of spectacular, but a part of him remained distant, and that was the part she wanted most.

She could suggest they meet at a restaurant to discuss her

new observation, but when their meal ended, he might excuse himself and say he had work to do.

Damn, seduction was no easy chore. She stopped at a light and snapped her fingers. If calling him might backfire, texting could be a better choice. Perhaps if she picked up a to-go order at Italiano's, she could say she needed someone to help her eat it. He'd see through her ploy to get him over to her house unless she told him she had information about the case. Once he arrived, she felt fairly certain she could stoke his fire.

CHAPTER SIXTEEN

TRENT'S SHIFT AT work was over, but he didn't want to leave, despite it being the start of the weekend. Something kept bothering him about the case. He hadn't been able to reach Richard Delaney, Elaine Goddard's brother, and he hated loose ends. Trent didn't understand why he was so focused on the man, but perhaps he wanted confirmation that Bill had been aware his wife had misbehaved at the party. But three years was a long time to be concerned about, or even remember, a kiss.

Trent wondered if he was trying to prove that Bill had been the one to frame Harmon, or did Trent seriously think Delaney had some insight as to who wanted to harm his brother-in-law?

Fuck if he knew. Of late, his head hadn't been on straight. For a brief moment, he debated asking Dan Hartwick to take him off the case, but Trent believed he could solve this murder despite the connection to his brother.

He leaned back in his office chair and let his inner demons battle it out. If he were honest with himself, he'd admit Charlotte had turned his world upside down. Ever since that week in the cabin where he'd protected her, he hadn't been able to get her out of his mind, and that loss of control worried him.

His phone buzzed, and he hoped it was Delaney returning

his call. When he swiped his screen he smiled. It was a text from Charlotte. He hadn't spoken to her since their amazing encounter, but she was busy not only with her parents but also needed to spend time at the Goddard household finishing her job, and he hadn't wanted to disturb her—or perhaps he didn't want to disturb himself.

He checked the message and then read it again. Learned something about Mrs. Goddard that I believe you'll find interesting. At Italiano's picking up dinner since I finished the job. Want to come over and celebrate with me?

He had to hand it to her. She knew what would entice him—a double lure. Offering him a tidbit about the case as well as herself. The sexual energy always sizzled between them, and the lovemaking was better with her than with any other woman. Charlotte was the first person he'd met who understood him. Her father being in the business had given her an insight no one else had.

He texted her back: Red or white? What time?

Seconds later, she responded. *Red. How about seven?*

He pressed the icon for a smiley face and actually grinned. He pushed back his chair and gathered his things, shelving his unease about leaving before he'd done all he could. Trent had close to an hour to return home, shower, and buy the wine before he had to be at her place.

On his way out, he called Vic who answered on the first ring. "You doing surveillance?" If Vic had been home, he might not have answered.

"Have been for two evenings, but the man is predictably boring. I'll have to hand it to John Samuels, he seems like a hard worker."

Dead ends sucked. "Give it another couple of days and see what he does on the weekend."

"Roger that."

Vic disconnected and Trent wondered if Vic had wished he'd asked Trent whether he was going to see Charlotte this weekend.

If he were Vic, he sure as hell would be concerned about who his daughter dated.

* * *

Trent had conflicting feelings about celebrating with Charlotte since mixing business with pleasure was never a good idea, but he couldn't seem to stop himself.

As he neared her apartment, he realized just how much he was looking forward to discussing the case with her. He had to be careful how much he told her, but he was interested in her theories. He wouldn't be surprised if she'd spoken with her father about Bill Goddard's death, but Charlotte would draw her own conclusions instead of depending on what her dad said.

He had no doubt that Charlotte would do everything in her power to seduce him, but he had to remain strong. She was slowly eating away at his resolve to keep his distance. Unfortunately, as soon as he kissed her hello, she'd be able to tell how much he wanted her, and she'd turn up the heat on her seduction.

With the bottle of wine in hand, he climbed the steps to her apartment. He wanted to greet her properly before asking what she'd found out at Mrs. Goddard's house.

Trent knocked and a few seconds later, Charlotte opened the door, only this time she was dressed in cute jeans and a rather loose blouse, instead of a sexy siren outfit. While she looked hot, it didn't appear as if she had invited him over for sex, and he refused to address the disappointment rushing through him.

"Let me set this down." Trent wanted to start the evening off on a less uncomfortable note than the last time he'd been here. He also wanted her to know that he hadn't come just for her information.

"Thanks for picking up the wine." She looked up at him with those beautiful blue eyes of hers.

That seemed to be his M.O. "Maybe I should just buy a case

and leave it here." Oh shit, he never should've said that. The implication was that he'd be at her place a lot, and while that might be nice, he certainly didn't want to lead her on.

"That would be great," she said, actually looking a little uneasy.

Trent definitely was out of practice when it came to dating. "Congratulations on finishing your first Rock Hard job."

Before giving her the chance to respond, he gathered her in his arms and kissed her. Trent had to use all of his control not to rub his hands over her glorious body, but the moment she delved into his mouth, his cock went ramrod straight and every hormone in his body flooded his system. For their sake, he had to step back.

"Wow," she said. "You sure do know how to kiss a girl."

Not just any girl—you.

He didn't want to talk about his feelings as they were still too unclear. "Didn't someone promise me dinner?" Trent raised his brows and inhaled the rich scent of tomato sauce.

"I did. If you open the wine, I'll serve the food."

This time the two of them moved about the kitchen without getting in each other's way. It was almost as if they knew what the other person was about to do.

He retrieved the glasses and the corkscrew, and had the wine poured just as she brought the food to the table. For a moment, he imagined what it would be like coming home to this every night, but then he worried she'd have the meal all ready to go and he'd have to call for the umpteenth time and say something had come up at work. Disappointing Charlotte would eventually wear on him—and on her.

Trent brought the wine over to the table and waited for her to be seated before he sat down. Instead of going straight into cop mode, he dove into his meal. She'd tell him about Mrs. Goddard when she felt like it.

The first taste hit the spot. Only then did Trent remember

he'd forgotten to take lunch and had eaten something rather unhealthy out of a snack machine. "This is really good," he said.

"If I didn't think I'd gained a ton of weight, I'd eat at Italiano's every night. The food there is fantastic." She finished chewing and taking a sip of her wine before she leaned back in her seat. "You're not going to ask me about Mrs. Goddard?"

Trent laughed. "I figured you'd tell me in your own time. I didn't want to come off as being insensitive." She smiled, but he didn't want to ask what that was about.

"I'm thinking that Mrs. Goddard might have been abused by her husband."

Trent's hand stilled. He'd run a slew of scenarios in his head, some including Mrs. Goddard in the staring role, but not one of them had her being an abused wife. "Care to elaborate?"

Charlotte told him about touching Mrs. Goddard's shoulder and how she'd winced. Then when the woman was climbing onto the chaise lounge, Charlotte had spotted the week-old bruises.

She waved her fork. "I tried to think of what might have caused them, but having bruises on both sides of her body confused me."

"Your theory has a lot of validity, but I need more facts before I can pursue that line of thought." Even now he was thinking about how to gather more information. Perhaps her brother could chime in about whether he thought Bill had been the kind of man to hit or shove his wife, or else the neighbors might be willing to spill the beans, assuming they had any idea. "Did you get the sense that Mrs. Goddard would have allowed this manhandling to happen?"

"Allow it to happen? As in she begged him to rough her up?"

Trent realized his mistake instantly and held up a hand. "No, I didn't mean it like that."

"What did you mean?" Charlotte's posture turned defensive, and he couldn't blame her.

"I'm betting that if anyone tried to hurt you, you'd either

inflict some wounds on him or else go to the police and charge him with assault."

"Damn right I would." Charlotte's lips were firm.

"Good. Do you think Mrs. Goddard is the type of woman to go to the police?" Sadly, not every woman was.

Charlotte looked off to the side. "No. She'd have too much to lose if she helped send her husband to prison. From what I could tell, Mrs. Goddard likes nice things and she enjoys being a lady of leisure. Without her husband's income, she might not have what she desires. Have you looked to see if there was a pre-nup?"

Trent chuckled. "You are something else, Charlotte Hart. And the answer to your question is yes I did look, and no, there was no pre-nup."

She sipped her wine. "So, if she divorced her husband, she could have received half of his possessions."

"It looks that way."

He'd also asked about a life insurance policy. While substantial, half of Bill's wealth was probably more. Charlotte continued eating, but from the way her eyes were roaming around, she was thinking hard.

She looked up at him. "Maybe her sister's husband decided to do something about the abuse."

Or Elaine's own brother. "It did appear as though she and her sister were very close, so it's possible the sister's husband would want to put an end to Elaine's pain."

Charlotte wiped her mouth with her napkin. "There appears to be a lot of suspects. How do you plan to narrow it down?"

"Good question. I have to keep an open mind. Mrs. Goddard said she was with her sister at the time of the murder, but it's possible the sister was covering for her. On the other hand, statistics show that women are not prone to stabbing their victims. Poison is more their game, or shooting them."

"What about Mr. Goddard's partner at the investment firm?"

"Frank Hamilton. What do you think his motive would have been?"

She held up both palms. "The oldest in the book. Money."

He loved the way she thought. "Being the only partner left, Frank might end up with more income, but only if the person who took Bill's place can do as good a job."

She narrowed her eyes as if he was purposely throwing roadblocks in her way. "Who else do you suspect?"

Trent smiled and waved a finger at her. "Can't discuss the case."

Her mouth opened. "That's rich. What have we been doing?"

"I've been interrogating you, not giving you details of the crime or telling you who I suspect."

She pointed a finger at him. "You are a clever man, Trent Lawson."

"I'm smart because I know who to listen to."

She pressed a finger to her chest. "Little ole me?"

He laughed. "You have good instincts."

She grinned. "If only you knew."

He wouldn't touch that line for all the wine in Rock Hard.

CHAPTER SEVENTEEN

CHARLOTTE WAS STOKED that Trent took her theory about Mr. Goddard possibly abusing his wife so seriously. She totally understood that Trent couldn't act on it without more proof, but sometimes even one piece of seemingly irrelevant information could make a case. She'd learned that much from her father.

Sitting at dinner, talking about the suspects, and tossing out theories, stimulated her in more ways than one. It helped put her seduction into perspective. From her actions, Trent must be well aware of her interest in him, and she figured it was now his turn to put some energy into them being together. Deep inside, she needed to know if he was interested in her.

When they both finished their meal, she stood and picked up her plate. "I imagine you'll want to get back so you can work on a new strategy for figuring out who killed Bill Goddard."

Trent stilled, clearly not expecting her to say that. Part of her plan was to let him take the initiative. Men liked it when they believed they were in control.

"Let me help you clean up." Despite his parents having divorced when he was rather young, someone had taught him how to be polite. She appreciated that about him.

Charlotte noticed that he didn't address her comment about

needing to leave, and that avoidance mechanism might be his way of regaining his balance.

After she dumped the empty containers into the trash and placed the dishes in the dishwasher, she faced him. "Did you give the books to Harmon?"

He clenched his fists for second. "Yes, I'm sorry I forgot to tell you. He plans to find a good home for them."

"Perfect. I didn't feel right about tossing them."

"You're a good person, Charlotte, and I really want to thank you for being so considerate of me and my family." Trent grabbed her by the waist, drew her close, and when he dragged a knuckle down her cheek, her hormones shot to life. "A lot of people wouldn't have given Harmon the time of day. Whether he committed his crime or not, the fact he spent three years in jail is going to make a lot of people uneasy being around him, but not you."

She wrapped her arms around his neck and leaned back, enjoying the way his expressive eyes spoke to her. "There's a gentleness about Harmon that I immediately recognized. If he was caught up in his job, he's served his time, and that's good enough for me. I'm sure my father has done a lot of bad things in his life, but he's a good man underneath."

"That he is."

Lust pooled in Trent's eyes and a second later his mouth captured hers, causing pinpricks of delight to skitter over her skin. His touch, smell, and taste ignited every part of her body, and as much as she wanted to ravish him, she had to let him take the lead.

As his tongue plunged into her mouth, his hands slid under her shirt and cupped her breasts. If that wasn't a signal that he wanted to make love with her, she didn't know what was. The mere pressure from his palms rubbing across her nipples sent moisture straight between her thighs. She hadn't meant the groan to escape, but she couldn't help it. Trent was everything she wanted and more.

He broke the kiss, and his breath came out rapid. "I'm trying to behave because I don't want you to think that I only want you for sex."

Yes! As much as she wished to question what he did want her for, right now conversation was the last thing on her mind. "I know."

If she said anything more, he might feel the need to explain. He could talk all he wanted after they made love. To show him she was fine with his expression of passion, she slipped his shirt from his pants and rapidly undid the buttons. God, she loved his chest and how the slight wisp of hair tickled her palms.

Trent lifted her blouse off and tossed it on the kitchen counter. When he unhooked the back of her bra, the relief was divine. As he dragged down the straps, excitement sizzled through her. She hooked her thumbs into his waistband and puffed out her chest, silently begging him to touch her.

His lids half closed as he dragged off her bra. "I can't seem to stop myself."

The second his mouth nabbed her nipple, she leaned against the counter and grabbed the edge. Lust swirled inside her, and the delicious ache sent electric pulses straight to her core. Worse than anything, she wanted to rip off his clothes, but she needed to refrain. This was Trent's show.

"I love your tits."

She worked hard not to laugh. "You're such a guy."

"Oh, yeah?" He punctuated his comment with a tug on each tip, and her breath caught. "Wait 'till I show you just how much of a guy I really am."

"I'd love to see it." She nodded to his cock.

He tapped her nose. "That's off limits until I enjoy you first."

While he caressed and licked each nipple, his tongue heightened her desire. Much more of this exquisite torture, and she'd have to take control and strip. To hurry the process, she kicked off her shoes.

Needing to touch him, she dragged her fingers over his head, loving the softness of his hair. While he kept it short, the top had grown in, and it was like playing with silk. Since he was working hard to undress her, it seemed only fair to help him out of his jeans. As soon as she undid the buttons, it was like the race was on to see who could undress the other faster. He lifted his head and kissed her hard, all the while dragging her jeans down her hips.

This time, Charlotte broke the kiss and burst out laughing.

"What's so funny?" he asked.

She shook her head. "You are."

"I have no idea why you think so, but I'll show you funny."

In a flash, he lifted her up onto the kitchen counter. He then slipped off her jeans and panties and dropped them behind him before stepping out of his pants and briefs.

"You sure did show me, but I have to be honest, there's nothing funny about that." She nodded to his rigid cock.

Trent smiled, picked up his jeans, folded them in half, and then placed his pants behind her. "Lean back on these. It'll be softer on your elbows."

Could he be any more considerate? She did as he asked, and he then placed her feet on the counter. With her legs wide open, anticipation made her inner walls cramp. He then had the nerve to run his tongue along his lips, and she could almost feel the lick that was sure to come.

"I hope you have a lot of staying power, as I plan to enjoy you for a long time," he said.

She laughed. "Me? I think you're the one who can't hold out."

He lowered his chin, clearly ready to take on the dare. She probably shouldn't have challenged him like that as she knew very well she'd be the first to cave, but there was nothing wrong with having multiple orgasms.

"As long as I don't let you touch me, I'll be good. Or so I hope," he said, sounding wonderfully tentative.

Reaching underneath her, he clasped onto her thighs, his thumbs close to her opening. Trent leaned over and ran his tongue above her folds, but not giving her what she really wanted. The man sure did understand the art of building sexual tension.

Because Charlotte was leaning on her elbows, she was unable to touch him, but her time would come. When she finally grabbed hold, she'd make certain Trent would have no doubt that he'd met his match.

He reached up and flicked his thumb over her distended nipple, and spikes of passion spread across her breast, heating her up. He'd only begun his seduction, and yet she was already close to bursting. It wasn't fair.

Trent opened her folds with his free hand and very gently rubbed his thumb across her clit, stimulating her, but it wasn't enough. She wanted it harder and faster.

"What are you waiting for?" She wasn't really trying to tell him what to do, but it probably sounded like it. Aw, hell. *Just ask.* "Lick me."

He glanced up at her. "In due time. I need to get you ready."

"I don't think I could have any more desire for you than right now." Charlotte believed in honesty because it lessened misunderstandings.

"I need you to be desperate."

If she came before he planned, he'd know just how desperate she'd been. Charlotte scooted closer to the edge of the counter, wrapped her legs around his neck, and drew him near. Her butt lifted up enough so that her pussy was close to his mouth.

"That's cheating." Trent swiped his tongue across her wet slit, and she had to grip his jeans to keep from toppling over the erotic edge.

"No, it's called getting what I want," she panted.

Trent's fingers alternated between her breasts, plucking, teasing, and basically shooting her need level into the stratosphere, while sucking on her clit. Pride prevented her from coming right away, but when he slipped a finger into her wet hole, she gave up the fight. Charlotte dropped onto her back to free her hands and grabbed his head. Pulses of desire beat against her from the inside out as her orgasm claimed her.

"Yes, yes."

As amazing as that experience had been, she needed more. Much more.

"You really were ready." Trent ducked from under her legs and slid her off the counter.

"It won't take much to make me come again," she said.

He cupped her face and kissed her, his cock pressing against her belly. Bliss and joy slammed into her as she dragged her palms up and down his corded back, loving the way their passion flared. She couldn't get enough of him.

Trent lowered his hands to her hips, flipped her around, and dragged her hips away from the counter. "Hang on."

Charlotte wiggled her rear. "Hurry."

"God, you're beautiful."

He slipped one hand under her and cupped both of her breasts while he guided his cock between her thighs. He then drove straight into her, and her breath lodged in her throat. Despite being wet, the friction drove her wild. Trent dropped his chest onto her back and held on tight. For a few seconds, he remained still, as if he needed a moment to compose himself.

He lifted off her. "Oh, shit, I forgot a condom."

"I'm on the pill," she blurted.

"I'm clean, I swear."

She trusted Trent more than anyone she'd ever known. "Take me."

Trent kissed her neck then pounded into her. Her fingers tightened on the counter as waves of ecstasy set her on fire. He lightly pinched a nipple, sending sparks of need in every direction.

As much as she wanted to wait until Trent had been fulfilled, each thrust made it more difficult to remain in control. Her groans turned into near screams, and Trent's moans became louder and louder each time he plunged into her. His fingers tightened on her breasts and his mouth roamed up her neck to her ear. When he dragged his teeth along the outer shell, chaos descended.

Trent drove into her one more time, and she tightened her muscles to keep him there.

"Charlotte!" Heated pulses shot out and filled her.

The stretching and expanding shoved her over the climactic edge, as waves of ecstasy washed over her. Her pulse soared, making it hard to even take a breath.

Trent dragged his hands down to her hips and leaned back. "Each time I make love with you, I'm amazed that it's better than the last."

Charlotte was totally blown away. She never expected that admission to come from him. He slipped out, found a towel in the drawer, and wet it. He turned her around and cleaned her up.

"I don't know what comes over me, but every time I'm near you, I have to make love with you. I swear I didn't come over here for that," he said.

She cupped his face. "You are a sweet man, Trent Lawson. I'm flattered."

His face slightly reddened as he grabbed his pants off the countertop. As if he'd received a call from the precinct, he dressed quickly. Not wanting to be the only one naked, Charlotte did the same thing.

There always seemed to be that one moment of awkwardness between them, and this was that time. She thought about asking him to stay the night, but she believed it was a little too soon. Men like Trent needed to be the one to make that decision, and crowding him would only push him away.

"So what's next on your agenda?" Charlotte asked, as she zipped up her pants.

"You mean about the case?"

"Yes." Though if he wanted to talk about the two of them, she wouldn't have minded.

"I need to interview Mrs. Goddard's brother to see if your

theory has any validity, but even if he denies Bill Goddard abused his wife, it could just mean that Elaine Goddard kept that information from him."

She had to agree it was a long shot. "If you learn anything you're allowed to share, I'd love to hear it."

He clasped her shoulders and smiled. "You can count on it."

CHAPTER EIGHTEEN

TRENT COULD HAVE waited until Monday to catch up with Richard Delaney, but after hearing Charlotte's theory about Mrs. Goddard's possible abuse, he was anxious to speak with the man. It was a good motive for murder. While Delaney had not returned any of his calls, Trent decided to drive by his house in the hopes of catching up with him Saturday morning.

Luck was on his side. Someone's car was in the drive and he hoped it belonged to Delaney. Trent parked his Jeep on the street and headed up to the front door. He still hadn't figured out exactly how we wanted to broach the topic of Elaine's bruises, but when he did, he doubted he'd get a very welcoming response.

Trent rang the bell, and it seemed forever before someone answered. It was Delaney.

"Detective Lawson, I've been meaning to return your call. I'm sorry, but I've been very busy." The man's chin tucked in and his shoulders straightened, as if he was preparing to do battle.

Delaney didn't seem remotely contrite. Most people he interviewed were able to come up with a better excuse than that. "Do you have a moment? I just need to ask you a few questions about your brother-in-law." Trent watched for signs of nervousness, but Richard Delaney didn't display any obvious signs of guilt—no twitches, sudden perspiration, or eye contact avoidance.

"Come in." While the man didn't act uneasy, Trent doubted Delaney was happy he was there.

He showed him into the living room and pointed to a rather uncomfortable looking straight-backed chair while Delaney sank into the sofa.

Trent pulled out his notepad and flipped through some blank pages. "I believe Detective Benson asked you about Bill's death."

"Yes, and like I told him, I didn't kill the son of a bitch."

Okay, the hostility had not been in Cade's report. "We're not accusing you of anything, Mr. Delaney. I believe you told Detective Benson you were home alone the night your brother-in-law was murdered."

"Yes, and since I was alone, I can't prove I didn't drive over to Bill's house and kill him."

"You seem to have a lot of anger toward the victim. Why's that?"

"No use hiding it. I figured you guys would have spoken to my ex-wife and found out how much I disliked the man. When you find the real killer, let me shake his hand."

While Trent didn't have many murder investigations under his belt, he could honestly say none of the men who'd been guilty ever claimed they wanted the victim dead. As for speaking with Delaney's ex-wife, Trent hadn't considered doing so. "Care to elaborate?"

"I think it's obvious. Bill's firm blabbed my company's secret. I lost my job and my wife because of it." Delaney tapped his chest. "And did my S.O.B brother-in-law lend me hand? Fuck no."

Trent didn't need to mention that Delaney's big mouth that created the problem. At least he wasn't bad mouthing Harmon.

Trent had uncovered all of the information about Delaney's

dismissal shortly after Harmon had been sent to prison. "Who else beside yourself wanted Bill dead?"

"Anyone with common sense."

So much for learning names. "I want to ask you about the night of the Christmas party when Jayson Kendall told you about my brother and your sister kissing. Did you tell Bill about her indiscretion?"

Delaney looked off to the side, probably debating what to tell. "Why would I? I loved my sister. Besides, Elaine said Bill suspected her of being unfaithful."

Now that was news.

Delaney continued. "Your brother wasn't the first man she'd kissed, and he probably won't be the last."

Relief washed through him. Trent took some notes, but they were minimal because he was confident he wouldn't forget one word. "I take it your sister was unhappy in her marriage?"

Delaney's fists clenched. "Yes. Bill was incapable of affection. The man was a sociopath."

Many in his field were. It was probably best that Harmon wasn't in that business any longer. While Trent doubted he'd get an answer, he needed to see the man's reaction when he asked if Bill ever harmed Elaine. "Were you aware that Bill abused your sister?"

His head jerked back. "No, but I suspected it because she was always applying makeup a little too heavily, especially around her neck, and upper arms, but how did you know?"

"It's my job to know." He certainly wasn't going to tell Delaney about Charlotte's observation. "Did you ask her about it?"

"Fuck, yeah I did, but she always denied it. She knew if I found out that I'd do something about it."

Trent wasn't certain how much he wanted to push this line of questioning. Too much, and Delaney might approach his sister. If she had killed her husband, Trent didn't want to tip his hand.

Trent stood. "Thank you for your time. If you think of anything, please let me know."

He left and headed home to think. This case was getting more complicated by the minute. As he neared his house, his cell rang.

It was Vic. "You got something for me?"

"Possibly. Guess who stopped by to visit Elaine Goddard this morning?"

Considering Vic was being paid to follow John Samuels, the man who'd moved up to Bill's position, and not Elaine, the answer was easy. "Samuels?"

"Yup."

"Anything interesting happen?" Trent asked.

"I wasn't standing outside the house with my face pressed to the window, but Samuels was in the house for about an hour and a half."

Trent tried to think of a reason he'd be in there that long. "He probably was asking her about some of her husband's clients."

"Did you get the impression that Elaine Goddard was privy to what Bill did?"

"No."

"So what makes you think it was an innocent interaction?"

He thought back to what Delaney had just told him about Mrs. Goddard's interest in other men. "Are you thinking there was something going on between them?"

"It's possible, which was why I called Charlotte and asked her where the master bedroom was located."

Trent could fill in the blank. "Don't tell me you saw them head in that direction."

"Bingo."

His mind raced as he pulled to a stop at a red light. Trent hadn't seen that coming. "Let's suppose they were having an affair. Her brother told me that Bill suspected Elaine of having a few. Would it be enough to kill Bill over it?"

"Anything is possible, but if John Samuels wanted her, he might have tried to talk her into leaving Bill. When she wouldn't, he killed her husband, and furthered his career at the same time."

Trent had thought jealousy could have been a motive, but then dismissed it. "Divorce is less messy, but that assumes she wanted John over Bill."

"She might have asked Bill, and he said no. It would look bad for business, not to mention what it would do to his bank account."

"Damn. Watch Samuels for the next couple of days to see what he does. The fact Mrs. Goddard threw out all of Bill's possessions implies she wasn't overly fond of the man."

"I'd say you're right."

"Keep in touch."

Trent disconnected and headed home, more confused than ever.

* * *

IF HISTORY WAS any indication, Trent wouldn't call her today. Charlotte had no idea if he felt guilty every time they made love, or if he truly had too much work to do. Regardless, she was going to take advantage of the weekend.

She arrived at the shop around one and went straight to work putting the final touches on her store. She planned to open on Monday. Once she had some clients lined up, she'd put a sign on the door that said, by appointment only. That way she wouldn't have to hire someone to man her place when she was at a client's home.

She'd been hard at work for about two hours when her cell rang, and she hoped it might be Trent calling. Most likely, it was her mom asking how things were going. She nabbed her phone and checked the number, but didn't recognize it.

"Hello?"

"Is this Charlotte Hart?" The man had a deep, soothing voice.

"Yes, it is."

"My name is John Samuels. Mrs. Goddard gave me your name and highly recommended you."

Excitement jumped her pulse into the red zone. Charlotte had to work to keep the thrill out of her voice. "Fantastic. How may I help you?"

"I'm looking to redo my master bedroom."

Bedrooms were one of her favorite rooms. "Would you like to come to the store to look at some samples, or would you feel more comfortable if I brought some materials to your house?"

"I think it would be best if you stopped by my house so that you can see the layout of the room. It's a bit odd."

That sounded fine. "Is tomorrow convenient for you? I'm officially opening my business on Monday, and I need to be here."

"Perfect."

"So that I know what to bring, how would you describe your style?"

"Style?" He truly sounded confused. The man must not be married.

"Modern, contemporary, western?"

"Ah, I don't know."

She smiled. "That's all right. I'll bring a bit of everything."

They discussed the time, and he then gave her his address along with some directions.

When she hung up, she leaned back in her seat and smiled. She couldn't wait to tell Trent. Coming to Rock Hard just might have been the best thing to happen to her.

Energized by this new job, Charlotte put the finishing touches on her store and gathered the samples she thought would be suitable for a bedroom and headed home for the evening. She thought about stopping at her parents' place, but then decided she didn't want to become accustomed to going over there all the time. After five years of being divorced, they deserved to have some time alone together.

Wanting to spend the entire evening creating a few proposals for tomorrow's meeting with Mr. Samuels, she stopped at the Valley Café for a to-go order. Charlotte could only hope Mr. Samuels was as easy to work with as Mrs. Goddard.

CHAPTER NINETEEN

CHARLOTTE HAD NO reason to be nervous, but she was. It wasn't very often she worked for a man, though more than likely, he'd be like her dad—someone who really didn't care what items she picked.

She'd never be so rude to ask, but she suspected there might have been a Mrs. Samuels who had recently left or possibly died. Maybe that was why Mr. Samuels and Mrs. Goddard had spoken. They were both experiencing a loss.

With her samples in her arms, she traipsed up to the front door and rang the bell. A wrought iron lamp hung above the doorway and the stained glass door was exquisite and spoke of money.

The door opened and a tall man about forty-five greeted her. He was dressed in khaki pants, a starched white shirt, and loafers —not the usual Sunday fare. In fact, she couldn't remember seeing a man dressed like that in Montana—with the exception of Dan Hartwick, who seemed to live in a suit.

"Ms. Hart?"

Given she was laden down with samples and had arrived at the appointed time, it was a good guess. "Yes."

As soon as she stepped inside, she perused the large area,

trying to sense his style. To be honest, she didn't know what to call it. The sofa was contemporary, but the coffee table and TV stand bordered on the antique. The light dining room table and straight back chairs had a Scandinavian flair.

Mr. Samuels chuckled. "It's a mess isn't it?"

Everything was neat, so he was probably referring to the eclectic style. "It could use a theme."

"I like you, Charlotte Hart. I'm glad I listened to Mrs. Goddard."

Her cheeks heated, even though she found it interesting that he'd hesitated a second before he said Mrs. Goddard's name. Perhaps he was used to referring to her as Elaine, not that it made a bit of difference.

"Mind if I walk around a bit to get a sense of your style?"

He lifted the heavy samples from her arms and set them on the side table in the entry. "Absolutely, but let me first show you the bedroom, and you'll see why it needs to be redone."

Given how the living room furniture was scattered randomly around the room, she was surprised he'd even asked her there, unless it was Elaine Goddard who'd said his place needed a total overhaul. The eighteen-foot by eighteen-foot master bedroom had a plain queen-sized bed and a rather ratty dresser. While there were blinds on the window, there were no drapes, making the room cold and sterile. The home on the outside spoke of money. The inside did not.

"Can you give me a hint what you're looking for?" she asked. "Something cozy and romantic, with a sitting room perhaps? Or do you want a more masculine feel to the room?" His answer would give her a clue about whether there was another woman in his future.

"I'll leave it in your hands."

That directive was almost worse than him being too specific since there was a big chance he wouldn't like what she designed. "How about I show you the samples and perhaps something will strike your fancy."

After gathering her things from the hallway, he led her into the dining room where she spread them out.

"What did you do with the things in Bill's office when you redecorated it? I only ask because I'd like my furniture to have a good home, too."

That made sense. "I threw out a lot of things, but the paintings, furniture, books, and assorted artwork were donated. Mrs. Goddard could have put them on consignment, but she seemed anxious to move on."

"Donating my stuff sounds good, too. As long as they land in a good home, I'll be happy. Did you know I used to work with Mrs. Goddard's husband?"

That was a rather random thing to tell her. It caused her pulse to soar and a trickle of fear to drip into her belly. "No, she never mentioned it." Or him, for that matter.

He leaned back in his seat. "I only mention it because there were several books that Bill had that belonged to the firm. I was hoping they'd be returned, but I guess they never will. There were also some missing client files. Do you recall finding them?" His brows rose. "It's okay if you trashed them, I just didn't want them out in public."

She had to think what was in the desk and the file cabinets. "Most of his drawers were empty. Perhaps you should ask Mrs. Goddard if she did anything with the items." She could ask Harmon about the books and what he'd done with them, but she didn't want to mention them in case he'd already given them away.

"I will. I normally wouldn't be concerned, but perhaps you've heard that we had an incident a few years ago that nearly brought down the firm."

He was probably referring to Harmon's insider trading. "I didn't know. I just moved to town." She'd learned from her dad about how sharing too much information could come back to bite her.

"Well, it's not important."

She figured he'd been fishing.

For the next half hour, they discussed what might look good in the bedroom, and she had to admit he was just as easy going as Mrs. Goddard.

Charlotte pushed back her chair. "You said you wouldn't mind if I look in a few of the other rooms?"

He waved a hand. "Go ahead, but I don't think you'll be able to figure out my style from any of those rooms either. My mom passed away and left me a lot of her furniture. With an ex-wife who had a much different taste than I did, I ended up with a mess. When I stopped over at Mrs. Goddard's house to drop off some papers, I saw her new retreat. That style really appeals to me."

She smiled. "I'll keep that in mind."

Charlotte spent a few minutes looking in the other rooms and then met him back in the dining room. He was right. She wasn't able to figure out his style. She picked up her samples and he escorted her to the door.

"So what's the next phase?" he asked.

"I'll draw up some plans, complete with color pallets, and I'll show them to you. I'm opening my store tomorrow so I can't promise when I'll be back, but I'll make it as quick as possible."

"Thank you."

As she left, she realized he hadn't asked her how much this renovation would cost, but given where he worked, maybe he didn't care.

* * *

Trent was actually enjoying a moment of peace in his home for the first time in weeks. Okay, peace may not have been the right word, but he wasn't at the office nor was he battling with his dad or counseling his brother. He'd been able to carve out a few hours of his day to lay out what he knew about this case. On the dining room table, he'd placed a separate file for Elaine

Goddard, one for Bill's partner, Frank Hamilton, one for Elaine's brother, Richard Delaney, and one for John Samuels, the man who took over Bill's position at the firm. All of them had a motive for wanting Bill Goddard dead, but Frank and John probably had the least issue with the man. On the other hand, Trent would never learn what really went on behind closed doors.

Then there was everyone else who worked at the investment firm, any client who ever lost money, and possibly Elaine's sister's husband. It wasn't like Trent hadn't been in this bind before, but it wasn't a fun place to be. He just needed to find that one piece of information that would send him in the right direction.

His cell rang, and for a split second he debated not answering it, except that it could be the precinct. Hopefully, it was Cade with that elusive missing part. Given he was tailing Elaine, Cade might have learned something.

He picked up his phone. It was Vic, not Cade. "Hey. You got something for me?"

"Did you fucking send my daughter into Samuel's house?"

Whoa. Every cell in his body shot to high alert. Vic was highly pissed, an attitude he could handle, but when Vic mentioned Charlotte was at Samuel's house, an ember burned a hole in his stomach. "What are you talking about? Of course, I didn't send Charlotte in there. He could be our killer."

"I've been watching his house since ten this morning. At two this afternoon, who drives up but my daughter with a bunch of samples in her hand."

"Just calm down, Vic. Charlotte is a designer, and she just finished redoing Elaine Goddard's house. Perhaps Elaine recommended her to Samuels."

"She was in Elaine Goddard's house, too?"

Crap. "I guess Charlotte didn't tell you."

"No, she didn't."

"Her being in his house could be innocent."

"I doubt it. Did Charlotte have any idea who she was dealing with?" Vic asked.

Trent went over the conversation he had with her about Mrs. Goddard and her brother. "I don't remember mentioning Samuels' name. This is an ongoing investigation, so I've been very careful about not telling her too much. Is she still in his house?" The acid burned deeper.

"No, she left a few minutes ago. Thankfully, she drove in the opposite direction from me, so I don't think I've been made. She would have called if she'd seen me."

He let out a long breath. "Let's hope Samuels is only interested in a redesign. Do you know if either Samuels or Mrs. Goddard is aware Charlotte is your daughter or that she and I are... friends?" He wasn't about to say lovers to her dad. At least not yet.

"I can't be certain. I didn't know either one of them before the murder, however I'm only one of a few private investigators in town. It's possible they know who I am."

Frustration charged through his veins. "Harmon may have spoken to some people about Charlotte and me, too. It's also possible Samuels or Mrs. Goddard could have spotted you with her. Damn. I'll speak to her and see if I can convince her to be more cautious or tell her not to do the job at all."

Vic huffed. "If you tell Charlotte not to do something, I guarantee that she'll do it in spades. I raised a very stubborn daughter."

That wasn't news to him. "Let me see what I can find out, and I'll get back to you. Don't worry. With you on the lookout, she'll be safe."

"If only I could mic her, I'd feel better. I now need to rent a car so she won't spot me hanging around Samuels. That would really piss her off."

"Smart."

Trent disconnected and fixed himself some coffee, needing a moment to come up with a plan. Knocking on her door on a Sunday evening might look a bit suspicious, not to mention, they'd probably end up in bed. If her life weren't in possible danger, he would have enjoyed another interlude.

Trent mulled over his options. He wanted to take her out on a date anyway, in part because he didn't want her to think he was just interested in getting her into bed. Sitting at a restaurant might allow for a calmer interaction, as he suspected she'd be upset with his suggestion of keeping her distance from Samuels.

Trent needed someplace quiet where they could sit and not be overheard. The only restaurant that came to mind was the Steerhouse.

The hardest part would not be leaking any information about the case, while at the same time, asking Charlotte to take care. He could always say that a divorced man might be interested in more than her decorating skills.

Pleased with this plan, Trent called Charlotte, hoping she was free.

She answered on the second ring. "Hey, Trent. I didn't expect to hear from you. Is everything okay?"

He liked to believe she worried about him. "Just working on the case and thought maybe you'd like to grab some dinner tonight."

She hesitated for a moment, and he wondered what that was about. Had she been uneasy around John Samuels and wanted to mention something?

"I'd love to, but I can't stay out too late. I'm opening the store tomorrow."

Damn, perhaps she did believe he only wanted her for sex. "I understand. I have to be in early tomorrow, too. How about I pick you up at six?"

"Where are we going? I need to know what to wear."

"Steerhouse."

She sucked in an audible breath. "You don't have to take me there. I know it's expensive."

Because he rarely spent money, he had saved quite a lot. Besides, when Harmon was in the investment business, he'd given him some good advice. Now, Trent had a nice little nest egg.

"You're worth it," he said, and Charlotte giggled. It was a sound he'd come to enjoy.

"Okay. I'll share some news with you when I see you."

He leaned back against the sofa. "Oh yeah? What's that?"

"You'll just have to wait until tonight to find out. I'll see you then."

She was such a tease. "Later."

He hoped she'd be in as good a mood after he told her about Samuels.

CHAPTER TWENTY

"WE'LL HAVE TO park behind the restaurant," Trent said.

He'd driven around the block, and all of the parking places in front had been taken. Because the skies had suddenly darkened, bringing with it cold air, Charlotte was glad for the shorter walk. "Fine by me. It looks like it's about to rain."

"Or snow." Trent found a spot, jumped out of the Jeep, and went around to her side. After opening her door and helping her out, he plucked an umbrella from the back and waved it. "Preventative measures."

She smiled. "We can only hope."

Wrapping an arm around her waist, he sheltered her as they walked down the alley between the restaurant and the hardware store, the buildings thankfully blocking some of the wind. His protective action stirred something deep inside her. This was where she wanted to be.

Once inside, Trent gave his name and asked for a booth near the back, and they were immediately seated. The fact he'd made a reservation thrilled her. She hoped he wanted to have a romantic conversation, but she wouldn't let her hopes rise. Right now she needed to focus on her store and making her new client happy.

No sooner were they seated than the waiter arrived for their drink order. "I'd like a bottle of champagne," Trent said then looked over at her.

Stunned, she leaned forward on her elbows. "What are we celebrating?" Her mind spun. "Oh, my God. Did you arrest Mr. Goddard's killer?" she whispered.

His eyes widened briefly. "I wish. You said you had something to tell me. I thought it might be cause for another celebration."

She had asked him to her place to celebrate her first client. Now, she felt a bit guilty that her news wasn't worthy of a bottle of champagne. "You are the sweetest man alive."

He froze for a fraction of a second before smiling. "Not always. So tell me about your news."

"It's not that big of a deal, but I have another decorating job." When she told him the name of her client, she had a feeling he'd be unhappy, given the man's connection to Harmon's former firm, but she wanted to share everything with him.

"That's fantastic. Was it a referral from Mrs. Goddard?"

"It was." She loved that he acted so pleased. "His name is Mr. Samuels. He knows Mrs. Goddard because he worked for her husband."

His lips thinned. "Really? Did you know this before you took the job?" His words came out tight, though he didn't seem angry.

"No. It wasn't until I was in the middle of the job that he mentioned his connection to Ardton Investments. He asked about some of the books and papers Mr. Goddard had in his office and wanted to know if I'd tossed them."

Trent fiddled with his napkin, looking as if he was trying to figure out what to say. "What did you tell him?"

"I told him the file cabinets were already empty and to ask Mrs. Goddard what she might have done with the contents."

His fingers relaxed and he let go of the knife he was holding. Her answer must have pleased him. "Was he nice?" he asked.

That was an odd question, and since Mr. Samuels still worked at the firm, she bet Trent had interviewed him. "What was your take on him?"

"I asked you first." His tone sharpened, and she imagined this was how he sounded when he interrogated a witness.

Clearly, he wasn't in the mood to play around. "He was very easy-going. As soon as I walked into his living room, it was clear that he needed a decorating intervention as nothing in his house matched. He asked me to redo his master bedroom, and I could see why. It was a nearly empty shell of a room with no personality. If he ever brought a woman there, she'd run."

His shoulders sagged. "I'm glad to hear it, but you know what I'm going to ask of you next."

He sounded too much like her dad. "Yes. Keep my eyes open for anything strange and be careful."

"So he's divorced?"

"Yes." Most likely Trent knew that.

"He's old enough to be your father, you know."

His implication shocked her. "Are you kidding me? He's a client."

"Who conveniently has you redecorating his master bedroom and just might be looking for the next Mrs. Samuels." His jaw was so tight she feared it might break.

A bit of anger speared her, but then humor edged its way in. "Trent Lawson, I'm ashamed of you. Trust me when I say I only have eyes for you." She probably should have kept her intense interest to herself, but Trent had to know how much she liked him. The tension on his face evaporated, but she couldn't judge his level of relief.

"I've met John Samuels and he's a good-looking man."

All she could do was shake her head. "So are you. Remember, I'm a professional. Now can we talk about something else?" Here she thought he'd say the man might have been involved with Mr. Goddard's murder, and all Trent was worried about was a man nearly her dad's age putting the moves on her.

Before he could answer, the waiter came by with the champagne and two glasses. He poured their drinks then slid the bottle into a bucket of ice. As soon as their server left, Trent lifted his glass and she followed suit.

"Here's to a successful opening of your store and to many more clients to come," he said as he tapped his glass to hers. All remnants of the Mr. Samuels' conversation seemed to have been forgotten, pleasing her to no end.

"I'll make a toast, too. May your case end soon."

"Here, here."

As she lifted the glass to her lips, the bubbles tickled Charlotte's nose, and she giggled. While they'd eaten out together before, she considered this their first real date, and she wanted to enjoy it the best she could. "So tell me about your most exciting case."

"I already did. The whole incident with your father and the terrorists was one that will forever be burned in my brain. We had to use every resource at our disposal to find out who was behind the potential attack, and we identified them with only a day to spare."

She was pleased that her dad was involved in something that affected so many people. "Do you think you'll always be a detective?"

His chin tucked in. "As opposed to what? A private investigator?"

She shrugged. "I don't know. You ever see yourself being in charge of an entire unit, like Dan Hartwick, or do you want to pound the pavement searching for clues?"

"The latter. I enjoy the mystery of it all. I inherited much of my drive from my dad, though I don't aspire to be like him."

That didn't bode well for him wanting a family, but she wouldn't be discouraged. The waiter stopped back and after they placed their order, Charlotte decided to relax and not dig too deep into Trent's psyche. He'd already explained that his life growing up hadn't been easy, so there was no use unearthing more pain. "What's your fondest memory with your brother?"

"I can see this is twenty questions night."

She laughed. "You afraid?"

"Hell no."

She smiled. "You should be."

He glanced at the ceiling and said nothing for a moment. "I think my favorite memory with my brother was when he taught me how to ride my bike. Harm was really patient and didn't make fun when I kept falling off."

Harm? Cute nickname. "I can remember when my dad helped me learn, too. He wasn't home very often, but one time after he'd finished a job, he bought me a pink bicycle. He made me wear a helmet, which I didn't like, but when I fell off, I was glad I had it. I remember thinking Dad was pretty smart." She leaned back against the seat. "It was one of the happiest days of my life."

Trent polished off his glass of champagne and poured a second one. "I'm pleased you had some nice memories of him."

"Me, too, though I was angry with Dad after he left. I'd like to think I've grown up since then. I know Dad did what he thought was right, and I can appreciate that now. He says he regrets a lot of things in his life, and we're working toward a better relationship."

"I believe all relationships are a work in progress." He tossed back his glass as if that was yet another touchy subject.

Not wanting the dinner to be a downer, she changed the topic to one dear to her heart—decorating. "If you could have your ideal home, what would it look like?"

His eyes widened. "I haven't a clue. I'm never home long enough to worry about it. What I have now suits me fine, even if it is a bit bland."

With the right decorations, his place could be cozy, even for two. Fortunately, the food arrived, giving her time to come up with another topic. "How often do you think I need to practice shooting in order to become proficient?" She figured he'd like to talk about weapons.

"I don't see why you need to improve. It's not like you're a police officer or anything, but if you're asking on a theoretical basis, I'd have to say about three times a week in the beginning."

"Good to know."

Besides impressing Trent, she wanted to be proficient mostly because she liked having the control and power.

They chatted a bit about Harmon, and then talked about a few of his other cases. About halfway through their meal, the rain came down in earnest, making their corner retreat all the cozier. Twenty minutes later, the storm passed, and the sky cleared.

Trent picked up the umbrella. "Told you this was my good luck charm. Are you ready?"

"Yes. There's nothing worse than being cold and wet." She was anxious to return home and finish some last minute preparations for her opening. For once, she wasn't going to let her inner desires rule and ask Trent in.

He paid the check and escorted her outside. Just as they stepped into the alley he stopped. "Fuck."

A lake had formed the length of the alley. "That's not good."

He handed her the umbrella. "No, it's not. Why don't you wait here, and I'll head around back and pick you up in front. You'll ruin your shoes if you walk in the water."

She had dressed in her good boots, and they probably would be damaged. "What about you?"

He lifted his booted foot. "These have been through mud and rain and survived. Don't worry about me, I'll be back in a moment."

With the umbrella in hand she headed back around the corner and leaned against the front wall. She had thoroughly enjoyed being with Trent tonight, and while the conversation had started out a bit uneasy, once they found a safe topic, an easy rhythm developed between them.

As she was thinking about how he'd ordered champagne, popping sounds floated toward her. At first, she thought she was imagining the opening of the bottle, but then the noise registered. They were gunshots reverberating down the alley, coming from the back, and every one of her senses shot to alert. All she could think of was that Trent had been shot.

Her muscles froze for a moment before she was able to move. Heart pounding, she dropped the umbrella, stuck her hand in her purse, and retrieved her gun. Not caring that she was about to ruin her shoes, she raced through the near lake-like alley, all the while keeping her eye out for on any movement coming from the parking lot area. Her throat nearly closed and a tight band squeezed her chest, making it hard to breathe. She prayed Trent would emerge from the back any second and say he'd shot some wild animal about to attack a small child. That was a stupid thought, but fear had blocked all logic.

As much as she wanted to call his name, keeping her presence hidden for as long as possible would be best for both of them.

She was about ten feet from the back parking lot when a large hooded figure charged around the corner. As he came toward her, she pressed her back against the wall, hoping the darkness would hide her from view, but the dim bulb on the wall across from her cast too much light. Indecision swamped her. Run or stay put? Her muscles screamed for her to run, but she'd never escape the large man.

He closed the gap between them and her stomach cramped. Her breath lodged in her throat as images from the last time she'd been shot at entered her brain—from the loud report to the shattered car window.

Then the scant light reflected off the gun in his hand. Oh, no.

Shoot him.

What if he hadn't harmed Trent but was running from the person who had? He was wearing a ski mask, but it was cold, so it made some sense.

No sooner had she dismissed the thought of him being evil,

than he was upon her. Before she could move out of his way, he slammed an elbow into her face and an ache the size of the lake exploded. The force caused her head to smash against the wall, adding a wrenching pain to vibrate through her. Shock took over as time stood still. Having no say in how her body reacted, she slowly slid to the ground, losing her focus.

Shoot him. This man is evil.

As if on autopilot, she lifted the gun, and pulled the trigger just like Trent had shown her. Before Charlotte could see if she'd hit her target, she blacked out.

CHAPTER TWENTY-ONE

JUST AS TRENT kicked the dirt from the heel of his boot on the rocker panel of his Jeep, he spotted something in his peripheral vision. His first thought was that Charlotte had followed him down the alley since it was something she would do. As he turned to check who or what it was, all he noticed was the barrel of a gun pointing straight at him, and his cop instincts clicked in. He reached across his body for his weapon, only to realize he wasn't carrying. Shit.

Trent ducked a split second before a bullet skidded across the top of his Jeep, whizzing and pinging over his head. The shot that followed failed to do any personal damage, but adrenaline still rushed through him. He dove into the car and reached across to his glove compartment. He wrenched it open, withdrew his spare, and clicked off the safety.

Footsteps sounded across the lot, and Trent slid back out of the car, keeping just below the window. As the man headed away from him and toward the alley, all Trent could think of was that the shooter was running toward the front where Charlotte was standing, and fear jacked up his heartbeat. Acting on instinct, Trent took aim and fired, but when the man didn't falter, he figured he'd missed. Damn.

The assailant then disappeared around the corner. Faster than Trent had ever moved before, he sprinted after the man, his gun aimed at the retreating figure's back. As he chased him down the water-filled alley, Trent was so focused on catching the shooter that he barely caught sight of the darkened lump near the ground. Had it not been for the moan, he might never have looked down.

It was a person, and Trent's mind fractured. He tried to watch which way the man turned when he reached the street, and at the same time check on the injured person. As he stepped toward the prone figure, the light from the wall shown on her face, and all thoughts of capturing his attacker flew out of his mind.

It was Charlotte. Trent dropped to his knees and the cold water seeped up his leg, but he barely noticed the discomfort. "Charlotte?"

Not knowing if she was seriously injured, he didn't want to move her, yet he couldn't leave her for long sitting in the cold.

She lifted a hand and placed it on her bloody cheek then scooted back toward the wall. "Don't hurt me."

Fuck. "Charlotte, it's me, Trent. Are you okay?" That was a stupid question as clearly she wasn't. Only then did he recall hearing another gunshot after the man sped down the alley. "Are you shot?"

His throat nearly clogged awaiting her answer. Even after he'd been hit in the leg chasing the terrorists, he hadn't been this scared.

"Trent?" Thank God his presence registered. Her voice sounded a lot stronger, and she wasn't crying in pain, which gave him hope.

Trent wanted nothing more than to hold her, but he needed to be cautious. "Yes, it's me. Can I help you up?"

"You're okay! I heard shots." Her voice sounded far away.

"I'm fine. What about you?"

"He hit me." She nearly choked out the words.

Heavy dread instantly filled him. "Where are you hurt?" Trent pulled out his phone and called 911. She clearly needed help regardless of the extent of her injuries.

"In the face."

She had a small cut on her cheek, but from the size, it didn't come from a bullet. The dispatcher answered and asked him the nature of the emergency. Trent relayed his location and that a woman had been injured, possibly shot. They assured him they'd be there as quickly as they could.

Keeping an eye on the alley, he blocked Charlotte's body from view. Who the fuck was trying to kill him? He wanted to question Charlotte why she was even in the alley, but now wasn't the time. He had to make certain she remained safe until help arrived.

When she pressed her hands against the wall and tried to stand, Trent rushed to her side. With one arm around her waist, he slowly lifted her up and then gathered her against his chest. "Where are you hurt?

She rubbed the back of her head. "I heard the shots and I ran down the alley. This man in a ski mask charged me."

Her evasive answer worried him. "Charlotte. Look at me." She turned her head to face him and winced. "Where exactly are you hurt?" he asked for the third time, but damn it, he needed to know.

"I told you. He smashed my face with his elbow and then I hit my head against the wall."

No, she hadn't said that. "Tell me what happened." Reconstructing the order of events might take her mind off her injuries.

"After I hit the wall, my vision blurred and my knees just crumbled. As I was slowly falling, I got off a shot, but I don't think I hit him."

A kaleidoscope of emotions spun through him, one of which was anger, but he tamped that down. "I heard that shot." He was relieved Charlotte had been the aggressor and not the other way around. "Did you black out?"

"I think so. Yeah."

Damn. That meant she had a concussion. "The ambulance should be here soon." No sooner had he said the words than a siren sounded. Trent gently lifted her into his arms and sloshed through the water toward the front. Lights glared down the alley as the vehicle turned in, forcing Trent to move to the side.

"I can stand," she said.

Even with a concussion, Charlotte was Miss Independent. "I know you can, but I like holding you."

The ambulance stopped twenty feet in front of them, and then the passenger side whipped open along with the back door. A minute later, two paramedics came toward them pushing a gurney. As they neared, the light from the building shone on Stone Benson's face, but Trent couldn't identify the other man.

"Trent," Stone said. "Want to tell me what happened?"

Trent placed Charlotte on the gurney.

She lifted her forearm. "He wasn't there. I was." She gave a brief description of the man hitting her. Clearly, Charlotte Hart was a force to be reckoned with.

After she told him what she remembered, Trent stepped back to let the two experts do their job. As they moved their hands up and down her body, they asked her a series of questions about her injuries. They then rolled her to the ambulance.

Once she was securely inside, Stone faced him. "We'll have the doctors check her out. She has a concussion and possibly a broken cheek."

His heart tripped. "I'll follow you to the hospital," Trent said.

Stone placed a hand on his friend's shoulder. "She'll be okay."

He could only hope.

The drive to the hospital seemed to take forever. Trent kept replaying the series of events, trying to decide where things had gone wrong. He'd told Charlotte to stay put, and yet she hadn't listened, and that worried him. His ego should be boosted that she was willing to charge into the unknown to save him, but sometimes she just didn't think. He was the cop, damn it, not her.

Aw hell, it wasn't really her fault. If he hadn't asked her to dinner in the first place, none of this would've happened. This incident only confirmed that her being with him could put her in danger at any time.

With his cell phone on speaker, he called Cade, and his partner answered quickly. "What's up?"

As factually as he could, Trent relayed what happened, including him failing to chase after the shooter. "The moment I saw Charlotte, I had to stop."

"You did the right thing."

"But the shooter escaped. I'm on my way to the hospital now to be with her."

"Good. I'll put out an APB for the man. Can you give me a description?"

"That's the problem. The man wore a mask and it was dark. All I can say is that he was about six-feet tall and moved easily."

"Not much to go on. Looks like we can rule out Elaine Goddard, assuming the perpetrator was someone involved with Bill Goddard's death. She hasn't left her house all evening."

"She could have hired the person."

"You worry about Charlotte, and I'll work on locating the whereabouts of each of our murder suspects."

"Vic is keeping tabs on John Samuels. I'll ask him where he was tonight." Trent had to call Charlotte's parents anyway to let them know what happened.

"I'll stay in touch."

The hospital came into view and Trent pulled his Jeep as close to the front entrance as possible. After scanning the lot for someone in a ski mask, and not spotting anyone, he jumped out and ran toward the front entrance. Despite flashing his badge, he was asked to wait until the doctor finished examining Charlotte.

Pacing one corner of the waiting room, he called her dad. Vic had already blamed Trent for sending her into John Samuels's home, so he could only imagine his reaction to this fiasco.

"Hey, Trent."

Vic sounded in a good mood but that would end shortly. "I'm afraid Charlotte had a little incident." He filled him in as best he could, leaving out the part about how disoriented Charlotte had been. "I'm at the hospital now waiting to hear what the doctor has to say."

"El and I are on our way now." He disconnected.

While Vic hadn't asked him more than one or two questions, Trent was certain there would be plenty to come.

Within a few minutes, Stone appeared from down the hall. "Charlotte's in room number three if you want to go in."

"How is she?"

"She'll soon be headed in for an X-ray to check on her face. Hopefully her cheek isn't cracked."

Guilt assaulted him again. "Will she have to spend the night?" Knowing Charlotte, she'd be really upset, especially with needing to open her store tomorrow.

"That's up to the doctor."

Trent ached for her. He rushed to her room, pulled back the curtain, and stepped inside. Seeing Charlotte in bed, with pain lacing her face, broke his heart. She looked so small under the sheets. Her hair was tangled and her face pale—and it was all his fault.

"Hey," he said as he stepped over to the bed.

She tried to smile then stopped. "Face hurts."

"You don't have to talk. I'm really sorry you got messed up in this stuff."

"It wasn't your fault," she said not moving her mouth much. "You told me to stay by the front and I didn't listen. When I heard the gunshots, I panicked, imagining you were lying on the ground bleeding. I don't know what I thought I was going to do when I found you." She glanced off to the side then turned back to him. "Truthfully, I wasn't thinking at all."

He agreed but no good would come from confirming her statement. He picked up her hand and gently squeezed it. "I appreciate your concern." Telling her that she should always do as he instructed would only make matters worse between them.

She asked what had happened, and he told her what he knew. He was in the middle of questioning her about her condition when voices sounded down the hall, one of which belonged to an irate Vic Hart. Seconds later her parents barreled in. Her mom appeared both angry and frightened and her dad looked as if he was ready to kill someone. Hopefully, it wouldn't be him.

Her mom rushed over to her side. "Oh, Charlotte, how are you, honey?"

"I'm fine. Just a bit sore."

Charlotte would downplay the near tragedy. Feeling like an outsider, Trent stepped toward the exit. Now probably wasn't the time to ask Vic about John Samuels, but he needed to know if Charlotte was in further danger. Whoever had shot at him and injured Charlotte might believe she recognized him, even with him wearing a mask.

"May I speak with you outside" Trent asked.

"Make it fast. I want to be with my daughter."

Trent could totally understand. They edged down the hallway, out of Charlotte's earshot. "By any chance were you watching John Samuels this evening?" He would like to be able to cross one name off the list.

"I was until about two hours ago. El called and asked if I would help with something at home. I was tempted to say that I needed to remain on the job, but then I realized that was what I kept telling Ellie all those years ago. It's taken me a long time, but I've finally realized that my wife has to come first from now on."

Trent was a bit disappointed at the lack of surveillance, but he totally understood. "I can't expect you to follow him twenty-four hours a day. I appreciate you tailing him for as much as you do. Where was he?"

"At home. And no, Elaine Goddard wasn't with him." His expression turned even harder, if that was possible. "Excuse me. I need to take care of Charlotte."

Vic headed inside, anger rolling off him in waves, implying Trent was no longer capable of taking care of his daughter and that stung because he might be right.

CHAPTER TWENTY-TWO

TRENT CHARGED OUT of the hospital, anger and frustration colliding. Charlotte didn't deserve to be mixed up in this mess, yet she had been. While he wasn't positive the attack was related to Bill Goddard's death, it was his only murder case. Add in the fact that no one else was in the parking lot, and he had to conclude the shots were aimed at him.

As much as he wanted to be with her, Trent had no doubt that she'd be more comfortable surrounded by her mother and father. With her dad there to protect her, Charlotte would be safe.

Once in the car, he headed toward the station. He'd fired his weapon, and not only did he need to turn in his firearm, he wanted to start on the extensive paperwork. Going home and being alone was the last thing he wanted or needed.

Trent found a spot in front of the precinct and rushed inside. For a change, the station was rather quiet, even for a Sunday night. Cade's office was dark, implying his partner was running down the location of the assailant as promised.

Trent gathered the necessary papers and began filling out his report. A wicked ache churned in his gut when he wrote how he'd found Charlotte. A few minutes later, Dan Hartwick appeared in front of his desk. The man must never sleep or relax.

"How about coming into my office where we can talk?"

The command speared his heart. No one was around, so they could have spoken at Trent's desk, but asking for a delay was not an option. "Sure."

He had no doubt that Dan wouldn't be pleased that Trent had let the shooter escape. He pushed back his chair and followed his boss down the hallway. When he stepped inside, Dan pulled up a chair and motioned Trent to sit while he sat behind his desk. "Heard you had a little incident at the Steerhouse."

Fuck. Dan seemed to know everything that went on in town. What Trent wouldn't give to have that talent. "I was with Charlotte Hart when it happened."

"I know. Tell me everything."

Trent detailed the series of events, but even in the retelling, nothing became any clearer.

"Any idea who it might have been?"

"My best guess was that it was either Bill Goddard's brother-in-law, Bill's business partner, or someone who worked at the firm. It's possible his wife hired someone to take me out, but if she'd hired a professional, I probably would be dead."

"Don't forget any irate clients."

"Don't remind me."

"If someone is trying to take you out, I'm guessing you're getting close to finding the killer, which is why I'm taking you off the case."

Surprise and indignation swamped him. Trent always prided himself on keeping his cool, but this time he lost it. "With all due respect, sir, you can't do that."

Dan stared at him for a few seconds. "Listen to yourself. You're already too emotional. The fact Charlotte was injured seems to be clouding your vision. I always suspected this case might be related to your brother somehow, but since I had no concrete evidence, I let you remain on the case. After tonight, I can't do that in good conscience. I won't have your death on my hands."

A bit of Trent's anger deflated. As much as he didn't want to believe it, Dan might be right. While he could take care of himself, he didn't want whoever was after him to take it out on his family. As for Charlotte, Trent truly believed she'd been in the wrong place at the wrong time.

"Who are you putting in charge?"

"Cade will take the lead. I've asked Devon to follow Frank Hamilton and Connor to watch Richard Delaney. If he's still willing, Vic Hart can continue with John Samuels."

"What about Elaine Goddard?" Trent was pleased Dan was willing to schedule overtime to find the killer.

"Cade will continue to watch her."

"What would you like me to work on?"

"Fill out the paperwork, hand it in, and then take a few days off." Dan pulled out his top drawer and extracted a pen, acting as if this conversation was over.

Trent wasn't finished. He needed to find some relief from the elephant sitting on his chest. "I screwed up bad."

Dan set down the pen. "Because you took care of a woman you're very fond of and didn't chase after the perpetrator?"

His observation convinced Trent that Dan could read minds or else his boss had been in the same spot before. "Yes."

"I can't tell you how to live your life, because God only knows I've messed up mine many times, but if a cop doesn't show compassion at the right time, he won't be any good at his job. You did the right thing stopping to help Charlotte."

"I know, but I should have suspected something like this might have happened. Look how that crazy man came after Vic and put his family in jeopardy."

Dan shrugged, but it didn't come across as callous. "It's the hazard of the job. Why don't you head up to your dad's cabin and take some time to think about your priorities. If you're

going to remain in this business, you have to know what's important to you."

He had his priorities straight. Hadn't his boss just told him
that? "Is that an order, sir?"

"It is. You haven't taken vacation days in forever. Besides, I
want you safe. Now go fill out that report."

There was no use arguing with the man. While he didn't like
being on forced vacation, Charlotte would be safer without him
around. He just hoped she'd understand.

* * *

DAD HAD INSISTED she stay in the hospital for a few more hours
in case there were complications from the mild concussion. Sure,
her head ached, but her vision was fine and she didn't feel nause-
ated. The results of the X-ray confirmed Charlotte's cheek wasn't
cracked, despite the amount of pain she was still experiencing.
After a very long wait, the doctor arrived and provided her with
some pain medication. He said she was fine to be home alone,
but if she experienced any nausea, she was to return.

All Charlotte wanted to do was take a long soak in the tub,
and then drop into bed so she'd be refreshed to open her shop
tomorrow. She'd have to work at covering up the bruise that was
sure to come, but she refused to let this get her down.

She retrieved her phone from her now damaged wet purse to
check if Trent had called or texted. He hadn't. "Dad, did you say
something to Trent?" *Like to stay away from me?*

Trent was no more at fault than her dad had been when her
mom had been stalked.

"No."

Before she could ask her mother what she thought of Trent's
behavior, the nurse came in with her discharge papers. It was a
little after midnight and Charlotte was anxious to leave. Not
only did her face hurt, her heart ached for Trent and what he

might be going through right now. She understood what it was like to have someone want her dead.

Her mother helped her out of bed. "Are you sure you don't want to stay with us? What if you get sick?"

Her mother had always said that even though Charlotte was a grown woman, she'd always think of her as a little girl. "I'll call you if I'm feeling bad, okay?"

"You better."

The nurse wheeled her out while her dad retrieved his car. Even though she wore her coat, the scrubs the hospital gave her provided little warmth.

In no time, Dad was parked in front of her apartment, and Charlotte patiently waited for him to open the car door and then let him guide her up to the front entrance. She could have insisted her parents stay in the car, but she understood their need to help.

"You make sure to call us if anything happens, okay?" her mom said, pulling Charlotte's coat closed.

She wanted to tell them to stop smothering her, but she wouldn't. They were merely being cautious. "Promise. I'll call you tomorrow after the opening."

Both hugged her goodnight and left only after she'd safely entered the building. On the ride home, she'd asked her dad if he thought she was in any danger from her attacker, and he said he didn't believe so, but to keep her sidearm close by just in case. He thought she might have to file a report with the police stating she'd fired a shot in the city limits, but she'd worry about that after speaking with Trent.

Charlotte was not paranoid by nature, but when she stepped into her apartment, she turned on the lights in each room and checked to make certain no one had been there. Then she ran her bath and undressed.

She was almost afraid to step into the bathroom and look in the mirror to see the damage to her cheek. In the end, she decided it was better to face it now rather than tomorrow morning.

The right side of her face was swollen, but with a little artfully placed makeup, she could minimize the distortion. For a brief moment, she debated taking a selfie and putting it up on Facebook to show her friends back in Kalispell, but then she worried her attacker might see it and conclude she knew something, when in fact she didn't.

Once the tub was full, she eased in and groaned in pleasure. The wicked sensation reminded her of the joy she and Trent had experienced in her apartment. She wished he could be here right now. On second thought, it might be better if he weren't. The man would fuss at her more than her mom had and then forbid her to ever go out again. His protective nature was admirable, but sometimes he took things too far.

Trent kept saying it had been his fault the man had run past her and pushed her down, but she didn't see it that way. She'd been wrong in wanting to be a hero. That had been dumb, dumb, dumb. As soon as she heard the gunshots, she should have called the cops and let them handle things. Live and learn.

Tomorrow after opening her store, she'd spend some time working on Mr. Samuels' design and then call Trent. If he saw that everything was back to normal, he just might forgive himself.

After she finished her long bath, she crawled into bed, but as much as Charlotte tried to sleep, the image of running down the alley with fear pummeling her heart bombarded her. It was bad enough that she couldn't stop picturing Trent shot, but then that evil man had to attack her. She could still visualize his gun and remembered the fear clawing at her belly.

As the night progressed, her sleep became more and more erratic. She'd doze for a bit, then relive the scene, even making up a different ending in which she'd raised her arm and shot the bastard.

In hindsight, she shouldn't have been so indecisive. When

she'd described to her father what had happened, he'd said she'd done the right thing in not shooting him until after he'd assaulted her. She, however, wasn't so sure.

* * *

SOMEHOW, CHARLOTTE HAD survived the night, but in the morning, the soreness had returned. The side of her face had doubled in size and her head still throbbed, but thankfully there was no bruising—yet. Wanting to make a good impression on any potential clients, she took care dressing, hoping that if anyone stopped in, they wouldn't be upset at her injury.

After choking down a rather bland breakfast, she headed out to her first day at work. While she was excited, she was also scared that no potential clients would stop by. It didn't help there were snow flurries this morning.

Once she opened, to keep occupied, Charlotte focused on Mr. Samuels' bedroom design. She had her phone close by in case Trent called, as well as her gun in a nearby drawer.

Unfortunately, Trent didn't call. Most likely, he was at work filling out the paperwork, but she was disappointed he hadn't wanted to find out how she was doing. For as long as she'd known him, he'd been caring, so this behavior was not like him. She could only conclude that he was trying to keep his distance so she'd be safe.

Stupid man.

She would just have to show him she wasn't afraid of being with him, that this incident didn't sour her on dating a cop.

Shortly after lunch, two women came by to check out her services. While neither of them hired her, Charlotte had a good feeling that if they ever required decorating services, they would give her a chance to show them her designs.

By five o'clock, Charlotte decided it was time to close shop. She thought about stopping at her dad's office and seeing if Sharon wanted to go out to dinner, but then thought better of it.

She wasn't in the mood to run into her dad and have him lecture her on her bonehead move. Again.

Charlotte snapped her fingers. Because she didn't want to bother Trent, she went with the next best thing—Harmon. He might know what his brother was up to. From the way Trent talked, the two of them were fairly close.

It was a little after five, and she had no idea if Harmon worked at the restaurant tonight or if this was one of his two nights off. The only way to find out was to call him.

They'd exchanged numbers after that first night she'd driven him home. Because he didn't have a car at the time, she'd offered to give him a lift if he ever needed one.

She stood at the front door of her shop and tapped in his number.

He answered immediately. "Charlotte? How are you feeling?"

"I guess you heard?"

"Yes. Trent came over to my place last night and told me everything."

"How is he?"

"He's upset." She wished she could see Harmon's expression in order to tell how much of the truth he was telling her.

If he was so upset, why hadn't he contacted her today? She would have asked Harmon but she didn't want to keep him on the line if he was at work. Bosses never appreciated personal calls. "Are you at Italiano's right now?"

"No, but I'm working from eight until closing. Do you need to talk?"

That was one of the things she liked about Harmon. He seemed to understand where she was coming from. "Yes."

"Well, I'm always up for company. I'm just making some spaghetti and meatballs. If you hurry, I'll save you some." He gave her his address.

"I'll be right there." Maybe now she could find out exactly what was gong on in Trent's head.

CHAPTER TWENTY-THREE

NOT WANTING TO keep Harmon waiting, Charlotte rushed over to his apartment. He must have heard her coming up the steps, because he had the door open as soon as she reached the top.

"Hey, come in." No sooner had she entered than Harmon lifted her chin. "It doesn't look too bad, but I bet it hurts."

"As long as I don't touch my face, I'm okay. My headache went away a little after lunch."

"That's good. Are you hungry?"

"Very." Her appetite hadn't returned until about an hour ago. "What can I do to help?"

Harmon smiled. "I'm the cook, remember? Have a seat at the table and I'll bring the food in."

He stepped into the kitchen and pots and plates clanked and scraped. "Has Trent contacted you today?" he asked.

"No."

"I figured. His boss took him off the case and told him to go up to Dad's cabin for a few days to think about things. I imagine he's rather preoccupied." He walked out of the kitchen carrying two plates.

"Oh, no. He's off the case?"

"'Fraid so, and he's not happy about it."

She could only imagine what Trent was going through. "Didn't he object?"

Harmon chuckled. "Let's just say he voiced his opinion rather strongly, but his boss said we're all safer with him out of town."

That made sense, but now it would be harder to convince Trent that she should be in his life. Harmon held up his fork but didn't eat. He must be waiting for her.

Between the divine aroma and her cramping stomach, she was ready to scarf up the whole plate of food. "This looks delicious. Thank you."

"I'd offer you wine, but I'm guessing you shouldn't have any."

"Unfortunately not." She was still on some pain meds.

"I brewed some coffee. Want some?"

"I'd love a cup."

Harmon was so easy to be with. She should have set her sights on this brother. Not really. She wanted Trent.

Harmon brought out the drinks and sat down. "So what's on your mind?"

"You can't guess?"

"You sustained a fairly serious injury, and could have been killed, and yet Trent walked out on you while you were still in the hospital, and then he didn't bother to check on you today. You're hurt, as well you should be."

"You're perceptive." Almost scarily so.

"Actually, Trent told me how bad he felt for leaving you, but he thought you wanted to be with your parents." He waved his fork. "Trent cares about you. A lot. He's worried that something will happen to you if he stays around. He believed that before his boss confirmed it."

As much as Charlotte was happy to know the truth, it wasn't what she wanted to hear. At least Harmon hadn't said that Trent didn't care for her. "My life's in danger just by being my father's daughter. I understand the risks of being around a cop, and I'm willing to take them."

Harmon chugged part of his wine then took a mouthful of

spaghetti. He was probably trying to give himself some time to think what he wanted to say. "Have you told Trent about your feelings?"

"Yes, but he has a lot of hang ups about protecting me."

Harmon nodded. "Once he returned from serving his country, he changed. My brother became the noble one—maybe overly so."

Just Charlotte's luck. Her dad had been the same way. At least her father had figured a few things out. Unfortunately, he waited until he was fifty to do so. "What do you suggest I do?"

"I'm probably not the best one to give advice. It seems whenever I talk to Trent about stuff like that, he gets upset."

Harmon was no help. "What do you think he would do if I just drove up to his cabin?"

"What do *you* think he would do?"

She could picture it now. She'd knock on his door and when he answered and saw who it was, his face would be taut with controlled anger. Being polite, though, he'd ask her in, then demand to know why she was there.

She had no doubt that Trent would not react favorably to her just showing up. After all, he'd been taken off the case, which to him would be like a slap in the face. He wouldn't want her to see him like that. Not only that, he was feeling guilty for how he'd reacted to her injury.

"He'll probably tell me to turn around and go back home, that being around him wasn't a good idea."

Harmon chuckled. "I think you nailed it."

About the only way for Trent to relent would be to seduce him—again. When they made love, she was able to reach deep inside him and almost touch his heart. "Is there anything I can say to make him change his mind?" she asked.

"You mean about letting you into his life?"

She liked that Harmon spoke his mind. "Yes."

He scooped up the last of his meal, ate it, and then placed his fork on his plate tines down. "I think you have to make him realize he'll be miserable without you. You can talk until you're blue in the face and tell him you're willing to risk it all for him, but he's such a self-sacrificing son of a bitch that he'll turn you away and then immediately regret it."

He didn't paint a very rosy picture. "How do I make him so miserable when I'm not around that he'll relent?"

Harmon grinned. "A pretty young thing like you? I'm sure you can think of a few ways."

Why yes, I can.

Charlotte and Harmon talked a bit more, but then he had to go to work. During that time, they'd come up with a plan. Tomorrow after he finished at Italiano's, he'd pick her up at her place and drive her up to his dad's cabin. Once he was certain his brother would let her in, he'd take off, and she could face the beast alone. By dropping her off in the evening, Trent would have to let her spend the night. That was when she'd put the real plan into action.

On the drive back to her apartment, she came up with how she could spend a day or two with Trent and have her store operational. Her mom worked a few days a week at a local gallery, but she didn't work Wednesdays or Thursdays. Charlotte hoped her mom wouldn't mind sitting in the store the day after tomorrow to answer the phone and let any client who happened to walk in know she'd be back soon.

Charlotte thought about stopping over at her parents' tonight to ask her mom about the favor, but dad might be there, and he'd probably forbid her to go up to the cabin, especially with what happened the last time she'd been there. Hopefully, Mom would be more receptive.

Happy that things could potentially go her way, Charlotte made plans for what was left of the evening. Not only did she have to pack, she wanted to add a few more touches to the design she'd nearly completed for Mr. Samuel's house.

One of her goals was to prove to Trent that she was an independent woman who could handle his long hours and dangerous job.

As soon as she stepped into her house, she pulled out her phone to check if she had any messages. Not that she expected Trent to call, but a girl could hope.

Nada.

Pushing aside her disappointment, she went straight to work finding the sexiest outfit she owned. While she could do nothing about her slightly swollen face, she could entice him with the way she dressed. By the time she finished with him this weekend, he wouldn't know what hit him.

* * *

WORK THE NEXT day went by incredibly slowly. Even though Charlotte had several people stop in and ask about her services and pricing, she kept checking the time, waiting for five o'clock to roll around. The trip to the cabin would take a little over an hour, and Harmon suggested they leave around seven that evening since he didn't get off work until six. After work, she planned to drop the office key off at her mom's and hope she was willing to help. As soon as the last person left her store, Charlotte called her.

"Are you feeling okay?" Mom asked as soon as she answered.

Why couldn't people just start with a simple hello? "I'm fine. I was wondering if I could stop over. I have a favor to ask of you."

"Of course, hon. I'm always happy when you stop by."

"Is Dad home?" She hoped not.

"No, he's working."

Perfect. Since she had about two hours before Harmon picked her up, she thought it would be nice if they had dinner together. "How about I grab something to eat for the two of us?"

"I'd love that."

"I'm leaving the store now and I'll be there shortly."

As soon as she disconnected, Charlotte called in an order for pizza then gathered her things. In case she became too preoccupied with Trent, she contacted Mr. Samuels to set up a time to show him her new designs. She really hoped he liked them. After discussing a few options, they decided on Thursday at six p.m. That would give her almost two days with Trent.

"Perfect. I'll see you then," she said.

Happy to have that chore out of the way, Charlotte locked up and headed over to Italiano's and parked in the To-Go Lane, wondering if Harmon would be the one to make her meal.

She didn't have to wait long, and soon was headed over to her mom's with food in hand. As she slipped into her car, she crossed her fingers that this burning seduction would work.

* * *

TRENT HAD SPENT the day settling into his dad's cabin, but the space didn't hold the appeal like it had in the past. He was still pissed over the whole dismissal thing and could taste the bitterness on his tongue. He understood why Dan wanted him off the case, but it didn't mean he had to like it. On the other hand, if the murder had anything to do with Harmon, it wouldn't be smart to keep investigating as it might put his brother in danger.

The biggest downside was there was no way to know what the person might do if he realized Trent was no longer in town. The unstable man might take out his frustration on Harmon, or worse, Charlotte. While Trent had warned Harmon to be careful, he wasn't a trained officer of the law. Charlotte wasn't either, but Vic would keep her safe—assuming she didn't go against her father's wishes and go off on her own. If anyone went after his dad, they'd end up the loser.

If Trent could learn what had caused the sudden attack, he might figure out who had tried to kill him. He agreed with Dan. His team had to be close to finding the killer.

Trent tossed the paperback on the coffee table in disgust

then clenched his fist. Despite being on this forced vacation, nothing was keeping him from staying in the loop. He located his phone and called Cade.

"You going nuts yet?" his partner asked with way too much cheer.

Cade knew him well. "Yes, and I sure hope you have something for me. I have a ton of questions and no answers."

"As a matter of fact our grieving widow seems to be entertaining Mr. Samuels at the moment."

That was interesting. This added to the picture that Vic had first painted. "You're sure? Did Vic contact you?" Vic was keeping his eye on John Samuels while Cade was assigned to watch Elaine Goddard.

"Yup. I told him I'd watch both of them, so Vic could catch supper. He informed me of the location of the bedroom. The light went on about half an hour ago, and then just clicked back on. From the looks of it, they were doing the nasty in there."

He didn't need the visual. "Neither is married, and having sex with someone doesn't mean they're guilty of murder. We have no proof they conspired to kill Bill."

"I know, and short of bugging their homes, I don't know how we'll find out what's truly going on."

It appeared as if John Samuel's had no physical interest in Charlotte, which brightened Trent's dreary day somewhat. Most likely Elaine complained about the condition of his house and suggested he make it nicer when she visited. "Even if you bugged every room, do you really expect Samuels to blurt out that he tried to shoot me? Assuming he was the one. Or say he murdered Elaine's husband?"

"No."

Which meant they had squat. "Has the tech department found anything on Bill's erased computer?" Trent asked.

"Not yet, but they're working on it."

He felt like he was swimming in quick sand. "So what's your plan?" Hartwick would never allow his men to watch the citizens of Rock Hard for long without something happening—not to mention it would cost the town too much money.

"Didn't you mention that Charlotte is redecorating Samuel's house?"

Trent didn't like what Cade was about to suggest. "I did."

"If I got a warrant to bug John Samuels's house, do you think Charlotte could slip something in the bedroom and perhaps place another bug in the kitchen?"

His protective anger shot up. "No way. I'm not putting Charlotte in further danger."

"She's already going to be inside, so I don't see how it could makes things worse."

Cade wasn't thinking. "It won't be an issue unless she's caught. If John is our killer, it could cost Charlotte her life." This whole case was starting to unravel. "What about Connor and Devon? Have they learned anything?"

"When Devon called in, he said Frank Hamilton had spent last night at the office until about ten. Looks like he's not your shooter."

Trent wasn't ready to jump to that conclusion. "Given where Frank's office is located, all Devon could do was watch his car. There's a back entrance to the building. Frank could have high-tailed it over to the Steerhouse, waited for me to leave the restaurant, taken the shots, and been back in his office with no one the wiser."

"Damn, you're right."

"What about Richard Delaney?" Connor was supposed to follow Elaine's brother.

"Connor hasn't been able to locate the man," Cade said. "He asked at Richard's workplace, and they said he was on vacation."

It was possible Elaine's brother was lying low, though Trent saw no reason why Richard would want to take him out. He hadn't been back to question him, so there was no reason for the man to run scared. "What about the casings from the two shots?"

"We retrieved both of them. They came from a 38 caliber, but because we have nothing to compare them to, we have no idea who the shooter was."

Trent stabbed a hand through his hair. Bill Goddard's killer was going to get away with murder. Christ. They needed a break. And soon.

CHAPTER TWENTY-FOUR

CHARLOTTE CHECKED HER hair in the mirror, smoothed her hands down her sweater, and then faced Harmon. "Wish me luck."

She hoped the turquoise top brought out the little bit of green in her blue eyes. Wanting to make undressing easy, she went with a knee length stretchy skirt. The UGG boots were more for warmth than fashion.

"You don't need any luck," he said. "Once my brother takes one look at you, he'll be putty in your hands."

That was sweet of him to say, but she wasn't as confident. Trent would most likely be mad, but hopefully she could soften him a little with a few kisses and a lot of well-placed touches.

With the engine running, Harmon stepped out of the car and retrieved her suitcase. He then set it on the front stoop and returned. She slid out and inhaled, her nerves jangling.

"As soon as he answers, I'm taking off. I don't want to give Trent the chance to send you back."

"Thank you for everything. I'll never forget this." She stood on her tiptoes and placed a light kiss on his cheek. It was too dark to see if he blushed, but from the way he cleared his throat, she'd embarrassed him.

As Harmon slipped back into his seat, Charlotte marched up to the front door of the cabin and knocked. Trent must have been looking out the window, because he opened up within seconds.

As promised, Harmon drove off, and Trent stared at the retreating car. "What's going on, Charlotte?"

"May I come in?"

Trent picked up her suitcase and motioned her inside. Memories came flooding back of the time they'd spent at the cabin all those months ago. Tomorrow, she'd inspect the front of the house to see if any evidence of the fire remained.

"Can I get you something to drink?" he asked. While he sounded calm, the small tic around his eyes told her otherwise.

"Water is good." She took off her coat and hooked it over the back of the kitchen chair.

He shook his head. "I wasn't expecting you."

He might not be happy she was there, but at least he hadn't suggested he drive her home right away. "I know, but I was worried about you."

She could only imagine what he was experiencing—the guilt, the frustration, and the embarrassment of being taken off the case.

"I'm fine." Trent walked into the kitchen, retrieved a beer and a glass of water.

"You look like shit, you know." Not really, but he hadn't shaven, and it seemed as if he'd slept in his clothes. She was merely trying to lighten the mood.

A slight smile lifted his lips. "Believe it or not, I feel worse than I look." His shoulder sagged as he walked with her over to the sofa. They both sat down and he twisted to face her. "How are you feeling? I'm sorry I didn't call."

She waited to see if he'd explain, but he didn't. "I'm sore, but I'll heal."

He nodded. "I need to apologize."

She'd expected him to say that, but she didn't want to hear it.

"What's done is done. It was stupid of me to follow you, but I was worried. You know why?" Having secrets between them after all they'd been through wouldn't do either of them any good.

"Because you care?"

At least he wasn't oblivious to her feelings. Charlotte set down her water and clasped his hand in hers. "I more than care. It's probably stupid of me to open my heart because everyone says I should play hard to get, but that's not who I am. In the beginning, I was drawn to the fact that you were this hot, sexy protector."

"Charlotte, you don't understand." He glanced to the side as if he couldn't handle the compliment.

She wasn't going to give him a chance to respond further until after she said her piece. "I do understand. Your job means everything to you, and that's very commendable, but there will come a time in your life when you need someone to hold and care for you. Perhaps your father didn't provide the love you expected, and I know your mother was taken from you at an early age, but I want you to know that I love you for who you are, and have no intention of changing you." She held up her other hand. "Before you go and say that you don't want to put my life in danger, or that you can't promise you'll be there when I need you, I want to tell you that I'll take what I can get. It's because you are so noble that I love you. I want to make this work between us."

Her heart was pounding so fast that she let go of his hand and took a drink to wet her mouth and try to calm her nerves a bit. She certainly didn't expect him to say he loved her back, but she hoped he'd at least give them a chance.

"I don't know what to say."

That might be a first. "You don't have to say anything. I'd like to spend the night here and not have to worry if you're drinking yourself to death, or if the person who shot at you and knocked me down is going to come after me."

Trent cupped her face and his pupils dilated. "You are such a loving and giving person, I don't deserve you."

That was the nicest thing anyone had ever said to her. "How about you let me worry about that?" His green eyes shimmered with what she hoped was akin to love—or at least lust.

"I can do that. Would you like me to light a fire?"

She was already burning hot inside with need for him, but a fire would create a nice romantic setting. "I'd love one."

"I like your outfit, by the way. You look hot." He winked then stepped over to the small stack of wood. His mood had almost turned cheerful.

"I was hoping you'd appreciate it."

"Hold that thought. I'll appreciate it more in a moment."

Yes!

He stacked a few pieces inside the fireplace, wadded up some newspaper, and shoved it under the logs then lit it. Once the papers caught, the flames licked the logs. He turned off all but one light in the living room and sat next to her—closer this time. "If you're going to pursue this crazy notion that you can handle my job, you must realize that I can't always be around."

"I know."

"For my peace of mind, I'll need to insist you take shooting lessons at least twice a week for a few months. You said you were willing to practice, but I want to be assured that you know how to use a gun should the need arise."

Excitement sizzled inside her. "Does that mean I can stay around?"

Trent wrapped an arm around her shoulder. "If you're good and do everything I say, you can."

"Oh, I can be good." Doing everything he said was a totally different matter.

"Show me."

* * *

Trent's head swam. He never expected Charlotte to drive up to the cabin, nor did he think she'd ever say she loved him. He should have taken her home right away and explained that she could do so much better than a cop, but stubborn Charlotte would never have listened. No woman had told him she loved him since before his mother died. He'd always pushed people away because he feared there was something wrong with him and that he was unlovable.

Now, he realized he'd had it all wrong. Cade seemed happy and able to balance his job with his family. Even his stoic boss said that a man could learn to do both. Trent wanted to take a chance on Charlotte, but he was afraid he'd mess it up.

Somehow, though, he had the sense that no matter how many times he failed, Charlotte would be there to help him up.

At least for tonight, Trent wanted to forget everything about the case. He was with a woman who had turned his life upside down, and who was willing to take him as he was.

"Would you like to sit by the fire?" He wasn't certain how long they'd actually be sitting, but he thought his idea was a good segue into making love with her.

"It will probably be a little hot. I hope you don't mind if I kick off my boots."

"I'm hoping I can convince you to take off more than that."

A huge grin spread across Charlotte's face, and his pulse ticked up a notch. "What are you waiting for?" she asked.

He laughed, stood, and then held out his hand. When she grabbed hold, he pulled her to her feet. If he kissed her right now, he might not be able to stop. "Grab a couple of pillows and bring them over to the fireplace."

He lifted two, and as he stepped near the hearth, he flicked off the remaining light. The flames cast a yellow glow over the entire room, entombing them in romance.

They arranged their pillows side by side, and then she dropped down in front of the fire. Trent took a moment to admire her pretty features, her lush curves, and her gold spun hair. He hoped he could be the man she wanted him to be.

After he removed his shoes, he dropped trou, leaving on his briefs and his shirt. He'd let Charlotte do the final honors.

She looked up at him. "If I'd known that a fireplace made you undress, I would've looked for an apartment with one."

Her openness excited him. Game playing and secrets were a turn off. "It's being with you that makes me want to be naked."

He dropped next to her and slowly lifted her sweater over her head. The sight of the purple push-up bra made his cock peek out over the elastic waistband. "I didn't stand a chance, did I?"

She grinned. "Nope."

"How about stretching out on these pillows so I can enjoy everything you have to offer?"

"It's only fair to let you know that I plan to tease you way past your limit."

"You can try." He loved how she wasn't timid when it came to making love. He spread out on the cushions and guided her alongside him.

She flipped onto her side, supported her head with her hand, and dragged a finger down his chest until she banged into his cock. "I'll more than try. I'll succeed."

He believed her. "I guess I'm about to fall into some serious trouble."

Before Charlotte had the chance to do real damage to his control, he unhooked her bra and dragged down the straps. When her breasts bounced free, his hormones shot to life. Lust, desire, and need soared through him, and as much as he wanted to impale her right there, he wanted to taste her first.

Trent slid down on the cushions until his mouth was level with her delicious tits. He cupped both of them then lightly licked each nipple.

"That tickles," she said.

"Better get used to it, because I plan to be here a long time."

Wanting better access to her, he rolled her onto her back, and then straddled her. Pressing his face into her breasts, he inhaled her delicious scent that reminded him of the flowers his mom used to grow.

He swirled his tongue around her right nipple while he strummed the left with his thumb. Charlotte grabbed his head and tugged on his hair. Her breaths came out rapid and his cock ached to take her. He'd purposely not removed her skirt to prevent him from losing his cool, but he was slowly sinking into the abyss of desire.

He nipped and tugged on each nipple, loving how the perfect tip turned taut.

"How about getting me naked?" She slipped her hands under his shirt and dragged her nails down his back.

"Don't you like what I'm doing to you?"

"That's the problem. I like it too much."

The moment she was naked, he'd have to have her. "You asked for it." In one quick tug, he whipped off her skirt and panties, and his breath caught at the sight of her, the light from the fire shimmering over her skin. "You are so beautiful."

"I bet you're more beautiful, but I can't tell because you have on too many clothes."

Trent laughed. "Subtlety is not your strong suit tonight."

"I thought I made it clear that I always speak my mind. I want you. I need your body, and I long for you to possess me."

Her words caressed his heart and stole his soul. He'd give her anything she wanted. While part of making love was the sensual nature of undressing each other, he couldn't wait any longer to have her. He lifted off his shirt and dragged down his briefs. "Did someone say something about trying to push me to my limit?"

He wouldn't have allowed such torment if he didn't want to give her everything she desired.

"You are so going down, Trent Lawson."

CHAPTER TWENTY-FIVE

CHARLOTTE HAD NEVER been more excited in her life. Not only was this amazing eye candy overwhelming her senses, her heart was near to exploding. She'd told Trent that she loved him and to her amazement, he hadn't turned her away. He was even giving her the chance to show him that he rocked her world.

"How about you get on your back so that I can enjoy you?" she asked, stroking his face and loving the roughness of his beard. He was all man, and all hers.

Touching and rubbing more than he probably needed to, Trent exchanged positions with her then wrapped his hands behind his head.

"I have to control myself. If I put my hands on you, I could go all he-man on you, and I'm not sure you're ready for that," he said.

Sure she was. She could handle anything Trent doled out. "I'll be careful." Careful to stay out of his reach, that was. She planned to use every trick in the book to drive him wild.

She scooted onto her belly and slid between his legs. When she grabbed his thick shaft, her mind spun with possibilities. Even thinking about his cock had her inner walls clenching with desire and need. Using her forefinger and thumb, she lightly stroked his dick. He lasted all of five seconds before he growled, but she wasn't worried. Charlotte could tell how far to push him.

Before she tasted him, though, she rose onto her knees and dragged her breasts across his cock.

"That's not fair," he said.

"It is by my rules." She squeezed the sides of her tits, sandwiching his thick shaft, then rubbed her breasts up and down his length.

"You've got ten seconds to put it in your mouth or I'm going to *git* you."

He was so full of it, and his accent was just as phony. In case he was serious, she slipped down onto her belly again, and encased his cock with her mouth. He groaned louder and she didn't know how this was any better, but she wanted to make him regret asking her to change her seduction routine. Slowly swiveling her tongue around his dick, she lightly pumped her fist up and down.

He unfolded his arms and threaded his fingers through her hair and tugged hard. "Times almost up."

She hadn't thought his limit would be so low, but perhaps all of the day's tension had caught up to him. She sucked hard and then lifted off. "You are so easy."

As if she'd pushed him too far, he sat up, deposited her onto the cushions, and then loomed over her. "I will make you regret those words."

His mouth was on hers in a flash and his palms gripped her shoulders.

The dizzying and erotic nature of the kiss had her swooning. Their tongues twisted and entwined as if they desperately wanted to become one. She couldn't get enough of him so she dragged her palms up his back, pressing on his bulging muscles.

His cock notched open her slit, and bolts of electricity chased up her spine. She tried to scoot lower for more penetration, but he held her tight.

Trent broke the kiss then licked his lips. "I love the way you taste."

"I have someplace else you might like to lick."

He laughed. "I know my way around. Just give me some time. I plan to enjoy all of you."

She loved his sentiment, but her climax was about to take hold and she needed him now. He slid lower and captured her breasts with his hands, lifting, squeezing, and massaging them, sending blissful lust straight to her core. Charlotte pressed her hips upward hoping he'd impale her, but he seemed too intent on making her nipples tender and rigid.

Each swirl of this tongue heated her insides, causing lustful sparks to skitter across her skin, and she wasn't sure how much longer she could last. "Lick me now, please." Trent had more willpower than she did, so she didn't mind admitting defeat.

He slowly shook his head and a smile formed. The light from the flickering flames made his green eyes shine. "Now who's easy?"

This wasn't a competition. "Me."

He grinned and slid lower. When he opened her folds and licked her slit, she grabbed the edges of the pillow below her and sucked in a deep breath. Streaks of pleasure engulfed her as he rolled his tongue and slid partway into her wetness. The nubby texture sent sparks of need deep inside her, but she wanted more —so much more. Her breaths came out faster as her pulse raced. He must have sensed her urgency, because he replaced his mouth with two fingers. When he curled them and hit her G-spot, she could no longer contain herself.

Her inner walls tightened and she let loose a feral sounding scream. Her orgasm descended and swamped her with overwhelming lust.

Trent sat up and slowly crawled on top of her, balancing on his elbows. "I can't wait any longer," he whispered. His eyelids half closed and his mouth opened.

The fire crackled and the flames danced. All thoughts left

her head as she focused on the marvelous man in front of her. "Love me."

He could take her comment anyway he wanted, but all she could think of was becoming one with him.

As if she'd pressed some inner button of need, he forged into her, driving his cock to the hilt. His wide girth stretched her, but it only served to turn her on even more. Her inner walls coiled and tightened, gripping him hard.

Trent let out a strangled cry. "Don't. Please. I'm so close."

His plea sent her soaring. He slowly withdrew his cock and kissed her with more passion than she'd ever experienced before. It was as if he was trying to gain some control before he plowed back in. Not wanting him to use any restraint, she grabbed his hips and thrust upward.

Her pussy convulsed as erotic bliss infused her body, and goose bumps sped up her spine. Trent held her tight and pummeled into her over and over again. It was as if they were on a runaway train and couldn't stop. His hands roamed everywhere, touching and rubbing while she dug and scraped her nails across his skin. Their breaths merged as their bodies joined, and she nearly came apart at the seams.

When he gently bit down on her bottom lip, his loving nature pushed her over the edge and her climax consumed her again. Stars burst in the back of her lids as her breath caught in her chest.

As she grunted out his name, his hot seed filled her and his cock pulsed and expanded to the beat of his heart. Somehow he managed to roll them over while keeping them joined.

Only after the fire began to die, did he slip out and wipe her clean.

Trent kissed her forehead and then her nose. "Remind me to thank Dan."

It took her a second to understand what he meant. If it hadn't been for Dan taking him off the case, Trent wouldn't have come to the cabin, and she wouldn't have had the chance to plot her seduction. "Perhaps in the future, you should consider more vacations."

"If you promise to come along, I just might."

She had never heard more wonderful words.

* * *

AFTER HAVING ACCOMPLISHED her mission, Charlotte was willing to head back to Rock Hard with Trent the next day. As they neared town, Trent glanced over at her. "Given someone took pot shots at me and failed, he might try again."

Shivers ripple of her arms. Why was he trying to scare her? Perhaps she hadn't been aware how much danger he and her dad were in on a daily basis. "If that's the case, you should hole up in your house. You said you can't go into work for a few more days anyway."

"I was thinking about you, that you should stay sequestered until we find the killer."

If he hadn't looked so serious, she might have laughed. "What are you talking about?"

"Someone was angry at your dad, and instead of attacking him directly, they came after you and your mom. The same thing could happen to you now that we're together."

She was pleased he considered them a couple, but he was missing the point. "No one knows we're together. Besides, you do remember I have a shop to run, right?"

"I'm not so worried about you during the day, but what if he comes after you or Harmon at night?"

Either he was being overly protective, or he was having second thoughts. "Remember, I agreed to take shooting lessons."

"I appreciate that, but it doesn't mean they can't harm you first."

She twisted in her seat and tucked a leg under her. She'd had enough of his excuses. "No one can remain safe all the time no matter the precaution. Someone could pull out of a street and ram into your car. A bolt of lightning could strike you, or you could have an allergic reaction to a bee sting and die. That's life."

His fingers tightened on the wheel. "It's not the same as having a target on your back, but I'm a reasonable men. How about until we arrest the murderer, you stay at your parents' place?"

She could think of a hundred reasons why that wasn't such a good idea. For starters, her parents had just remarried, and they needed their space. "Who's to say Dad isn't involved in a dangerous job right now, huh?"

The lines around Trent's eyes tightened. "I'll give you that. Would you consider staying at my place then?"

Now that was a request she'd love to honor, but it might not be as safe as he thought. "It has appeal, but if this person is out to get you, wouldn't it be safer if you stayed with me?" She had an exterior door and a set of stairs to climb before the person could reach her apartment. Trent's house was open to the sidewalk where anyone could peer in.

"I want to keep you safe, Charlotte, and if you feel more comfortable with me at your place, I'm fine with staying over."

She loved the idea of having him there, and while he wouldn't be working for a few days, she suspected sitting on the sofa all day wasn't his style either.

"Thank you."

"I'll drop you off at your apartment as I'm sure you'd like to pick up your car so you can stop by your shop, but call me when you close up. I'll head on over."

"I can't wait." She meant that whole-heartedly.

He pulled in front of her apartment. "Want me to come in and make sure it's safe?"

He was going a bit too far. "I'm good." She leaned over and brushed her lips against his. Anymore, and she'd be dragging him upstairs and having her way with him.

Trent clasped the back of her head, pulled her close, and delivered a toe-curling kiss. This time she pulled back. "If I don't go now, I'll never make it to the shop." *Because I'll be stripping you naked.*

"Fine, but be aware of your surroundings at all times."

She saluted and he smiled. Once Trent drove off, she gathered her designs from her place then headed to her store. She parked in back and let herself in with the spare key. As she stepped into the main showroom, she called to her mom.

"In here." Her mom twisted around and smiled. "How did it go?"

How did one tell one's mother that she'd seduced the man she loved? Most likely her mother had done the same thing with her father, but Charlotte didn't want to think about that. "Mission accomplished, thank you."

"Does that mean you two are officially a couple?"

"I think so." She detailed how Trent was worried about her safety, and how he suggested he stay at her place. It wasn't quite accurate, but she didn't want her mother to sacrifice her time with Dad and say it was okay if Charlotte stayed with them.

She placed the designs she made for Mr. Samuels on the counter and unrolled them. "Want to see how I'm going to redecorate my client's bedroom?"

Her mother stepped over to the counter. Once Charlotte explained everything she had planned, her mother placed a hand on her arm. "I might be able to paint, but you are the one with the true talent."

Charlotte beamed. "Thank you. I hope he likes the design."

"I'm sure he will."

"The shop won't close for another two hours, so feel free to head home. I can handle the hoards of clients from here." She'd be lucky if anyone stopped in.

"Mind if I stay? I have a feeling that in the near future I won't be seeing much of you."

"I'd like nothing more."

Until closing, they chatted about Hawaii and then about

Harmon and Trent. Charlotte filled her mom in with what she knew of the case after Trent's shooting, which wasn't much.

"If you need me to sit in the store at any time, I'm sure I can take time off work."

Charlotte had the best mom ever. "It'll be fine."

At five, she closed the store and drove home to change since she wanted to appear a bit more sophisticated for Mr. Samuels. At a quarter to six she headed out and was pleased to spot his car in the drive—or at least what she thought must be his car. The last time she'd been there, he must've parked in the garage.

She gathered her things and hiked up to the front door. As she was about to knock she noticed the door was ajar, and figured he wanted her to go in. He was expecting her, after all.

"Mr. Samuels?" she called loud enough for him to hear.

No answer. She knocked again and waited, shivering from the winter air. Perhaps he was in his bedroom moving things around and couldn't hear her. She pressed on the door and stepped inside. "Mr. Samuels?" She raised her voice.

Charlotte stilled, trying to heighten her senses. This was very odd. His car was in the drive and the front door open. As soon as she put those two pieces of information together the hairs on the back of her neck rose. Could there be an intruder in the house? Her pulse raced and her mouth turned dry. Trent's paranoia that something bad might happen must be coloring her thoughts.

Charlotte set her designs on the entry table, slipped her hand into her purse, and clutched her weapon. As quietly as possible, she eased farther into the house.

The refrigerator hummed and the heat pouring out of the vents hissed. She debated leaving and returning another day, but she really wanted to start on this project today. Releasing her grip on her weapon, she withdrew her phone and dialed his number. If he was in the house, she should hear it ring.

The faint tingling sound came from the direction of the bedroom, and she exhaled. He was in there, waiting for her.

Charlotte picked up her designs and headed into the bedroom. When she reached the open door, she knocked on the jamb, and entered.

While she prided herself on her ability to stay calm, the sight before her made her scream.

CHAPTER TWENTY-SIX

NOT ONLY HAD Trent packed in preparation for his move in with Charlotte, he'd checked in with each of the four men who were watching the possible murder suspects. Staying out of the loop had been impossible. What had Dan Hartwick been thinking taking him off the case? Charlotte had done more to help direct his priorities than when he'd sat on his ass in the cabin thinking about what was important.

As for remaining safe, Charlotte was right again. Even if he wore full combat gear, something not connected with the case could harm him. He was ready to return to work. All he had to do now was convince his boss to reinstate him. Trent didn't mind seeing the shrink about discharging his weapon at the restaurant, but once he jumped through the department hoops, he'd insist on returning to duty.

On the drive down from the cabin, he'd asked Charlotte to call him when she arrived home after work tonight so he'd know when he could come over, and he was still waiting for that call. As if he were psychic, his cell rang and he snatched it off the table. Darn. It was Vic again.

"You got something?" Trent asked. He'd just spoken to him a few minutes ago.

"I know you're not on the case, but you should know someone just murdered John Samuels."

Trent's gut contracted, and his mind spun in disbelief. "No way. You sure?"

"I'm looking at him."

Fuck. Once Samuels began asking questions about Bill Goddard's computer, and then made the moves on the dead man's wife, Trent had elevated him to his number one suspect. Now he'd been murdered, too. The detectives had kept an eye on those connected with the case during the day, so how could this have happened? "When was he killed?"

"We're waiting for the coroner now, but the body's been in rigor for a while. That's actually not why I called. You'll never guess who found him." Bitterness tinged his tone.

It could only mean one person, and a tight band squeezed his chest. "Charlotte?"

"Afraid so. She came here to show him her designs for his bedroom and found him."

She hadn't mentioned she was stopping by his house today. Had she thought he'd object? Hell, maybe he would have. Hopefully, she'd merely forgotten to mention it or hadn't made the appointment yet when he'd dropped her off.

Trent was off duty, but he truly believed Charlotte would want him around. Knowing her dad, he'd be working the scene, even though he was just a hired private investigator. "Who else is there?"

"Hartwick and two others. Cade, Devon, and Connor are still watching the other suspects, or so Dan said."

"What's the address?" Vic hesitated but then told him. "I'll be right there." Trent disconnected.

Hartwick would probably be pissed that Vic had called him, but too bad. Charlotte was a brave woman, and while she'd handled being shot at with composure, seeing a dead body was different. He hoped this wasn't the first time she'd viewed a corpse up close and personal, because the first was the worst.

As he entered the neighborhood, sirens raced up behind him, forcing him to pull to the side. No doubt they were going to Samuels' home.

Within a minute, Trent was parked as close to the house as possible. He jumped out, his head about to explode. It was difficult not to draw conclusions about why two prominent men from the same company had been murdered, but he needed to keep an open mind. Mrs. Goddard had nothing to gain by John Samuel's death, unless John demanded more than she was willing to give. Frank Hamilton had just lost one partner. Surely, his firm couldn't afford another. As for Elaine's brother, he wouldn't have had much cause to interact with Samuels. Shit. It was looking more and more like an irate customer was the offender—but which one?

Trent nodded to the officer at the door and strode in, spotting Dan Hartwick conferring with Thad Dalton, another detective near the kitchen. He hoped like hell Dan wouldn't tell him to turn around and go home. Trent was needed, damn it, but because Charlotte had found the body, Dan might think Trent was still too close to the case.

"Couldn't keep away, could you? Dan asked, thankfully sounding more amused than angry.

"Vic contacted me about the murder. Told me Charlotte found the body, and I just came to make sure she's okay."

"How did the *short* vacation go?"

He didn't know why he was asking about it right now, but he answered him. "Figured a few things out." One was that he wanted Charlotte in his life.

"Glad to hear it. I could use you if you can keep your head on straight. You'll have to promise to see the shrink real soon, though, about the shooting."

"Absolutely." Relief thrummed through him. "I'll do my best, sir."

"I've spoken with Charlotte, but she's rather upset. Maybe

you can find out more information from her. She's in the living room with her dad." Dan nodded behind him.

"Thank you." Men were rushing around, but once he spotted Charlotte around the corner, he made a beeline toward her. Vic was holding her hand, but it was her tear streaked face and puffy cheek that broke his heart.

As soon as she noticed him, she twisted to the side and opened her arms. Even though he was back on duty, he couldn't deny her. Trent sat down next to her, nodded to Vic, and then hugged her.

"I was so scared," she huffed out. "I didn't know what to do." She sucked in a breath and then cried on his shoulder.

He felt helpless, but then relied on what he did best—asking questions. "Can you tell me what happened?"

She sniffled and sat back. "I told Mr. Hartwick all I knew."

"Sometimes telling it again can jar your memory. Even the littlest detail can help."

"Okay. Before Harmon drove me to the cabin, I'd made a date with Mr. Samuels for six o'clock to show him my designs. When I arrived a few minutes early, his car was in the driveway —or at least some car was in the driveway."

So she had known about visiting him, but he wasn't about to call her on it now. "The Cadillac belonged to Samuels."

"Good. When I made it up to the front door, it was open, but I knocked anyway and called his name. When he didn't answer I stepped inside the foyer. I thought he might be working in the back of the house."

Trent forced himself to sit still. If Samuels' murderer had been in the house, Charlotte could have been killed, too. He closed his eyes for a second, trying not to let that horrible image distract him. "What did you see?"

"Nothing."

He glanced around. "Nothing was out of place?"

She looked down at her hands and wound her fingers

together. "I wasn't looking very carefully. If you're asking if there had been some kind of fight, I saw no evidence of it."

Her voice had risen as if she was becoming more agitated. If she hadn't touched anything, the forensic team would figure out what had gone down. Trent clasped her hands in his. "Then what did you do?"

"I listened to see if I could hear him moving about. Other than the heat being on and something mechanical running in the kitchen, the house was silent. I grabbed my gun, because I had the sense something was off. People don't leave front doors open in the middle of the winter."

Trent leaned back against the seat. "That was smart of you."

A brief smile lifted her lips. "I called to see if I could hear his phone ring and I could. The sound came from the bedroom. I walked in there and found him dead. I didn't know what I was supposed to do, but then I asked myself what would Dad do?" She looked over at her father and he nodded. "I called 911 and rushed outside. I didn't want to take the chance the killer was still inside."

Trent was relieved she'd acted sensibly. "You did the right thing."

Vic cut in. "I saw Charlotte run out of the house, and fearing something bad had happened, I showed myself. When she told me what happened, we waited in my car for the cops to arrive. While I wasn't in favor of her returning inside, Dan wanted her to describe where she was when she found the body."

Trent asked her a few more questions, but Charlotte didn't seem to remember much more. "Why don't you take her home, Vic? I need to stay here."

"I can do that. With Samuels dead, I'm officially off the case." He wrapped an arm around his daughter's shoulders. "How about staying with us, hon? I can work from home."

She looked up at Trent, her eyes shimmering, and indecision flooding her face. "What do you think? You said you'd stay with me."

Guilt swamped him. "Your dad can take better care of you than I can right now. I bet he'd even be willing to go to the shop with you during the day."

Vic nodded and Charlotte's shoulders slumped. "Can I see you?"

Both Dan's words and Charlotte's reverberated in his head. Before this weekend, he'd have said he had a job to do. Now, he realized there was something more important—Charlotte. "Absolutely. How about I pick you up in the evening from either your dad's place or the shop depending on when I'm free, and then take you back to your apartment. I'll spend the night with you."

Vic tightened his grip on her shoulder. "We'll see how it goes."

From the ache in Vic's eyes, this wasn't about a father being worried his daughter would be sleeping with him, but more if he and Ellie would be able to handle any emotional collapse better. Trent didn't argue, as he wanted what was best for her.

* * *

WHILE THE NEXT few days were hell, Trent's evenings were filled with the wonderful Charlotte. For the first couple of nights, they sat in her living room talking. She still harbored some resentment about her dad's work with the FBI and how it had affected the family, but she was trying to understand his reasons for basically abandoning her and her mom. Trent had never met a more forgiving woman in his life—or a braver one. For the first time, he was given a glimpse into why his mom might have left his dad. His father had put his job first—not his wife or his children. Now he could see how wrong that had been.

Trent had held off making love with Charlotte because she still had nightmares about finding Samuels' body, and Trent wanted to be there for her and give her comfort instead. When the time was right, if she hadn't come to grips with what happened, he'd suggest she seek counseling. He could still remember the first dead body he'd come across, and the image would be forever burned in his head.

In the mornings, Trent would drive her to the shop where she called her dad to meet her. Trent could only hope the forced time together would help mend things between her and Vic.

Once he was certain she was safe, Trent headed on in to work. Once there, the tension built. With so many of the detectives watching—or perhaps protecting—Elaine, Frank, and Richard, it was up to Trent and Dan to figure out what they'd missed. By concentrating on these three, he feared they'd been barking up the wrong proverbial tree.

By the time Samuels' viewing rolled around on Tuesday, they'd made little headway. They could only hope the killer would show up and give something away. Mrs. Goddard had cremated her husband and hadn't wanted a service, but John's family, who lived in town, decided to honor him differently.

A few hours before they were to leave for the funeral home, Harmon called Trent at work, something he never did. His brother understood that when Trent was on the job, he didn't want to be disturbed.

"Hey," Trent said, praying nothing was wrong.

"You'll never believe it. I think I know who set me up."

CHAPTER TWENTY-SEVEN

"WHAT DO YOU mean you know who set you up?" Trent asked.

"Remember those books from Bill Goddard's office that Charlotte asked me to give away?"

Please say there was information inside them. "Yes."

"When I picked them up to move them, I dropped one, and a bunch of photos fell out."

Trent went straight into cop mode. "What kind of photos?"

"Surveillance photos of *me*." His brother had an annoying way of stringing out the information. "I think Bill wanted them so he could set me up."

Trent didn't understand. Nor could he figure out why Bill would have photos of Trent's brother, unless Harmon was speaking with his client or maybe Richard Delaney outside of the office. "What were you doing in the pictures?"

He hoped Elaine Goddard wasn't in them. If she were, it would mean his brother had lied to him about being with a married woman.

"Nothing. Don't you get it?"

Apparently he'd been sifting through clues for too long and his neurons had overloaded to the point where he wasn't capable of understanding anything. "No."

"I started thinking about that night at the Christmas party when Elaine kissed me. I'd gently told her I wasn't interested, and she never put the moves on me again, but I'm thinking that Bill found out. It's possible Elaine said something to him, or Jayson, my coworker, mentioned it. Looking back to the time between the Christmas party and when I was accused of insider trading, Bill suddenly began acting a lot friendlier."

"How does this imply Bill was the one who set you up?"

"I don't have proof," Harmon said, "but it made me remember some of the little things that had happened. A couple of times, I found Bill on my computer when I stopped back at work late at night to pick up something, and again when I arrived earlier than usual. Now, I'm thinking he was pretending to be me and was informing my client about the information on his brother-in-law's company."

Excitement pulsed through Trent's veins, even though supposition didn't prove guilt. "Did you ask him why he was there?"

"I'm sure I did, and he must've given me a satisfactory explanation, because I forgot all about it. After all it was his firm, and I was the new kid on the block. At the time, no accusations had been hurled at me."

Trent wasn't convinced there was enough evidence to prove Harmon innocent. "Did Bill exhibit any other odd behavior?"

"I know this sounds strange, but Bill was almost too nice when he found out I had supposedly told my client about the future merger at Richard's firm."

"Why was that suspicious?"

"Think about it," Harmon said. "My supposedly illegal action could have triggered an even more in depth investigation by the SEC than it did, yet Bill never acted all that upset. Sure he wasn't pleased, but he seemed more fatherly than like a boss. I'm thinking he didn't want me to think he could have been the one to turn on me."

Harmon was grasping at straws, but there was no use pointing that out. "I'll tell you what. When we find Bill's murderer, maybe we'll find the answers to what happened to you." It was the best Trent could do.

"Appreciate it."

Once they disconnected, Trent worried he hadn't handled the situation as sympathetically as he could have, but dammit, he worked on facts not wishes.

Trent had about two hours before he had to head to the funeral home, so he spent most of the time reading over the reports from Vic, Devon, Cade, and Connor. Unfortunately, no one's behavior looked suspicious. He leaned back and stabbed his fingers through his hair. This case seemed to have one dead end after another.

He and Dan had decided that just the two of them would attend Samuels' viewing. Having half the detective force there would prevent any false move by the killer—assuming he showed up.

Because Mrs. Goddard would be attending the service, Cade would be outside as backup. Most likely Frank Hamilton would be there, too, as his right-hand man was the guest of honor. Trent doubted that Elaine's brother would show, but if he did, it would be to support his sister. After all, it was her lover who'd been murdered.

Since Dan and the funeral director had gone to school together he was able to convince the director to allow the precinct to install cameras in each corner of the room, along with some well-placed microphones. Dan had to promise that nothing would be leaked or shown unless it became evidence in court.

Trent arrived a few minutes early at the funeral home and took a seat at the back of the room where he could watch who came in. He and Harmon had discussed whether it would be appropriate for his brother to show up, but Trent believed Harmon asked only because he wanted to confront Frank Hamilton about who'd set him up. The last thing they needed was that kind of disturbance. Because John Samuels had been hired after Harmon was sent to jail, it made no sense for Harmon to come. In the end, his brother agreed to stay home and not answer his apartment door unless it was Trent.

Dan arrived shortly after Trent did, but he didn't make eye contact. Instead, he acted the concerned officer by offering his condolences to John Samuels' relatives. Trent tried to note who had shown up, but other than those who worked at John's firm, he wasn't able to identify many of them.

Trent studied each of them as they spoke with John's relatives, to see if any exhibited any underlying hostility. If someone had lost a lot of money, he might want to see if Samuels' aunt and uncle were willing to fork over some cash. So far, all well-wishers had seemed sincere.

Frank was the only one with the information about which clients had made money with John and which ones had lost their life savings. If he'd been more cooperative, the investigation might have proceeded faster.

Fearing people might wonder why Trent was just watching everyone, he spent the next few minutes mingling. He spoke with Mrs. Goddard and Frank Hamilton, offering his sympathies, then moved on and spoke briefly with the other relatives.

Halfway through the viewing, a bitter tone emanated from the corner that caught his attention. He glanced behind his shoulder and spotted Mrs. Goddard with Frank Hamilton. Surely the death of John Samuels had to have brought up more feelings of abandonment for the poor woman, as both men in her life were now gone. Trent hoped the cameras were picking up the interaction, as her voice was getting louder and filled with emotion. A few minutes later, the two separated, and Trent was no closer to learning anything.

After three long hours, the viewing ended. Dan walked out with him and followed Trent to his car, probably to make sure no one could overhear.

"Pick up any interesting chatter?" his boss asked.

"No."

"Let's not become discouraged. I've instructed the surveillance tapes to be brought over to the precinct and examined, though it will take a while to go through them," Dan said. "Maybe we'll learn something, maybe we won't."

"We can only hope." Even if they didn't garner any useful clues, identifying those who'd come might help. While they would ask for a copy of the registry, probably not everyone bothered to fill it in.

Frustrated and tired, it was time to pick up Charlotte then head home and snuggle with her.

* * *

As much as Charlotte loved being able to spend time with her father, it was driving her crazy how he watched her every move. Once when she needed something from her car, he had to follow her outside. Sheesh. He was more of a protector than Trent and that was saying a lot.

They did have some good discussions, but it seemed as if every time they were at the deep emotional part, someone would enter her store. One benefit of having customers, though, was that her dad was able to see what she dealt with on a daily basis, and many times, expressed how proud he was of her. For those few words of praise, she was almost happy the killer had disrupted her life.

Right at five, Trent entered her shop, and her thoughts switched directions. As much as her father's presence made her feel protected, she wanted Trent and the safety and security of his arms—forever.

He'd come from the viewing and looked so handsome in his suit. She kissed him hello with a rather chaste kiss. "Give me a second to get my things, and we can go."

Her dad stood, came over, and placed a kiss on her cheek as well. "See you tomorrow, sweetheart."

Being with him for eight hours at a time was a bit much since her dad was wound rather tightly.

"Mom has tomorrow off. If you want to bring her around, it might be fun for the three of us to spend some time together."

Dad smiled. "Might not be a good idea. I'm not sure I'll be able to keep my hands off her if she were within reach."

"Da-ad." Some things were meant to remain secret.

He laughed and then left.

Trent watched her lock up and then escorted her to his Jeep. "Want to pick up something at the grocery store and cook dinner together?"

She loved the part about doing something with him. "I'd love that."

Given how overwhelming these last few days had been, she didn't know what she would've done without Trent by her side. They'd had the time to learn more about each other, and for that she'd be eternally thankful.

They hadn't made love because Trent didn't think she was ready. In hindsight, he was probably right, as every time she closed her eyes the horrid image of that man appeared. After a few days passed, her memory grew dimmer, and Charlotte felt it was time to celebrate them as a couple.

At the grocery store, Charlotte suggested they pick up something simple to make, because she wanted to get him into bed as quickly as possible.

They debated options and finally ended up with some pre-made fried chicken. She offered to steam some vegetables and heat up some rolls in the oven for sides. Easy peazy.

As had been Trent's practice since moving in, she was allowed to step into the entrance of her apartment and then had to wait for him to check each room.

"All clear," he said coming out of her bedroom.

Given how small her place was, she doubted anyone could have hidden, except in the bathroom behind the shower curtain.

As if they'd already established a routine, they began

preparing the meal. Trent handled the rolls while she fixed the vegetables.

"How was the viewing?" She had thought about going, in part to support Mrs. Goddard, but Trent had talked her out of it. Given he was in the middle of an investigation, she went along with it. Most likely her father would've nixed it anyway.

"Nothing out of the ordinary, except I noticed that Elaine Goddard didn't seem all that fond of Frank Hamilton." Trent dropped the rolls on the cookie sheet and placed the tin in the oven.

"Maybe Mr. Goddard and Mr. Hamilton never really got along, and the wife picked up on those feelings of resentment. I have no proof, of course, and Mrs. Goddard never mentioned it. Then again, perhaps she wanted a bigger piece of the company and Mr. Hamilton said no."

"Could be," he said.

There was probably more to the story, but she knew not to push. A few minutes later both the rolls and veggies were done. In relative silence, they chowed down. While she started a few conversations, Trent seemed preoccupied. Many women might have become concerned, but not her. She couldn't blame him for being frustrated. He hadn't come right out and said he suspected Mr. Samuels of offing Bill Goddard, but she had the sense that he'd thought it. He had to be wondering who was next on the list. She hoped no harm would come to his brother, since he, too, had worked at that firm.

Charlotte tried to figure out how to broach the topic of making love again, but she couldn't think of a subtle way to bring it up. She missed the comfort and the closeness it brought. While she might have periodic visions of seeing the dead body, she was ready to move on.

After they finished eating, she asked Trent to make them some coffee while she cleaned up the dinner dishes. This time he didn't complain and just complied. She wanted to shake the man, but that might only make him withdraw even more.

When she was done, she stepped over to the sofa where he was sitting. Instead of dropping down next to him, she lifted the steaming cup from his fingers, set it on the table, and then straddled him.

"Charlotte?"

She cupped his face. "I've missed you, Trent. I know you've been keeping your distance because you believed I was fragile and that I needed some time to process all that has happened, but I'm good now. I love you all the more for being so concerned for my well-being, but now it's time for us to be a couple again."

He ran his hands from her shoulders down to her wrists, gently lifted her palms from his cheeks, and brought her fingertips to his lips. "I don't deserve you, Charlotte. I'm off in my own world too much of the time, and here you're hurting because of my actions. I wish I weren't so selfish."

Aw. "It's not being selfish. It's called ambition and a desire to find a killer. I know you think he'll come after me, and that you have to protect me. For that I'll always love you. I'm not even going to tell you that nothing could happen to me, because I know it could. I just want you to talk to me."

As if he'd reconnected with her, a small sparkle came to his eyes. "I thought we had been talking. A lot. I've liked it, by the way."

"So have I, but I want us to continue to communicate. If you're worried about the case, I want you to tell me. I understand you might not be able to give me any details, and that's fine, but you can express your frustration. If you need time to yourself to concentrate on the clues, tell me. I want to make this work between us."

He ran his palms up to her shoulders and then cupped her breasts. "Are you sure?"

"I've never been more sure of anything in my life."

CHAPTER TWENTY-EIGHT

CHARLOTTE MUST HAVE said the magic words, because Trent stood with her on his lap. She lowered her legs and wrapped her arms around his neck. "Are you thinking of getting me naked?" *Please say yes.*

"Do you want me to?"

She loved when he teased her. "Only if you can be fast."

Before he had the chance to finish unbuttoning her blouse, she ditched her shoes and had his jeans undone.

"Is someone in a hurry?" His brows rose and one side of his kissable mouth turned up.

He was such a funny man. "I'm not sure yet. Perhaps if I see you naked...and hard... and desperate, I might consider making love with you. Slowly."

He smiled, something she hadn't seen in quite a while, and her heart soared.

"I guess I'll have to test that theory, won't I?"

Faster than she could draw two straight lines, he stripped her naked then removed his clothes. Without a word, he dropped to his knees, nudged open her legs, and threaded two fingers straight up into her pussy. A strong primal need shot up her body. She clasped his head and hung on tight as his tongue lashed back and forth over her bundle of nerves. The terror of the last few days receded and he made her forget everything but being with him.

Trent raised a hand and nabbed her nipple between his thumb and forefinger then twisted the tip back and forth, gently ratcheting her desire to a fevered pitch. Not having made love to him for days had made her even more desperate than usual.

She wanted to touch him with her fingers, with her tongue, and with her pussy. "Kiss me."

Trent slid his fingers out of her wet slit and looked up at her. "Have I turned you on yet?"

He knew the answer to that question. "Stand up and I'll show you just how much."

"I always have liked a woman who knew what she wanted."

There was no doubt what she desired—Trent Lawson. Once he rose to his feet, she wrapped her arms around his back and then clawed her way up to his shoulders. Her breasts pressed against his rock hard chest and she opened her mouth to receive him.

"I want you, Charlotte. Bad."

"Then take me."

As he captured her mouth, she jumped up and wrapped her legs around his waist. His hands supported her butt and as he squeezed each cheek, his tongue delved into her mouth. He tasted spicy and rich, and oh so sexy.

Electric tingles consumed her, and as she jockeyed for position, she forgot everything but him. Because he was supporting her, she slid her feet to his thighs and pressed upward, rubbing her wetness against his cock. The pressure on her clit was like a bolt of lightning straight to her heart. She needed him. She wanted him, and she damned sure was going to do whatever it took to have him.

Trent walked her backward until she hit the wall separating the living room and the hallway. She leaned against it for support, reached between them, and grabbed his dick.

Trent broke the kiss and closed his eyes. "I want you. Now."

Keeping a firm grasp of his cock, she slipped his hard shaft between her folds and sank down partway until his size made it nearly impossible to engulf all of him.

He moaned. "Jesus, Charlotte, you feel so fucking good."

He should be her. Trent eased out of her and then edged right back in again. The friction and the stretching heightened every sense to the point that tremors vibrated up her entire body. He dipped his head and captured her nipple, sucking and pulling the tip until shards of bliss exploded inside her.

She dug her nails into his shoulders, dropped her head back, and held on for the ride of her life. Trent plowed into her, nearly pushing her off her climactic edge, but she didn't want this joyous ride to end too soon. Being in his arms and touching him gave her immense pleasure.

He switched his attention to her other breast and she had to hold her breath to keep from coming. Each time he drove into her, the excitement grew, gaining speed until the joy blossomed.

"I don't think I can last much longer," she panted.

Trent clasped her waist and raised his head enough to lightly kiss her throat with such tenderness that she nearly cracked with desire. "I need you," he whispered.

Before she had the chance to respond, he thrust into her, holding her tightly. When the tip of his cock banged into her back wall, she clamped down on his hard dick. Just as her orgasm swept through her, his cock detonated, pushing her already racing heart into the red zone, where the glory and thrill consumed her.

She pressed her chest against his and held him, never wanting to let him go. This was where she needed to be.

* * *

THE NEXT MORNING at work, Trent was in a good mood, despite not being any closer to finding the killer. Charlotte had this amazing effect on him, though he still had a hard time believing she was willing to accept him for who he was, and be okay with him abiding by his rules of silence when he was working a case.

He leaned back in his office seat and thought about the delicious woman, and how she'd seduced him. Again. Charlotte had the uncanny ability to distract him and tempt him like no other. Every time he was around her, he had the urge to grab her thick, wavy hair and tug. Even fantasizing about her made his cock take notice.

His cell rang, jerking him out of his fantasy. He nabbed it and swiped a finger across the phone, the smile on his face quickly disappearing. "Lawson."

"It's Cade. Get over to Mrs. Goddard's house ASAP. Something's going down with Frank Hamilton."

Before Trent could ask any questions, his partner disconnected. He could only hope this was something that would lead them to the killer. Shoving his weapon into his holster and plucking his jacket from the back of his chair, he raced out of the precinct. Fortunately, he'd found a spot in front this morning and was on the road in less than one minute.

Sirens blaring, he raced through town toward Mrs. Goddard's home. He tried contacting Cade again, but his partner didn't answer. From the urgency in Cade's voice, whatever was happening, wasn't good.

When the traffic thinned, Trent cut the sirens, not wanting to give away his approach, though he didn't reduce his speed one bit. He spotted Cade's personal car a few blocks from Mrs. Goddard's house, pulled behind it, and parked.

Keeping a tight watch for any unusual activity in the neighborhood, he eased his way toward her home. Cade waved, motioning him to the other side of the big picture window. He wanted to ask what was happening, but he feared their voices would travel. He had to trust Cade.

From his angle, he could see a portion of the living room and some of the kitchen. Frank Hamilton was speaking with someone, probably Elaine, in the kitchen. Trent caught a face flash across the house through the opposite window.

Who's back there? he mouthed to Cade, hoping it was one of the other men.

Devon.

Before Trent could ask anything else, shouts sounded from inside of the house, and adrenaline flooded his veins. Because the front door was ajar, they both changed positions and stood next to the opening. What Trent wouldn't give for an amplifying mic right now.

They could enter the house, but barging in would prevent them from learning anything more.

"What did you see in Samuels anyway?" This bitter shout came from Frank.

Elaine's words were too soft to hear. Damn.

As long as Frank remained where he was, they would do nothing. It was only if they believed her to be in danger, would they enter.

"I've always wanted you," he said. "Bill messed around on you all the time, yet you stayed with him. Why?"

More mumbling came from inside the kitchen. Trent glanced at Cade hoping he'd caught something but his partner shook his head.

Frank stepped farther into the kitchen, and once he disappeared from view, Trent placed his hand on the doorjamb ready to enter. From where Devon was positioned, he probably had a better vantage point.

"I thought with Bill out of the way, you'd give me a chance." Frank's voice sounded more pleading than aggressive and Trent let down his guard for a moment.

Oh, shit. The puzzle pieces began to click into place. Even though he was married, it appeared as if Frank was interested in Elaine. Had Frank killed Bill and just admitted it? Even if he had, Elaine Goddard might not say a word. She'd said nothing when her husband abused her.

Loud footsteps sounded, along with scuffling sounds. When Elaine screamed, both he and Cade shot into action and barged in. Out of the corner of his eye, a blur shot by. Devon was heading their way.

When they reached the kitchen with their weapons drawn, Frank had a knife in his hand and his arm was raised.

Trent's instincts sharpened. "Police. Stop what you're doing, Frank," he shouted.

The man whipped around, the knife still clutched in his fist, his eyes wild and unfocused. "You don't know anything."

That made no sense, but he'd play along. "Why don't you tell us about it, Frank?"

As if he'd pushed aside the insanity, his faced calmed, and he set the knife on the counter as if it had all been a joke. He then held out his wrists. "I'm not saying another word until I speak with my lawyer."

Crap. Trent nodded to Cade who stepped forward and cuffed the man. "Come with me, Mr. Hamilton," Cade said.

His partner didn't announce why he was arresting him probably because there were too many offenses to list.

The fact Frank didn't claim he was innocent, spoke volumes. Devon rushed in and looked up at Trent. "Do you want me to go with Cade?"

"Yes, I'll see to Mrs. Goddard."

As soon as they left, Trent turned his attention to the woman who was shaking so badly, he thought she might collapse. "How about we sit in the living room?"

She looked up at him but said nothing, as if she was trying to formulate the words. Trent stepped over to her, placed a hand on her elbow, and led her out. When she was seated, he called the precinct and asked them to send over a forensic team. He wasn't sure what they'd find, but they needed to secure the knife.

Trent then returned to the seat across from her. "Can you tell me what happened?"

She cast her glance to the side and knitted her fingers together. "I'm not proud of how I've handled my life."

As much as he wanted her to talk, he needed her to focus on the recent events. "I'm not here to judge you, Mrs. Goddard. I'm only interested in what happened today and what Frank said to you."

Perhaps later he'd ask about the conversation at the funeral home, assuming their voices weren't picked up by the mic.

"Yesterday at John's funeral, Frank was acting his usual creepy self."

Creepy? "Can you be more specific?"

She inhaled deeply. "I've known for a long time that Frank has been interested in me. It didn't seem to matter that he had a wife or that I was married to his business partner. Bill wasn't perfect, but I loved him despite his faults."

Her thoughts came out a bit jumbled, but he understood the gist of what she was saying. Trent debated asking her about the origin of her bruises, but now wasn't the time. "Did your husband know of Frank's interest?"

She shrugged. "If he did, he never said anything, but I could always tell when he thought I'd stepped over the line." She rubbed her shoulder as if remembering Bill's violence against her.

Trent pictured the time when she'd kissed Harmon and wondered if it was worth bringing that up. While this wasn't about his brother, he needed to know. "Was Bill angry when he found out you kissed my brother?" He failed to keep his tone civil.

She jerked, almost as if his comment had come out of nowhere. "He never mentioned it."

"Was Bill a jealous man?"

"Only in that he didn't want anyone else to have what he did."

The possibility existed that Bill or Frank had framed Harmon because of his possible interest in Elaine, but without proof, his brother would never have his case overturned. Trent had let this conversation drift too far off course already and needed to discuss today's event. "What happened when Frank came here today? If you could run it by me step-by-step, I'd appreciate it." Trent pulled out his note pad.

"He rang the bell, and when I answered, he asked to come in. I knew what he wanted, but I wasn't interested, so I told him to leave."

Since his men had been sitting outside, they must've witnessed the exchange. "He didn't listen?"

"No. I tried to push him out, but he barged in anyway and wouldn't take no for an answer."

"Did he force himself on you?" Anger roiled inside him.

She shook her head. "I was able to calm him down by offering him a cup of coffee, but when I went into the kitchen to make it, he followed me."

That's when Trent had arrived. "Go on."

"He told me again how much he loved me, but that was a lie. Men like Frank and my husband only love themselves. He said that since Bill and John were no longer in the picture, there was no reason for me not to accept him as my lover. He had all the money I could possibly need. I said I still didn't want him, and that's when Frank grabbed the knife from the butcher block."

She must have been frightened out of her mind. "Did Frank mention if he'd harmed either of them?" His pulse raced. Trent didn't want to tell her they'd been listening outside the door.

She sat there as if her conscience was battling. "Yes. He killed both men for me—or so he'd said at John's viewing." She tapped her chest. "I never wanted that. Ever." She dropped her face in her hands and sobbed.

Trent wanted to console the poor woman, but he wouldn't. At some point, he'd ask her to come down to the station and make a statement, but he doubted she'd agree to it right now.

When she stopped crying, Trent continued. "Do you think Frank would have harmed you if we hadn't stopped him?"

She sniffled. "I don't know. He loved me, or so he said, but I think he just wanted what Bill had. When he raised the knife, I believed he wanted to kill me, but then you showed up." She swiped her eyes. "Thank you."

"You're welcome." In the end, it wouldn't matter if he meant to harm her or not. Frank Hamilton's other offenses would land him in prison for the rest of his life.

CHAPTER TWENTY-NINE

WHEN TRENT DIDN'T show up at five o'clock like he had these past few days to pick her up, Charlotte began to worry. "I think I'll call him," she told her dad.

"He's probably caught up at work. I'll drive you back to our house."

She spun to face him. "So you think I shouldn't disturb him?"

"When Trent is finished with what he's doing, he'll pick you up. Cops are busy."

She'd rather go back to her house, but that would mean Dad would stay until Trent arrived, and she had wanted to visit with her mom. "Okay."

They were halfway to her dad's house, when Trent called, and joy spread straight to her belly. She wanted to talk dirty to him over the phone, but with her dad driving, she didn't dare.

"Hey," she said.

"Sorry I didn't call sooner, but I got caught up at work. You'll never guess what happened today."

From the excitement in his voice, it was something good. "Don't tell me the killer walked into the precinct and confessed."

"No, that might have been nice, but we did find out who killed both Bill and John."

She glanced over at her father, and while he appeared to be listening, she didn't sense he knew what Trent was about to tell her. "Who was it?"

"I will, but only if you come over to my place."

Just contemplating what kind of celebration they'd have, sexy thoughts raced through her. "Now?"

"Yes. Can you have your dad drive you?"

She faced her father and asked him if he wouldn't mind dropping her off at Trent's.

"I can do that, but I know your mom wants to see you. She misses you."

Charlotte smiled. "If you'd brought her to work, we could have caught up. I promise to spend time with her this weekend."

"Fine."

A few minutes later, her dad pulled into Trent's drive, and the front door opened. He jogged down the steps toward the car, pulled open her door, and helped her out.

After a quick hello kiss, he then leaned in the car. "Thanks, Vic. In case Charlotte didn't mention it, you won't need to babysit her at work anymore."

"She told me you caught the killer. Who was it?"

He glanced at her first then back at her dad. "Frank Hamilton."

"Figured he was the one," he said with such confidence Trent almost believed him, but only for a second.

Trent laughed. "You are so full of shit."

Her dad grinned, saluted, and then took off. "So Frank Hamilton killed Bill Goddard?" she said. "Did he say why?"

"He lawyered up." Trent escorted her up the steps and into the warm house. "Elaine Goddard was the one who claimed he told her."

"Will her word be enough to stand up in court?"

"That remains to be seen. We've got him on a few other offenses, so he will serve time. I'm hoping the surveillance we have of him at the viewing will provide us with the proof we need." He slipped her jacket from her shoulders and set her purse on the sofa. "As much as I like to talk about work, I have something more important to discuss with you."

She loved the way his voice dipped when he said that. "Oh yeah? What's that?"

"Give me a second and I'll tell you. Stay right here."

"Okay."

Trent turned and jogged down the hallway toward his bedroom. She had no idea what he was up to, but whatever it was, she bet she was going to enjoy it. For a second, she debated taking off her clothes and surprising him when he returned, but he had something on his mind, and she wanted to let him take the lead.

The door to his bedroom opened two minutes later. "You can come back now."

Charlotte wanted to run to him, but instead she sauntered, thinking it wouldn't be good to act too anxious. When she'd reached his door, it was closed. Something was going on in there, but she loved the mystery of it all. When she twisted the knob and stepped inside, her breath caught at the sight. Trent was lying naked on the bed surrounded by ten flickering candles both on the nightstand and dresser.

"Wow. You always celebrate like this when you catch a killer?"

He lifted up on his elbows. "This has nothing to do with my job. It's all about you."

Probably for the first time in her life, Charlotte was speechless. Her heart was pounding and her breath came out shallow. She wanted to rip off her clothes, dive into his bed, and enjoy loving him for hours, but it was as if none of her muscles would move. Trent eased off the bed and came toward her—powerful, seductive, and virile.

He cupped her face and looked down at her. "Every time we make love, it seems like *you* seduce *me*."

That wasn't completely true, but for the most part she had instigated their lovemaking. "Does that bother you?"

"Hell, no. It builds my ego, but then I realized it's not fair for me to always be the one to receive all the loving."

"Are you kidding? I've loved every minute of our time together."

"I know, but it's different somehow. You've told me many times how much you love me, but I've been too fucking scared to say it back. I keep thinking all of this has to be a dream and that I'll do something wrong, and you'll end up leaving."

Tears shimmered in her eyes at the pain radiating off him. "Your mom didn't leave you. She left your dad."

"I know. I'm talking about us. I love you, Charlotte Hart."

The joy at hearing those words nearly made her break down. "You do?"

He swiped a tear about to fall from under her eye. "Yes, I do. All I ask is that you stand by my side when I make mistakes— like when I forget to call, or when I'm so wrapped up in my job that I don't mention you are the most important person in my life."

The tears fell in earnest, but they were ones of joy and wonder. "Okay."

"Hold still." Trent stepped over to his closet, withdrew something, and placed it behind his back. "I want to show you how much I love you."

Charlotte thought it best to keep quiet for once. He strode over to her, and when he waved a tie, excitement sizzled inside her. She'd always wanted to be tied up by him. "I didn't picture you as the bondage type."

His eyes widened. "I'm not, but I could be persuaded if it's what you want. I was thinking more in the line of blindfolding you. I want your senses to be heightened to the point where you will melt if we don't make love," he whispered.

She was already melting. Never had she imagined Trent being

so romantic. "How about if I just close my eyes?" That way she could peek.

"You're not trustworthy."

She grinned. "You know me too well."

She reached out to grab his cock, but he stepped out of her reach and laughed. "Turn around."

She obeyed. Trent seemed intent on seducing her, and this time she'd let him, while reveling in everything he wanted to give her.

He wrapped the tie around her eyes and knotted it in back. "Can you see?"

"No." That was the truth. She'd never been blindfolded before and it was kind of strange but exciting at the same time.

She expected him to drop to his knees, spread her thighs, and lick her. Instead, he lifted her blouse over her head then ran his palms from her shoulders down to her wrists and back up again, touching only the hair on her arms. The light pressure sent shivers straight to her clit. Never in a million years, would she have imagined a brushing could be so sensual.

His breath caressed her face. "I want all of you."

Who was this new man? He'd changed from the first time she'd met him, and she fell in love all over again. Soft kisses caressed her shoulder and trailed across her back and down her spine. No one had ever loved her like this before, and as much as she wanted to move and press her body against his, she was enjoying this new way of making love too much. It was as if they were truly learning about each other for the first time, and with each touch, her love bloomed.

From the light thud on the floor, Trent had dropped to his knees. "Kick off your shoes," he commanded.

He held her hand while she balanced on one foot and ditched her footwear. He then unzipped her skirt and lowered it. Once more holding his hand, she stepped out of it. She was now dressed in her matching black lace panties and bra.

"You came to seduce, I see."

"I came from work."

"I should have paid closer attention to what you put on this morning."

By the humor in his tone, he seemed pleased with her choice. With his teeth, he nipped her butt then dragged his tongue to the top of her thighs.

Anticipation soared through her and her inner walls clenched. She wanted to turn around so badly and have him play with her pussy, but she needed to let him be in charge. Her desire for him was so intense, though, it was hard to remain standing.

"I need you," she said. Just because he wanted to be the one to seduce her, it didn't mean she couldn't participate.

"Patience."

Trent clasped her hips and swiveled her around. "Let me love you my way."

Always. "Don't stay in any one spot too long."

He tapped her hip. "I'm in charge, remember?"

Is that what this was about? At the moment, she didn't care. Having his hands and mouth on her was what was important. In one quick tug, he divested her of her panties and then threaded his tongue between her folds. Good Lord in heaven. She nearly shot to the roof. Never had she thought having her eyes closed would change the way she experienced lovemaking.

She reached down, and when she cupped the side of his face, his bristles tickled her palms. The next swipe of his tongue had her bending her knees for more pressure. She thought about begging him to impale her, but he clearly was trying to make her even more desperate.

As she was thinking about taking off her blindfold, he swept her up in his arms and carried her to what she believed was the bed. A second later her back hit the mattress, and the blindfold disappeared. A grinning Trent loomed over her.

"I'm so fucking weak around you. I thought I could last for hours, but I can't. Forgive me for taking you so soon."

She almost wept for joy. Trent had managed to get under her skin and then invaded her heart. Now he was going to become one with her. "I was wondering what was taking you so long."

"Smartass." Trent released the clasp on her bra and dragged down the straps.

As if he'd never enjoyed her tits before, he tugged, nipped, and pinched each nipple until heated swirls consumed her. Charlotte thought it only fair to taste him so that he'd receive just as much pleasure, but he kept her on edge too much and her thoughts never cleared enough to ask him to stop.

"I have to have you," he grunted.

When Trent crawled on top of her and thrust his cock into her all the way to the hilt, chaos descended. Her climax brimmed, and the kiss that followed spoke not only of love, but of a future. As if they were ravenous beasts, they devoured each other. Needing him to stay inside her, she clamped down on his cock.

His eyes narrowed and his breath came out faster. "I love you so much," he whispered.

"I love you more."

"We'll see."

What ensued defied description. He kissed her lips, her eyes, her throat, and then returned to claim her mouth. It was as if he needed to sample every inch of her. With each expression of love, her orgasm loomed near.

As much as she wanted him to take control, Charlotte wouldn't be true to herself if she didn't show him her strong need. With her hands clasping his shoulders, she wrapped her legs around his waist and rode him with wild abandon.

When he reached between them and rubbed her clit, all thought disappeared. A tidal wave of ecstasy claimed her, and as she yelled his name, his hot seed spewed, anointing her with his love. He rolled them over, and all she could do was hold on.

Trent kissed her nose. "I guess now would be as good of a time to have our discussion."

She smiled. "What would you like to discuss?"

"I want you to move in with me."

Once more words abandoned her. She'd signed a one-year lease on her new apartment, but she was sure with the right amount of money, she could get out of it. "I'd love nothing more than to live with you."

"I promise you won't regret it," he said.

CHAPTER THIRTY

Four months later

"**D**O YOU THINK we have enough food?" Charlotte asked.

"Stop fussing," Trent said as he picked up the plate of steaks and carried it out to the back deck.

Charlotte followed with the tray of vegetables he planned to grill.

"Knock, knock. Where do you want me to put the beer?" Harmon had a case in his hands.

"Hey." Trent smiled, slipped the beer from him, and dropped the cans into the cooler. He then ran his gaze up and down his brother. "You don't look any different."

Harmon puffed out his chest. "I might appear the same, but inside I'm singing a different tune. It feels good to be exonerated."

Charlotte couldn't be happier for him. After four long months, Harmon finally had his day in court, and the conviction had been overturned. Not only had Frank Hamilton confessed that Bill Goddard had set up Harmon to get him out of the way so that he wouldn't tempt his wife further, Bill's computer had provided the conclusive piece of evidence. Goddard had sent emails to Harmon's client detailing the merger a week before he accused Harmon of breaking the law.

The videotapes, along with the microphones at the funeral home, had picked up Frank Hamilton telling Mrs. Goddard that he'd killed both men for her. The gun casings at the restaurant confirmed they belonged to Frank's gun. The man would never see the light of day again.

"So what are your plans now that you have no restrictions?" she asked.

Harmon shrugged. "Thinking about opening my own pizza shop."

He'd liked working at Italiano's, but he probably wanted to be his own boss. "That's fantastic. If you decide to do it, let me know if you want me to help decorate your new place."

"You got it."

The doorbell rang and Trent disappeared. A few seconds later, Cade entered with Stone, their wife Amber, and their fifteen-month old son, Trevor. No sooner had Charlotte oohed and awed over Amber's adorable baby, than Thad Dalton and his wife, Zoey showed up. Apparently, her other husband in their ménage relationship, Pete Banks, was out of town on business. Both couples brought appetizers, and soon there was little room to put the food. Max Gruden, the town's Fire Marshall who helped saved Charlotte's dad, and his wife Jamie had to cancel at the last minute because their newborn, Camille, had taken ill.

Not wanting to spend her time hustling between the front door and the back porch, Charlotte scribbled a note and taped it on the front door telling the new arrivals to come on back to the patio. She hoped the criminals in town didn't know that the majority of the detectives would be at their home. If they did, they'd have a heyday looting.

Late to the party were her mom and dad. From her mother's swollen lips, Charlotte could only guess what her parents had been doing. Oh, boy.

With everyone but Sharon there, Cade helped Trent grill while Charlotte made sure the rest of the partygoers had enough to drink. Harmon had stopped over a few days earlier and brought an old stereo system he'd hooked up for use outside, providing the party with a wonderful atmosphere.

"Food's ready," Trent announced.

Like a cattle stampede, the group descended on the meal. Once everyone was seated, Trent tapped his fork against his beer bottle and managed to settle down the crowd. Only when Harmon clicked off the music did the chatter stop.

"I want to say thank you to everyone who took the time to come to Harmon's celebration party. It's been a long time coming, and I know many of you here worked tirelessly these last few months to find proof that my brother was innocent of the crime perpetuated against him. For that I thank you."

The crowd clapped and Harmon held up his hand, looking like he wanted to disappear. Charlotte understood why Trent was making such a fuss. He was so happy with the outcome that he couldn't stop himself from shouting it to anyone who would listen.

As Trent opened his mouth to say something more, the doorbell rang, and Charlotte expected to see Sharon stroll on in. She'd said she'd be late. The only one to decline was Dan Hartwick. He said someone needed to stay at the precinct. When the bell rang again, Harmon stood.

"I'll get it. Be right back."

She let him play host since he seemed anxious to be out of the limelight.

"I have another announcement," Trent said, "but we'll wait until Harmon returns."

A bit of chatter started up and then died immediately when Harmon returned with his and Trent's father. Now that was a surprise. Her gaze shot to Trent, wondering how he'd respond. She met his dad a few times, but she'd never warmed up to him.

It was probably because she wanted him to love Trent as much as she did, and he'd never shown signs of doing that.

Trent placed a hand on her shoulder as if to gain control of his emotions. "Dad, you came."

Harmon guided him to an empty chair at a table near theirs. With some effort, he sat down then handed the cane to his son. "Didn't want to miss Harmon's celebration party. I have a lot of lost time to make up for, and I want to start now." He ran his gaze between Harmon and Trent.

If that were true, she couldn't be happier.

Trent's fingers tightened on her shoulder, and then he released his hand. "I'm glad you made it."

Charlotte could hear the sincerity in Trent's voice. She looked up at him and smiled, and he returned her look with a wink.

"Now that everyone's here, I'd like to make my second announcement. Actually it's not so much of an announcement as a question." He looked at Harmon and nodded.

His brother dipped a hand in his pocket, retrieved something, and tossed the small case to Trent, who caught it easily. He then pulled back her chair and twisted her toward him. When he knelt on one knee, Charlotte's heart nearly exploded. Her mother gasped and her father coughed. She didn't dare look at anyone else for fear she'd cry.

Trent lifted her hand and pressed his lips to her fingers. "There are no words to express how happy you've made me, Charlotte. I'm not going to discuss in public all the changes I've made because of you, but I will say that I want you in my life forever." He flipped open the velvet case to expose a sparkling diamond solitaire. "Will you, Charlotte Hart, be my wife?"

She didn't need time to think. "I will!"

He pulled her to her feet and kissed her. As much as she never wanted the passionate embrace to end, the whole group surrounded her and practically forced them apart. Her mother was already crying, and her father beaming.

"As your future brother-in-law, I think I deserve the first hug," Harmon said with pride in his voice.

She embraced Harmon, and whispered a thank you in his ear. She could only hope he found as much happiness as his brother had.

THE END

ALSO BY VELLA DAY

A WITCH'S COVE MYSTERY (Paranormal Cozy Mystery)

PINK Is The New Black (book 1)

A PINK Potion Gone Wrong (book 2)

The Mystery of the PINK Aura (book 3)

Box Set (books 1-3)

Sleuthing In The PINK (book 4)

Not in The PINK (book 5)

Gone in the PINK of an Eye (book 6)

Box Set (books 4-6)

The PINK Pumpkin Party (book 7)

Mistletoe with a PINK Bow (book 8)

The Magical PINK Pendant (book 9)

The Poisoned PINK Punch (book 10)

PINK Smoke and Mirrors (book 11)

Broomsticks and PINK Gumdrops (book 12)

Knotted Up In PINK Yarn (book 13)

Ghosts and PINK Candles (book 14)

Pilfering The PINK Pearls (book 15)

The Case of The Stolen PINK Tombstone (book 16)

The PINK Christmas Cookie Caper (book 17)

PINK Moon Rising (book 18)

SILVER LAKE SERIES (3 OF THEM)

(1). **HIDDEN REALMS OF SILVER LAKE** (Paranormal Romance)

Awakened By Flames (book 1)

Seduced By Flames (book 2)

Kissed By Flames (book 3)

Destiny In Flames (book 4)

Box Set (books 1-4)

Passionate Flames (book 5)

Ignited By Flames (book 6)

Touched By Flames (book 7)

Box Set (books 5-7)

Bound By Flames (book 8)

Fueled By Flames (book 9)

Scorched By Flames (book 10)

(2). **FOUR SISTERS OF FATE: HIDDEN REALMS OF SILVER LAKE** (Paranormal Romance)

Poppy (book 1)

Primrose (book 2)

Acacia (book 3)

Magnolia (book 4)

Box Set (books 1-4)

Jace (book 5)

Tanner (book 6)

(3). **WERES AND WITCHES OF SILVER LAKE** (Paranormal Romance)

A Magical Shift (book 1)

Catching Her Bear (book 2)

Surge of Magic (book 3)

The Bear's Forbidden Wolf (book 4)

Her Reluctant Bear (book 5)

Freeing His Tiger (book 6)

Protecting His Wolf (book 7)

Waking His Bear (book 8)

Melting Her Wolf's Heart (book 9)

Her Wolf's Guarded Heart (book 10)

His Rogue Bear (book 11)

Box Set (books 1-4)

Box Set (books 5-8)

Reawakening Their Bears (book 12)

OTHER PARANORMAL SERIES

PACK WARS (Paranormal Romance)

Training Their Mate (book 1)

Claiming Their Mate (book 2)

Rescuing Their Virgin Mate (book 3)

Box Set (books 1-3)

Loving Their Vixen Mate (book 4)

Fighting For Their Mate (book 5)

Enticing Their Mate (book 6)

Box Set (books 1-4)

Complete Box Set (books 1-6)

HIDDEN HILLS SHIFTERS (Paranormal Romance)

An Unexpected Diversion (book 1)

Bare Instincts (book 2)

Shifting Destinies (book 3)

Embracing Fate (book 4)

Promises Unbroken (book 5)

Bare 'N Dirty (book 6)

Hidden Hills Shifters Complete Box Set (books 1-6)

CONTEMPORARY SERIES

MONTANA PROMISES (Full length contemporary Romance)

Promises of Mercy (book 1)

Foundations For Three (book 2)

Montana Fire (book 3)

Montana Promises Box Set (books 1-3)

Hart To Hart (Book 4)

Burning Seduction (Book 5)

Montana Promises Complete Box Set (books 1-5)

ROCK HARD, MONTANA (contemporary romance novellas)

Montana Desire (book 1)

Awakening Passions (book 2)

PLEDGED TO PROTECT (contemporary romantic suspense)

From Panic To Passion (book 1)

From Danger To Desire (book 2)

From Terror To Temptation (book 3)

Pledged To Protect Box Set (books 1-3)

BURIED SERIES (contemporary romantic suspense)

Buried Alive (book 1)

Buried Secrets (book 2)

Buried Deep (book 3)

The Buried Series Complete Box Set (books 1-3)

A NASH MYSTERY (Contemporary Romance)

Sidearms and Silk(book 1)

Black Ops and Lingerie(book 2)

A Nash Mystery Box Set (books 1-2)

STARTER SETS (Romance)

Contemporary

Paranormal

Author Bio

Love it HOT and STEAMY? Sign up for my newsletter and receive MONTANA DESIRE for FREE. Click here

OR Are you a fan of quirky PARANORMAL COZY MYSTERIES? Sign up for this newsletter. Click Here

Not only do I love to read, write, and dream, I'm an extrovert. I enjoy being around people and am always trying to understand what makes them tick. Not only must my romance books have a happily ever after, I need characters I can relate to. My men are wonderful, dynamic, smart, strong, and the best lovers in the world (of course).

My Paranormal Cozy Mysteries are where I let my imagination run wild with witches and a talking pink iguana who believes he's a real sleuth.

I believe I am the luckiest woman. I do what I love and I have a wonderful, supportive husband, who happens to be hot!

Fun facts about me

(1) I'm a math nerd who loves spreadsheets. Give me numbers and I'll find a pattern.

(2) I live on a Costa Rica beach!

(3) I also like to exercise. Yes, I know I'm odd.

I love hearing from readers either on FB or via email (hint, hint).

Social Media Sites

Website: www.velladay.com

FB: www.facebook.com/vella.day.90
Twitter: velladay4
Gmail: velladayauthor@gmail.com

ABOUT VELLA DAY

Love it HOT and STEAMY? Sign up for my newsletter and receive MONTANA DESIRE for FREE. Click here

OR Are you a fan of quirky PARANORMAL COZY MYSTERIES? Sign up for this newsletter. Click Here

Not only do I love to read, write, and dream, I'm an extrovert. I enjoy being around people and am always trying to understand what makes them tick. Not only must my romance books have a happily ever after, I need characters I can relate to. My men are wonderful, dynamic, smart, strong, and the best lovers in the world (of course).

My Paranormal Cozy Mysteries are where I let my imagination run wild with witches and a talking pink iguana who believes he's a real sleuth.

I believe I am the luckiest woman. I do what I love and I have a wonderful, supportive husband, who happens to be hot!

(1) I'm a math nerd who loves spreadsheets. Give me numbers and I'll find a pattern.

(2) I'm addicted to taking pictures (I taught high school photo for 30 years). I plan to periodically post some of my favorites on my newsletter [so sign up!].

(3) I also like to exercise. Yes, I know I'm odd. Not only do I walk with different women each week, I teach Pilates twice a week at a local rec center, and lift weights the other days.

I love hearing from readers either on FB or via email (hint, hint).

SOCIAL MEDIA SITES

Website:

www.velladay.com
FB:
www.facebook.com/vella.day.90
Twitter:
@velladay4
Gmail:
velladayauthor@gmail.com
Google:
plus.google.com/u/0/116041077486216602121/posts
Tsu:
www.tsu.co/velladay